Allura and the

Hopeless World

Allura and the Hopeless World

Published by The Conrad Press Ltd. in the United Kingdom 2024

Tel: +44(0)1227 472 874

www.theconradpress.com
info@theconradpress.com

ISBN 978-1-915494-78-8

Cover artist Georgie Stewart
Map illustration by D'Arcy Roberts

Typesetting and cover design by Michelle Emerson
michelleemerson.co.uk

The Conrad Press logo was designed by Maria Priestley.

Printed and bound in Great Britain by Clays Ltd,
Elcograf S.p.A.

Allura and the

Hopeless World

Taylor Indiana Roberts

To Isabel

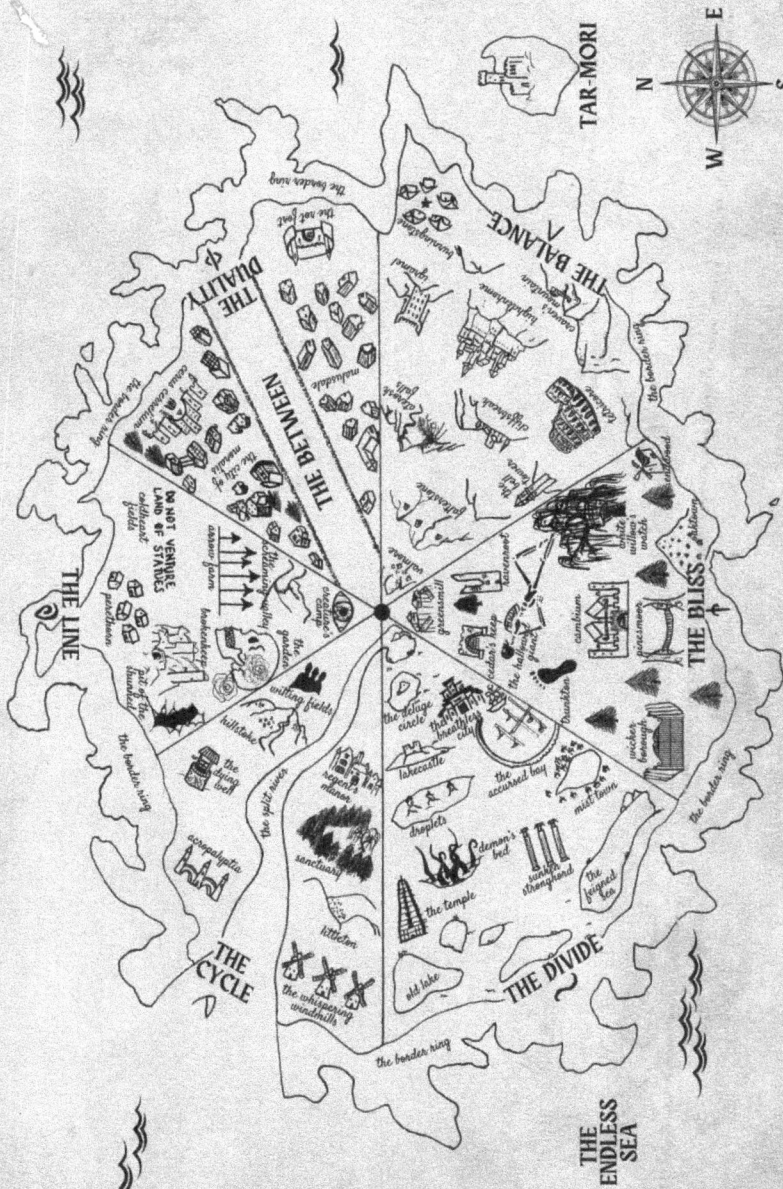

Map of Orterra from the pages of Ofelia Donnelly's sketchbook

1

The third death of Allura Saint-May

To the best of her memory, there had been three times when Allura Saint-May didn't think she would make it out alive.

The first was in August 2006, when at nine years old she found herself dangling from the roof of a three-storey house. Sinking her fingers into the muck and sludge that sloshed through the house's gutter was all that separated her from the concrete below as a torrent of rain tried to shake her loose.

Hearing her pained cries from their bedroom, Mr. and Mrs. Williams, her foster parents at the time, attempted a half-hearted rescue, grasping at her thrashing legs which hung a few feet above their window. Unfortunately, Mr. Williams seemed to take it quite personally when his hand was caught between her swinging foot and the brick wall. Although he would never admit it, Allura felt as though he was on the storm's side after that.

Whatever his true allegiances may have been, he was unable to grasp anything more than the scruff of Allura's trousers when a strong burst of wind and rain shook her from the rattling gutter. Her fingers slipped from the soaked metal and she fell for what felt like an age before hitting the ground with a sickening crunch.

It would have been a splat if not for the overgrown hydrangea bushes in the front garden doing their best to break her fall, but even they could not save her completely.

Ten long days of pain and boredom in a hospital bed passed like a slow and endless nightmare, leaving her with curious flowerhead scars across her back that would never completely fade.

But worse than that were the constant, 'what were you thinkings?' and 'how could you be so stupids?' from Mr. and Mrs. Williams almost every minute of every day. They simply could not understand how she had ended up on the roof that blustery night and would not realise for some time after that it had only been the first of many ill-conceived breakout attempts.

Yes, her year with the Williams family was to be an arduous one, but when Allura left the hospital, it was with a renewed sense that whatever came next would be nothing compared to her first death.

And so, the second time she was certain it was all over for her was in March 2008 when, as a rambunctious ten-year-old, Allura decided enough was enough and picked a fight with Mabel; the bully of Littlevale Primary School. Mabel was a terrible brute of a girl who enjoyed terrorising the smaller children, often shaking them by their ankles to see what fell out. Unfortunately, Allura was one of those smaller children.

She was downright weedy in fact.

It also did her no favours that Mabel had learnt to blindly mistreat those who looked or acted differently to her, believing that anyone who didn't wear their hair in tight pigtails or have skin as pale as milk deserved whatever they had coming to them. Needless to say, Allura Saint-May with her dark brown complexion and large mass of coiled hair made for an ideal target of Mabel's home-grown brand of terror.

For weeks Allura had tried to keep her head down and not make a fuss when Mabel would knock her tray from her hand in the canteen or trip her up in the corridor, but she could only take so much. Things finally came to a head when Mabel snatched Allura's favourite book from her in the playground.

It was a story about a knight who conquered a mighty dragon. Or at least it had been before Mabel started flicking through it and gleefully tore each page in two. Perhaps inspired by the hero whose story she had loved so much, Allura soon found herself kicking and clawing at the girl, only to quickly be knocked onto her back.

It was ironic really, Allura had ended up flat on the ground all because she had tried to stand up for herself. But in that moment, Allura didn't really care for irony (she wasn't even entirely certain what it was).

All she was certain of was that she was going to die.

Mabel's heavy shoes pounded mercilessly against her stomach until her vision was blurry with tears and consciousness slipped away from her like a runaway balloon.

The darkness crept in and she couldn't escape the dreaded feeling that she may never wake up again.

She might have been right as well, if not for the last-minute intervention of the teachers. Unfortunately, Mabel caught sight of them as they approached and feigned her own injuries, writhing around on the floor beside Allura as though they had hurt one another in equal measure.

Bruised and beaten, Allura awoke an hour later in the presence of the school nurse who provided her 'cure-all' remedy of a bag of ice and a stern telling off.

Meanwhile, Mabel gave the performance of a lifetime in the corridor, fake tears and all, but it didn't matter. Because, there and then, with her face swollen and ribs aching, Allura swore that she would never feel that helpless again.

Which brings us to the 19th December 2010, when at twelve years old, Allura's life as she knew it really would end.

It all began with darkness and someone named Mrs. Olderman.

In her three months with the woman, Allura had been sent into the basement of her miserable home at 13 Drudgers Row to 'think about what she had done' at least a dozen times. It was a truly awful place, filled with odd tools strewn across the floor, unexplainable stains and markings on the walls, low hanging beams, and most forebodingly of all, it was shrouded in complete and total darkness.

Of all the families Allura had stayed with, Mrs. Olderman was without a doubt her least favourite (which was saying a lot).

For starters, she demanded to be referred to only as 'Mother', with any variations ('mum', 'mummy' or 'mama') being strictly forbidden. Not that Allura wanted to use any of them anyway.

She also preferred to shout her orders rather than ask nicely, and if there was one thing Allura did not respond well to, it was shouting – or orders for that matter.

Worst yet, despite being one of the most untidy people she had ever had the misfortune of meeting, one of Mrs. Olderman's 'little quirks' was that she liked for every surface in the house to be dusted before the rest of the street had even begun to stir.

It used to take Allura nearly two hours to get the job done, but three months in, she prided herself on her ability to get the place spotless in just thirty minutes.

Yet no sooner had she finished her chores on that cold Sunday morning than Mrs. Olderman had set her the task of doing her Christmas shopping for her.

'And don't even think of running off again, cause you know I'll always find you. It's mother's intuition. Do you understand me?' she warned, just as she did every weekday before sending her off to school.

'Yes.'

'Yes what?' Mrs. Olderman asked sharply.

'Yes, mother,' Allura begrudgingly replied.

With that, she set off through huge crowds on the

main drag and empty shortcut alleyways to the bustling market that lived in the heart of a disused train station. One of the few things Allura actually liked about Drudgers Row was how close it was to the market which hummed with the collective chatter of bargaining customers and upselling vendors.

Red brick walls, stained brown by time, surrounded the space with cracked ornate windows allowing light and fresh air to breeze through. Thick pillars stretching all the way up to the curved glass ceiling were dotted about the place, each one wrapped in dazzling fairy-lights. Raggedy urban pigeons flew overhead as Allura passed through, waving to traders selling everything from huge slabs of meat to homemade wicker chairs to antique clocks to hand-carved trinkets.

With what little money she had been trusted with, Allura joyously haggled, bartered and negotiated her way through the morning and by midday she had filled a bag to the brim with gifts. A flat cap, a pipe and whiskey stones for Mrs. Olderman's father, a scarf and a second hand book about old cars for her mother, and a foot massager, a blanket and a pair of ugly sequined slippers for the old crone herself.

Then and only then, did she allow herself to rest, weaving her way through the market to a familiar little hiding place between two vendors at the back, where the stalls lined up neatly against the wall. Dropping to the floor with her back against the brick, she looked out at the scene.

Erasing all the stalls and the people in her mind, she then replaced them with massive steam trains on wide tracks. She thought of the places those trains would take her, far away from Mrs. Olderman and anyone else who sought to control her life.

But then where would I go? she reminded herself, rattling the daydreams from her head.

*

From there, the day trudged slowly on and as Allura made her way back to number 13, she spotted a few children from the neighbourhood kicking a football about on the fog drenched street. Among them was Charlie, a sprightly blonde boy from next door who looked particularly excited to see her.

'Hey,' he called out, punting the ball towards her, 'do you wanna join?'

She knew he would ask, he always did, but just like every time before she could already feel Mrs. Olderman's eyes burning a hole in the back of her head from the window above.

'Would love to, but I've really got to get going,' Allura replied, flashing him a warm smile and returning the ball with a powerful kick. 'Cheers anyway.'

'Oh come on, you always say that,' Charlie replied, once again rolling the ball towards her feet. 'Don't be nervous, there's no way you're as rubbish as our goalie.'

'Hey!' yelled the boy manning the net.

'Well, maybe just for a minute,' she said hesitantly before placing the bag on the floor. 'And just so you know, I've seen you lot play out here before, so trust me, I'm not nervous.'

But before she could even make her way into the street, she heard the upstairs window open behind her.

'ALLURA, DARLING!' Mrs. Olderman's voice rang out like a war-siren. 'COME INSIDE DEAR!'

'In a minute, please,' Allura called back to her.

'If you think that's wise,' Mrs. Olderman replied with a subtle sting in her sweet tone, like a needle in honey.

But Allura knew better than anyone that what was 'wise' was to come inside sharpish if she wanted anything to eat that evening. And so, she stepped off the makeshift pitch, picked up her bag and headed for the door.

'You know if she's ever being mean to you or anything, you're always welcome to pop round mine,' Charlie offered as she stepped inside.

'Thanks,' she replied, wondering as the door closed behind her if he had really meant it.

'Did you get all my gifts?' Mrs. Olderman asked, the house's gloomy lighting making her appear as though a spectre of death were descending the staircase.

'Yes,' Allura answered as she passed her, trying to avoid any further discussion.

'Don't just walk away from me Allura. We are having a conversation.'

Oh, so it's not 'darling' or 'dear' anymore, huh?

'Sorry,' she said meekly, turning on the spot and walking back down the stairs to meet her on the ground floor.

'I don't like you playing with those boys,' Mrs.

Olderman said as she ran her finger along the bottom of the table in the hall in search of the slightest trace of dust.

'Why not?'

'Because you are a lady and playing football in the street is not very ladylike.'

'What would you know about being ladylike?' Allura muttered under her breath, a little too loudly for either of their liking.

'What was that?' Mrs. Olderman asked furiously. 'Are you suggesting that I am somehow unladylike? That I'm some disgusting, unsightly thing?'

Yes, she thought.

'No!' she answered. 'What I meant was-' Allura tried to calm her down, but was immediately drowned out by the yelling.

'WHEN THAT AGENCY GAVE YOU TO ME, YOU HAD NOTHING! NO ONE! NOBODY WANTED YOU! NOBODY LOVED YOU! BUT I BROUGHT YOU INTO MY HOME! I GAVE YOU EVERYTHING YOU COULD EVER WANT AND *THIS* IS HOW YOU REPAY THAT KINDNESS! THIS IS HOW YOU TREAT YOUR OWN MOTHER?'

That was the final straw. Allura had held her tongue long enough.

'You are not my mother! You have never been my mother! In fact, I don't think I've ever hated anyone more than I hate you! So why don't you just let me leave and maybe next time that agency will give you a kid that can actually stand the sight of you!'

'LET YOU LEAVE? OH NO, YOU ARE WITH

ME FOREVER! BUT THIS BEHAVIOUR WILL NOT BE TOLERATED! DO YOU REALLY THINK YOU CAN TALK TO ME LIKE THAT? LET'S SEE YOU TRY THAT AGAIN AFTER A FEW HOURS DOWNSTAIRS!'

'NO!' Allura cried, but before she could turn and run, Mrs. Olderman pounced, grabbing a great big handful of her curly hair.

'GET OFF ME,' she screamed, but the wicked woman paid her no mind as she dragged her through the corridor and down into the basement.

'Stop it, please,' Allura begged, kicking and screaming, but to no avail. Instead, her cruel captor simply threw her down the last three steps into the blackness of the basement. Allura landed with a shout, twisting her ankle against the hard concrete.

'That sounded painful, if only your mother was here to look after you,' Mrs. Olderman sneered, her disgustingly smug face being the last thing Allura saw before the door slammed shut.

Muffled stomps echoed around the basement as the vile woman marched back upstairs.

Nursing her throbbing ankle, Allura relied on her usual tactic of sitting close to the sliver of light that emanated from under the doorframe, waiting desperately for her release. But as she did, she realised that the witch of a woman had gone too far this time.

One way or another, I am getting out of here, she decided.

The searing pain in her ankle continued to pulsate and swell as she shuffled further and further from the door, until eventually she reached a point where she couldn't even see her hand in front of her face.

It was a veil of darkness that she had never dared to pass through before.

The air was thick with the dust of crumbling bricks, but the sound of her rumbling stomach acted as a marching tune. It emboldened her to stand firm, certain in the knowledge that nothing in the basement could be worse than the thing that lived above it.

Stretching her arms out in front of her, she cautiously placed one foot in front of the other until she too disappeared into the dark. Unknown objects clanged against her shoes, each one making her heart do backflips, and with each step she grew more concerned that there was no end to this underground cell.

But she continued on, placing one tentative foot in front of the other until finally she felt coarse brickwork and cobwebs press against her hands. The wall's sudden and cool touch made her flinch, but once she composed herself, she realised that she had made it to the other side of the room.

Looking behind her, she saw that the light seeping under the door was still well within sight and that her entire odyssey had, in actuality, only been about twenty steps. But that did not change the fact that she had reached uncharted territory.

Clinging to the wall, she ran her hand against empty shelves and random nails driven into the brickwork, then stopped dead in her tracks as something unexpected brushed against her fingers – something soft and fabric.

Could it be?

Without hesitation, she seized it and pulled sharply with all her strength.

Suddenly, fresh beams of light burst into the room as a thick curtain fell away, revealing a small window above a rusted washing machine.

Although she was slowed by the immense pain, Allura's heart soared as she climbed carefully onto the hunk of old metal and used it to elevate herself. Undoing the latch hanging from the bottom of the window, Allura came to the terrible conclusion that the frame itself was just beyond her reach.

She took a deep breath, focusing on anything except the pain as she extended her toes and stretched her arms as far upwards as she could. Reaching higher and higher until every fibre of her body ached, she pushed herself further than she even thought possible.

But it was still no use.

She simply could not reach.

So close, she thought, unable to do anything but watch the legs of unaware people pass by on the pavement above. If the boys had still been playing in the street she would have called to them, but with them nowhere in sight, she would have to rely on the kindness of strangers.

Ready to call out to them, her words caught in her throat as she heard a terrible sound emanating from behind her.

'WHAT'S ALL THAT NOISE DOWN THERE?' Mrs. Olderman's voice called from behind the door.

A sickening pit opened in Allura's stomach as a

key slid into place in the door's lock. Panicked, she surveyed the room and spotted a plastic bucket lying at the foot of the machine. Scrambling to the edge, she grabbed it, placed it directly under the window frame and climbed on.

Click!

The key turned in the lock one more time and the handle began to twist. Allura's breath drew heavy and fast as she pushed against the glass, struggling to keep her balance on top of the bucket.

'Come on! Come on! Come on!'

Miraculously, the window popped open.

YES!

Grabbing onto the edge of the frame, she pulled with all she had as the door creaked open. Then behind her, a shrill voice cried:

'WHAT DO YOU THINK YOU ARE DOING?'

It was Mrs. Olderman and she was furious.

'YOU GET DOWN FROM THERE RIGHT NOW!' she barked like a mad dog.

Only Allura's legs were left hanging in the basement as the raging woman charged in and scrambled up onto the machine beneath her. Allura felt the tight grip of the woman's hands squeezing around her ankles as she struggled to reunite the two halves of her body in freedom.

'LET GO!' Allura cried, her legs flailing about frantically, but Mrs. Olderman's grasp only tightened, as though she wanted to grind her bones to dust.

'NOT A CHANCE YOU UNGRATEFUL LI'L...'

Thankfully, before she could finish her thought, Mrs. Olderman lost her footing on the rickety machine and came crashing to the floor.

Freed from her grasp, Allura crawled out on her belly onto the pavement and struggled to her feet. Dusting off the grit and dirt that covered her clothes and skin, she looked around, gathering her bearings on the pavement outside.

From the basement, she heard a yelp as the plastic bucket collapsed under the pursuing Mrs. Olderman's weight, sending her toppling to the floor once again. As much as she would have enjoyed watching her wriggle around on the floor like an upturned turtle, Allura knew that there was no time.

Thinking fast, she knocked desperately on her neighbour's door and waited with bated breath until it opened. It was Charlie who answered, looking at her in surprise as though he almost couldn't believe what he was seeing.

'Didn't expect to see you so soon? Are you alright?' he asked with a shocked smile.

'You have to let me in,' she said through heavy breath. Before he could ask why, Mrs. Olderman's screamed 'WHEN I FIND YOU, YOU ARE DEAD!'

'Please,' she begged the boy as his usually kind-eyes grew wide and worried. Charlie mumbled with uncertainty and Allura once again felt a pit open in her stomach, like the feeling of anticipation before a great fall.

'I didn't think you'd actually... I'm sorry,' he repeated, over and over again as he slowly closed the door in her face. 'I'm so sorry.'

'No no no! Please don't, please-'

The door clicked shut and waves of panic crashed down on her. She wanted to cry, to wail in despair that all her effort had been for nothing, but instead she did the only thing she could think of. She disregarded the pain in her ankle and pushed the fact that she had nowhere to go to the back of her mind.

Then, she ran.

Sprinted in fact.

Outright bolted down the street, before Mrs. Olderman could even make it to the door. She was done with Drudgers Row and she was never going back.

*

What was left of the day quickly turned to night and as the hazy winter sun vanished, London sprung to life with artificial lights and the sounds of rush hour traffic. But with the night came the cold, something that Allura's ripped shirt and torn shoes offered little protection from. Although Mrs. Olderman had been a great many terrible things, she had never skimped on the heating, a fact that Allura had never quite appreciated so much as she did now.

She had kept herself on the move for as long as she could, but eventually her shivering and limping took its toll and she collapsed onto a bench at the edge of a road. Other than the odd glances and murmured words about her, the passing crowds were oblivious to her presence or all too happy to ignore her as she rolled up the bottom of her trousers and examined Mrs. Olderman's parting gift: a dark, hand-shaped bruise plastered on her ankle.

Sitting there, cold, alone and in terrible pain, Allura noticed something across the road. It was a large window with its curtains spread open, revealing the brightly lit scene within. For reasons she couldn't explain, Allura found herself enamoured with that living room, taking in every detail.

A gorgeous metal fireplace sat against the wall beside a grand Christmas tree that stood tall in the corner. It was mostly adorned with large baubles of blue and silver, but there was one unique decoration that caught her eye.

It was entirely transparent, except for a white bear that stood like a noble king at its centre. She imagined the creature would appreciate what she was doing, that it would understand her need to be free.

At the top of the tree sat a beautiful gold angel with silver wings, while at the bottom were two very eager children, only a few years younger than herself. They poked and prodded at the mountain of gifts, until a man carrying two steaming cups emerged from the doorway.

Allura smiled as the children hurriedly moved from the base of the tree, pretending as though they hadn't left the sofa the entire time he was gone. The man planted a kiss on each of their heads and placed a cup into their hands as he did, before turning his attention towards the window.

Wait. Just a little bit longer, Allura begged as he slowly pulled the curtains shut, leaving her to linger on the life she knew she would never have.

She had been so lost in thought that she nearly screamed as a hand tapped her on the shoulder and she looked up to see a police officer standing over her.

He had a bushy brown moustache and distractingly dark bags under his eyes, yet his smile was kind and his voice was gentle.

'Allura?'

'Nope,' she said shortly, looking the other way as though that would somehow have made him forget her face.

'Allura Saint-May?'

She shook her head.

'You sure about that?' he asked, taking out his phone and turning it towards her. Briefly glancing over her shoulder, Allura saw a picture of herself staring back.

'Look it's alright. I understand that you probably didn't mean to cause such a fuss, but your mum is torn up about what's happened and she's been looking for you all day,' the officer explained as he sat on the other side of the bench.

'She is *not* my mum,' Allura replied harshly, stifling a laugh at the image of Mrs. Olderman trying to squeeze out even a single tear about her disappearance.

'That may be the case,' he said, 'but this isn't any place for someone to spend the night.'

'You think it'll be better there?' she asked with venom in her voice, shuffling further away from him.

'Do you not feel safe there?' he asked and she scoffed, giving him a look, as if to say 'you have no idea'.

'If she's mistreating you, we can look into it.'

'Yeah sure, I've heard that before,' she said dismissively.

'Come on now Allura, things can always get better. You can't just give up hope.'

She looked at him, part of her wanting to believe him. He seemed nice after all, but then again so had Mrs. Olderman at first. She had known exactly what to say and exactly how to act, until finally, when they were alone, her mask of kindness slipped, revealing the true and ugly face underneath.

No, Allura had seen what good hope had done her before, the image of Charlie closing the door in her face still fresh in her mind.

Never again, she decided as she leapt from the bench in a sudden sprint.

'ALLURA! WAIT,' he yelled, but it was too late.

Adrenaline pumping, she ran wildly across the road, narrowly avoiding a black taxi as she reached the central traffic island. Glancing back, she caught a glimpse of the officer flailing his arms about as cars continued to rush past.

She knew he would soon close the distance between them, but there was no way she was going back and no way she would escape if he reached her.

Focusing on the other side of the street, she saw a thin alleyway that split into different directions and she knew that was her way out. Like a sailor drawn to a siren's call, she ran without thought or trepidation, her feet pounding against the pavement.

All she could hear was the rush of traffic and the

officer desperately shouting: 'DON'T!'

Then, a harsh brightness consumed her, followed by a deafening horn and the screeching of tyres. She turned, all-too-late, to see a double-decker bus barrelling towards her.

The noise of the city faded into a steady breeze as the bright headlights swiftly morphed into a silvery hue that flowed and fluctuated.

What's happening? she thought for the last time on Earth.

In a flash, the speeding bus rumbled past, leaving the stunned officer to stare in disbelief at the empty space where Allura Saint-May had once stood. Except now there was no discernible trace that she had ever been there at all.

2

The labyrinth

Surging around her, the light whispered in a pained voice: 'Allura.'

Where am I? she wondered as the freeze of winter vanished.

'Allura.'

Am I dead?

'Allura.'

What is this?

Then the voice fell silent and the light seeped into her skin. As it faded, she could make out tall shelves stretching in every direction around her. Until eventually, the last flickers of the shining silver glow disappeared and the shelves came to life in their dark, wooden textures, each one overflowing with leather-bound books.

Allura had no idea where she had been transported to, but wherever it was, it was magnificent.

Large beams arched overhead, far grander and well maintained than the ones she was accustomed to in Mrs. Olderman's basement (or anywhere else for that matter), while golden chandeliers hung over her from absurdly long chains. Allura's eyes followed them all the way up to the top of the ceiling, the height of it all overwhelming her senses and making her legs feel like jelly.

As she admired it, she noticed the absence of the once searing pain in her ankle and rolled up her trousers to find no remnant of the enormous bruise.

That's impossible, she thought in astonishment.

'Hello? Is anybody there?' she called out, but the words merely echoed around her with no reply.

Where am I? she asked herself as she moved along the path of continuous bookshelves for several minutes before reaching a crossroad.

Routes to the left and to the right presented themselves, each one more or less identical to the other. Choosing the path to the left, she kept a brisk pace until she once again faced another intersection of bookshelves. This pattern continued at least a dozen more times with each direction leading her to yet another set of split paths.

'Hello?' she continued to call out, but there was still no answer.

Throwing her hands up in exhausted defeat, Allura leant against a panel and dropped to the carpet. There, she noticed an oddly titled book on the shelf opposite.

Plumes of dust dropped from it as she pulled the book loose, revealing the image of an enormous furry creature with shark-like teeth and horrible spindly fingers on the cover. Its giant bulging eyes seemed to peer back at her as she read the title once again: *Never Cross A Clawing Kross by Armandia Jackel.*

She had never heard of a clawing kross before, but based on the drawing, she did not care for it. Returning the book to its place, she quickly moved on to explore the rest of the shelf, her pile of discarded books growing bigger and bigger by the second. Is *Anybody Out There? An Exploration of the Endless Sea* was stacked carelessly on top of *Genesis of the Species: The Original Twelve* which itself had been dropped onto a first edition copy of *Tales From The Bliss*.

Once she had finished perusing one shelf, she moved to another and then another and then another. Allura considered herself an avid reader, making sure to get her hands on every book in every house she had ever lived in. She had finished Mrs. Olderman's entire 'library' in a matter of days (although what she referred to as the library was nothing more than a crooked shelf filled with celebrity autobiographies and gossip magazines).

Despite Mrs. Olderman's small offering, Allura had read or at least skimmed through more than her fair share of books in her life. Yet not once in this towering stack of literature did she find a single title that she had ever even heard of before.

Finally, she knocked the pile to the ground with an exacerbated shout.

The clattering of books and her own screaming echoed through the hallway then once again disappeared into what she had come to assume was nothing but an endless row of literature. It was as though she had died and been sent here as some cruel and twisted punishment.

But then, as though she had willed it into existence, an undeniable 'shush' rung out from somewhere in the beyond.

'HELLO? WHO'S THERE?' she shouted as loud as she could, her words carrying into the distance with no response. 'WHOEVER YOU ARE... HELP ME!'

More silence called back.

'PLEASE!' she bellowed.

A moment passed, then another, until suddenly an aggravated 'SHUUUUUSH!' came crashing towards her and this time she was certain of where it had come from.

Scrambling over the books, she sprinted through the library, taking sharp lefts and rights as she followed the sound back to its source. Then without warning, the shelves came to an abrupt end and she found herself at the top of a short set of stairs with more wings of the library stretching way off into the distance behind her.

At the bottom of the steps, a clutch of oak desks pressed against a smooth stone wall with large doors covered in elaborate patterns standing between them. Before she could run for a door, any door, she noticed a man sitting at one of the desks.

He was old and scrawny, with skin that stretched tightly over his bones and white hair that draped down the back of his neck. Although Allura had learnt through experience not to interact with such complete strangers, these were desperate times and so she crept down the stairs, approaching the man with slow and careful steps.

'Excuse me,' she said sheepishly, but he didn't so much as look up from his book as he let out an immediate: 'Shush!'

Allura was stunned, not only was this man her mystery 'shusher', but he was continuing to do so even now that she had found her way to him. Quickly, her shock turned to anger. Puffing out her chest and priming her finger for wagging, she readied herself for her best impression of the scariest woman she could think of; Mrs. Olderman.

'Now you listen here -' she started to say when he turned towards her and placed a single shaking finger against his lips to let out a final and definitive 'SHUSH!'

Against her own wishes, Allura's shout instantly simmered into a whisper before reducing further into nothing. She tried to scream, to ask him what he had done, but his attention had already returned to his book, blissfully ignorant of her as she panicked in furious silence.

Allura stomped her feet and clapped her hands together without a sound. Utterly confused, she grabbed him by the collar and forced him to look at her as she tried and failed to ask him what exactly he had just done.

Allura could tell that the old man's eyes were not nearly as good as they used to be, making it impossible for him to interpret her wordless outrage.

'What have you done to me?' she mouthed silently. 'What did you do?'

Collecting his books, he got up with surprising agility, but Allura refused to let him escape, sinking her nails deeper into his arm. He let out a screech and with his free hand he raised the heavy book over his head, ready to strike it down onto her when a tempered voice rung out:

'Enough.'

For a moment, Allura thought it was the old man talking, but soon realised that it had come from somewhere behind him. They both looked to see a shadowy figure stood in the doorframe, his features hidden by the light that emanated from it, reducing him to only a silhouette. Yet his very presence caused the old man to lower his book-swinging arm.

'What is happening here?' the figure asked.

'This little vagrant girl attacked me,' the old man answered in a raspy voice.

'Is that right?'

Allura attempted to defend herself, forgetting for a moment that none of it could be heard. The silhouette didn't even wait for her to finish before turning his focus back to the man and stepping away from the door.

Allura saw then that he was much younger than the man she had been fighting with, although his short and sharp hair peeking out from under his top hat was an even brighter shade of white, and he was adorned in far nicer clothes.

He wore a long, burgundy coat made of velvet, and the ruffled shirt tucked neatly underneath was so pitch black that it made his pale skin seem almost luminous in comparison. Running his fingers along the polished silver buttons of his coat and gently tugging at his flared cuffs as he entered, the well-dressed man walked towards them with a commanding presence, as though everyone else would simply have to wait until he decided they were worth approaching.

Then he stopped in front of the elderly man and spoke slowly and deliberately.

'Did you take her sound?'

Now that he was up close, Allura noticed that despite his impressive clothes and clean shaven face, there was an air of unkemptness about him, with old and rusted rings on the fingers of one hand and the dark shadow of dirt beneath his nails.

'Yes, I did,' the old man replied in a hushed tone, 'but she was being disruptive.'

'Today is her ascension, Arnold. She is Horas' replacement.'

Arnold looked at Allura, his jaw slacked.

'Wait until Cognitius hears about this,' said the dark stranger with a grim smile.

'Raven. Please, understand. I didn't know.'

'Return her sound,' Raven replied, narrowing his eyes.

Am I supposed to know what any of this means? Allura wondered, more perplexed than ever as Arnold snapped his shaking fingers. She still had no idea what was happening, but she was relieved to once again hear the sound of her own heavy breathing.

Clasping her hands together, she took great pleasure in the noise they produced.

'WHAT WAS THAT?' she blurted out, louder than she had intended.

Without so much as acknowledging her, Raven waved his ring-covered hand dismissively, as though to tell Arnold that he was done with him. The old man shuffled towards one of the doors as quickly as his frail legs could carry him.

'Wait, come back! What did you do to me?' she yelled as he walked away, but Raven moved to block her.

'I imagine you have a lot more questions than that, but I can promise you answers if you follow me,' he said calmly before heading towards the open door and stopping at the threshold. Only then did he turn back to see that Allura hadn't budged.

'I'm not going anywhere until you tell me what the hell is going on,' she said, crossing her arms in defiance as though she were rooting herself to the spot.

At the same patient pace as before, he walked back to her and crouched down to face her at eye level. He had a deep scar that ran from his nose down to the corner of his mouth and there was an unusual motion to his eyes, as though each one contained a spiralling black hole at its centre instead of a pupil.

'I understand that you're confused, but you must believe me when I tell you that never in your entire life have you been as safe as you are at this very moment.'

Allura was a particularly wary young girl when it came to other people, never quick to trust comforting promises or anything that sounded too good to be true. But there was something about the words Raven had spoken, or perhaps something about the soft way in which he had spoken them that, just for a moment, caused Allura to completely and whole-heartedly believe him.

Raven however, must have noticed the faint glisten in her eyes because he quickly dropped his kind demeanour and stood up straight, tugging at his coat as though the effort of talking to her had somehow creased it.

'So, unless you wish to return to that little hovel you crawled out of, I suggest you do as you're told and *come with me.*'

Cautiously following him to the door, Allura took one last look at the room, watching as one by one the entrances to the bookshelves began to close, leaving nothing but a smooth wooden wall in their place.

Raven's walk picked up into a determined strut as they entered a winding corridor, illuminated by torches and beams of impossibly bright moonlight that shone through small peekaboo windows.

Allura did her best to match his pace while keeping a distance between them, ensuring that he wouldn't be able to stop her if a reason to run away presented itself. At their brisk speed, she only managed to catch glimpses of castle walls and the world beyond them through the windows. All she could see were the treetops swaying in the wind and heavy rain, as well as a sliver of the moon before it was enveloped by clouds.

Has it always been so big?

Before she could think about it any further, the corridor led them to an arched opening in the wall where an uncovered bridge stood in the pounding rain. It was made from stones of various bland colours and rigid shapes, causing it to have an unevenness about it, with pools of water collecting in the resultant crevices. Along its sides were railings made from similarly mismatched stones with large gaps between the supports.

Raven stopped abruptly at the end of the corridor, the rain falling inches from his face as he took off his tall hat and tucked it under his arm.

'You'll want to be quick along here. Nothing good ever comes from hanging about in weather like this.' His warning was accompanied by a crack of thunder that made Allura shudder. Then in a flash of lightning, Raven was already on the other side, leaving only a puff of smoke hanging in the air between them.

He couldn't have made it across that fast, she thought, but that was not the first impossible thing she had seen that day and at this point she was tired of being forced to marvel at the unbelievable.

Covering her face with her arms, she took her first step into the biting cold, her attempt at a run quickly stumbling into an uneasy walk as she slipped along the soaked stone. Each freezing drop of rain nipped at her skin and she could already feel her fingers turning numb when a strong gust of wind swiped her legs out from under her.

With a yelp, she tumbled face first onto the floor and slid towards the edge of the bridge. Only then did she notice that the gaps in the railings were just big enough for her to slip through. She dug her fingers into the craggy stone to slow her momentum and barely stopped in time as her head slipped between two pillars.

The top half of her hung precariously over the side of the bridge and she froze at the sight of the hexagonal courtyard below, feeling like she was nine years old again, hanging from the guttering with the inescapable feeling that the next burst of wind would send her tumbling down, down, down.

Then a firm hand pulled her from the paralysing memory.

'WHAT ARE YOU DOING? I SAID NOT TO STOP!'

Raven looked at her with a rabid fury in his dark and rippling eyes as he dragged her the rest of the way, moving through the wind and rain as if it weren't even there.

They arrived on the other side and she pushed her damp hair out of her face, feeling the cool droplets run down her nose. Dripping to the floor, they formed a puddle at her feet and she watched it for a while, preferring to gaze at her own soaked reflection than into Raven's violent eyes.

'I got distracted,' she whimpered.

'Well let me tell you, the next time you decide to get 'distracted', don't expect me or anyone else to come to your rescue.'

'I'm sorry, but maybe you shouldn't have made me walk across there in the first place,' she spat back.

The raging tempest in his eyes expanded for a moment, then he returned his hat to his head and walked off, muttering 'foolish girl' under his breath.

She allowed the distance between them to double

before following, making sure not to look back to the bridge as she went. Further down the corridor they were met by an oak door so tall and wide that Allura could easily have stretched her arms out and not have been close to touching both sides of the frame.

Raven knocked on the door which, like everything else Allura had seen in the castle, seemed to not only be old, but ancient. As though the wood had been carved from a tree cut down millennia ago. There was a sturdiness to it, a noble dependability.

'This is where we part ways. I hope for your own sake that you learn to keep your focus from now on.'

As he spoke, Allura felt herself reach breaking point. She hadn't asked to be brought here. She hadn't asked to be dragged across a moss covered bridge in the middle of a rainstorm. She hadn't asked for any of this.

'I didn't want your help,' she said.

'Yet you needed it all the same.'

'I don't need anything from you. You're just another bully in a fancy suit and I just want to go home.'

'Believe me, no one would be happier to see that happen than me,' he replied with a devilish grin.

'Listen, I might not have any idea what is going on here, but what I do know for sure is that you are nothing but-' she would have been more than happy to go on, but quickly had to trail off as the door swung open.

A strikingly tall and muscular man with gristly stubble and a flat, crooked nose walked through, bumping his bald head against the top of the frame as he went (not that he seemed to notice).

'Is she ready?' Raven asked calmly, as though he had not just been in the middle of an argument with a twelve-year-old. The man nodded.

'Then my task here is done. Come Abraham, I believe Orville will be waiting for us.'

Without acknowledging Allura for even a moment longer than he had to, Raven walked away with the large man in tow, not so much as glancing back at her as he went. However, his companion seemingly couldn't help himself.

The burlap shirt that clung tightly to him creased as he turned his neck to look at her over his shoulder. Although he remained stone-faced, without even an inkling of a smile, Allura could have sworn by the warmth in his piercing brown eyes that he was looking at her fondly.

Then they both turned the corner and she found herself with only the open door and one immediate question rattling around her head.

If Raven was only my guide, then who has he delivered me to?

The thought haunted her as she entered the room, feeling woefully unprepared for any more surprises that may have been waiting for her. The room was filled with more tall bookcases and even taller marble pillars.

To the right of the door sat a green sofa smothered in pillows that glowed invitingly in the light of a stone fireplace. While at the centre of the room was a long table that was so well polished that she could read the words from an array of different languages inscribed on the ceiling off of its reflective surface.

At the head of it sat an old woman in finely woven robes with long-draping sleeves, who jumped to attention the second she noticed Allura.

'My dear there you are. I must admit I was starting to worry we might never find you, especially on a night like this,' she said as she approached and gently grasped Allura's shaking hands with a warm smile across her face.

'My poor girl you have had quite a day, haven't you? Please, sit and I will explain everything, starting with the greatest secret that Earth will never know.'

3

The doorway

The woman introduced herself as Cognitius – 'the Embodiment of Knowledge' (*whatever that meant*) – before offering Allura a choice.

'Tea or answers?'

Allura glanced at the plates and silverware on the table, then her stomach lurched violently. That was as good an answer as any.

The old woman nodded and with a click of her fingers, trollies carrying silver platters were wheeled in. The carts appeared to be moving on their own, but as they got closer Allura noticed what seemed to be a small bundle of twigs shuffling at their bases.

The trollies came to a stop in a neat line at the edge of the table and after she heard the manic pattering of feet against the marble floor, the door slammed shut.

'Let's see what they've brought us,' Cognitius said, rising from her chair. She opened one of the platters to reveal a mountain of the most golden roast potatoes that Allura had ever seen. Her mouth immediately filled with saliva and her hunger only grew more ravenous with each lid lifted.

There was sweetcorn dripping in butter, carrots roasted in honey, giant sausages wrapped in bacon, gallons of piping hot gravy and a crisp-brown bird, far larger than any chicken or turkey she had ever seen.

Once the last of twelve trays had been uncovered, the two tucked into the feast. Allura carefully stacked her food into a tower, fitting as much as possible onto her plate before gleefully tearing into it. The sounds she made were like those of a lion ripping into a gazelle or a pig loudly gnawing on an apple.

Usually she had better manners than that, but that evening her hunger greatly outweighed her sense of politeness.

'Some of your favourites if I'm not mistaken,' Cognitius said after finishing her plate and leaning back into her chair. 'The wood gnells did well, didn't they?'

Allura took her first break from the food to look inquisitively at her.

'Woo' 'ells?' she asked, her mouth still partially full.

'Yes. Our chefs.'

Allura swallowed the huge mouthful, her question still not quite answered.

'But what are they?'

'Harmless creatures of the forest and truly incredible cooks.'

'And they work for you?'

'Not quite. I helped this particular tribe out of a spot of bother some time ago and they felt indebted to me. I told them they needn't worry, but they insisted I give them a role in the castle. And so, I did, but only with the assurance that they would always be safe within these walls.'

Cognitius leant towards her and Allura was certain the candlelight dimmed as her smile dropped into a dour expression.

'You see Allura, the woods can be the most unwelcoming of places.'

*

Half an hour later, Allura felt more wonderfully sated than she had ever been before and yet, despite her and Cognitius' best efforts, the food looked as though it had hardly been touched.

When eventually the wood gnells returned to collect what had not been eaten, Allura was determined to get a good view of them. Unfortunately, not a single one was taller than the table.

Sitting high in her chair however, she managed to catch a glimpse as they went about their business. Their skin was made of bark, as though some part of a tree had simply grown legs and walked away and each of their heads twisted in unique patterns and shapes like roots.

Allura wanted to ask how they could even see with leaves over their eyes, but then she heard them speaking what sounded like nonsense to one another in high-pitched voices and decided it was best not to even bother asking. With their branched arms and twig-like fingers they each grabbed a trolley and wheeled it out.

Safe to say I'm definitely not in England anymore, Allura thought as they left.

After she had thanked Cognitius for the meal, they moved to the fireplace where Allura collapsed onto the plump sofa. Cognitius meanwhile leant against the mantle, silently swirling a glass filled with a mysterious purple liquid in her hand.

'So… am I dead?' Allura asked bluntly, expecting that her brazenness might catch Cognitius off guard, but instead the woman simply started to chuckle.

'No. I'm afraid that would be far less complicated.'

'Then what *is* happening? How did I get here? Who are you? Why am I here? And where the hell even is here for that matter?'

Cognitius sipped her drink, then poured the rest into the fire, reigniting the flames in a purple hue as she wandered towards one of the bookcases.

'You know, I often find in my moments of crisis that a good book can provide the solution. Wouldn't you agree?' Cognitius asked, thumbing through the titles.

'Not really,' Allura replied, but Cognitius ignored her answer and plucked a book entitled *Fables No One Believes* from the shelf. Returning to her place by the fire, she opened the book precisely on page 33 and read it aloud:

Fables No One Believes
The Legend of Lucy Lummens

Once, there was a girl named Lucy Lummens, who lived in a village at the base of a mountain. The mountain was so large and so tall that the peak stretched over the trees, above the birds and far beyond the clouds.

It was said that only the bravest person in the world had ever reached the top. And that they had made their home on the peak many years ago.

In Lucy's village, winter arrived and with it came a gang of outsiders. They took the villager's homes for themselves, exhausted all of their crops and stole their hard-earned coin. After months of their pillaging, Lucy decided she'd had enough. The bandits had taken too much, yet everyone else was far too scared to stop them.

Emboldened by the suffering of her people, Lucy decided to climb the mountain to enlist the help of the bravest person in the world.

Searching the house that had once been hers, little Lucy found nothing but a threadbare rope and a pair of old climbing boots.

She began to scale the mountain, rising higher than the trees, beyond the place where the birds made their nests and through the misty clouds. There, her skin froze and the air grew thin, yet still, she did not stop on her quest.

Until finally, she reached the top.

Through the blistering snow at the peak of all things, she saw a figure by a fire.

'Are you the one?' Lucy cried out. 'The one who climbed the mountain? The one who went higher than the trees and the birds and the clouds? Who conquered the cold and challenged the wind? Are you the one who embodies courage and bravery?'

The man turned towards Lucy with a smile and said, 'No, my friend. You are.'

With that, the book slammed shut.

'That's it?' Allura asked, thoroughly unimpressed and still very much confused.

'It's enough I thought. Why? Didn't you like it?'

Wasn't exactly a page-turner, she thought.

'No, it was good I just-'

'Prefer stories with more swords and monsters, I know,' Cognitius chuckled as Allura's brow furrowed.

How did she know that?

'If you're wondering how I knew that, it's the same way I know everything else,' Cognitius said.

Okay that was really weird.

'You wanted answers, well here they are. Much like how Lucy Lummens embodied courage, I embody knowledge. You see, this castle, this forest, this entire world exists alongside the one you know, but the difference is that a lucky few of us here are chosen to be embodiments.'

'Embodiments of what?'

'Everything. Anything. If it exists in the hearts and minds of the people of Earth and influences their lives, then someone here embodies it. Forces, feelings, emotions. All of it.'

Allura stared at her vacantly, throwing her theory that this was all the product of her dying brain out the window. She knew her own mind well enough to know that it would certainly not come up with this.

'I had hoped the story might help ease you into the idea,' Cognitius said as Allura's silence became concerning.

'Alright, seriously, where am I?' Allura asked again more firmly this time. The charm of this grand place and her generous host was no longer enough to keep her calm.

'You're in Cambium, a castle in the forest lands of Orterra. In other words, you're as safe as can be.'

Fighting every urge telling her to run as fast and as far as possible, Allura nodded along, pretending she understood what Cognitius was saying as she continued to explain. One thing that did ring true to her was that Raven was the Embodiment of Deception, while the colossal man she had glimpsed leaving the room earlier was Abraham, the Embodiment of Strength.

'What about the old man in the library? He made it so I couldn't make any noise,' Allura enquired.

'That'll be Arnold. The Embodiment of Silence. I'm sorry that he did that to you. Embodying these forces have their benefits, but that man is far too short tempered.'

'And everyone here is one? An embodiment?' she asked, feeling slightly silly for even acting as though any of this could possibly be real.

'Only those fortunate enough to be chosen, the rest are born and raised here with no influence on Earth,'

Cognitius replied while Allura stood up and began pacing around the room, struggling to process the utter insanity that she was hearing.

'So, let's just say for one minute that I believe you and you are the 'Embodiment of Knowledge'. What does that mean? If you stub your toe, does someone on Earth forget everything they ever learnt?'

'Not at all. We are merely vessels for that which we embody. We need only to exist here and the people of Earth continue to live and die, build and destroy, love and learn, dream and despair. Everything that makes the human experience. Good or bad. It all comes from us.'

Finally, Allura stopped her pacing and turned on her heel to face Cognitius as she asked the question she had been too afraid to:

'But what has any of this got to do with me?'

'Well you see, when an embodiment dies, the essence of what we represent needs to continue beyond us for humanities' sake. So, it leaves our body to find a replacement. Usually it chooses someone from Orterra, but sometimes it has to look... beyond this world.'

Allura felt sick as a dreaded realisation crept in.

Is she talking about that strange light? It couldn't have... I couldn't be...

Allura's thoughts were clearly reflected on her face as Cognitius' eyes lit up.

'You my dear embody one of the most precious forces on any world.'

She can't be serious.

'The thing that keeps people reaching for the light

in the darkest of times.'

This can't be real.

'Allura Saint-May, may I be the first to welcome you to Orterra as the new...'

Please don't say it.

'...Embodiment of Hope.'

I never should have left that basement.

*

Everybody makes mistakes and Allura was certain that was all this was. A giant mistake.

No, she couldn't be the embodiment of anything, let alone hope. She didn't even believe in it. There must have been a billion better candidates on Earth.

Perhaps the essence had meant a different Allura Saint-May? One that wrote in a dream journal and had one of those 'keep calm and keep on smiling' posters on their wall?

Yes, this was all an embarrassing misunderstanding. Of that, Allura was certain, but Cognitius was not so easily convinced.

'We often find ourselves unnerved when confronted with our destiny, but yours is here, right now. You just need to have the courage to seize it.'

Those words stayed with Allura as she rested in the guest room that Cognitius had left her in. Promises of further explanations in the morning had been made, but Allura already had all the answers she needed. She was certain (as always) that she did not belong here and now she knew exactly how to escape.

'So, if I'm the new Embodiment of Hope, what

happened to the last one?' Allura had asked on the walk from Cognitius' office.

Cognitius hesitated for a moment.

'He passed away. Earlier this very day in fact.'

'Oh, I'm sorry.'

'It's the way of things I'm afraid. We Orterrans live a fair bit longer than the people of Earth, and some embodiments can stretch that even further, but nothing lasts forever. We all perish just the same in the end,' Cognitius said, leaning against a window pane as she spoke.

'Speaking of Earth,' Allura said, expertly guiding the conversation where she needed it to go as she joined her by the window, 'can I ever go back?'

'Of course, you can. In fact, there's a doorway right out there,' Cognitius said, pointing out through the turbulent rain to a crumbling tower over the castle walls.

'But you certainly don't need to worry about that tonight, you wouldn't want to go out there in a storm like this. However, I feel I must tell you that if you were to return, your connection to Orterra would be severed. You would forget all about this place and another would be chosen to replace you.'

Perfect, she thought, ignoring Cognitius' foreboding warning. All she had heard was that there was a way back. Now she simply needed to get to it.

Springing from the bed, she moved to the desk and kick-started her plan into action. Searching the drawers, she found a quill and a plain piece of paper, then quickly scrawled on it.

Tucking the resultant note into her pocket, she

searched the grand cupboard and nearly emptied it of all its fine shirts and silk dresses before finding a hooded cloak and a pair of thick leather boots which fitted her surprisingly well.

Slowly cracking the door open just enough that she could hear people shuffling around the halls, she waited until all was silent and crept beyond the door. Clinging to the shadowy areas, she gingerly traversed the corridor, stopping dead in her tracks at the sound of approaching footsteps or creaking doors.

She continued onwards like this until she reached the top of a staircase at the end of the corridor where she heard a voice coming from below. Dropping to the floor, she crawled underneath a smooth marble bench as the voice drew nearer, talking to itself in a very prim and proper accent. Allura could hear footsteps growing louder and louder until finally they appeared.

Not one person, but two.

Two identical women with tied up hair and long, neatly buttoned white coats who spoke in identical voices, passing the conversation to one another like a baton.

'It's a strange pairing really, Orville and Darnigold-'

'-he's quite a bit older than her. You would think-'

'-Evelyn wouldn't allow it-'

'-but that's love for you, it can be utterly-'

'-unpredictable. That's for sure.'

They moved closer and all Allura could see was

their equally elegant black shoes when suddenly, they stopped.

'Did you-'

'-hear something? No. What-'

'-was it? I'm not sure. Almost sounded like breathing. It was-'

'-probably just the wind through the walls. I told you how I thought I heard-'

'-whistling in your room the other day. Yes, you are-'

'-probably correct.'

With that, they continued on down the corridor. Once Allura heard the distant slam of a door, she rolled out from under the bench and made for the stairwell. With no one around to stop her, she hopped onto the curving banister and rode it all the way down to the bottom.

Despite the underlying threat of being caught, she had to admit it was fun.

Her slide led her out onto a large hexagonal courtyard that she recognised almost instantly. Looking up, she saw the familiar stone bridge she had crossed earlier that evening, perched between two staggering towers.

The courtyard was littered with horseless wagons and small metal buckets overflowing with rainwater. Pitchforks and training swords were left upright against the walls and in the centre, an abandoned target sat with an arrow embedded inches from the bullseye.

The only people in the courtyard were two guards who stood on both sides of a giant gate adorned in brown leather armour with long swords holstered to their belts. Allura secured her hood firmly over her head and walked as casually as she could towards the gate, trying to project a sense of 'I belong here' with every step.

Approaching the guards, she readjusted her posture from a slouch to a strong, confident swagger and cleared her throat to produce the poshest voice she could muster.

'Please raise the gates,' she said firmly.

The guards looked at one another in confusion, then one stepped forward. He loomed over her, the hilt of his sword level with the top of her head.

Well, this is intimidating.

'There's a terrible storm tonight lass. You don't want to be going out there.'

'It's urgent,' she said, handing him the folded note she had written, which read:

My darling Lucy,

I pray that you are doing well at Cognitius' estate and that, as one of her most esteemed guests, the staff have been treating you kindly.

I wish I was writing to you with more fortunate news, but I'm afraid your brother has fallen terribly ill. As soon as you receive this letter, please arrange a transport through the woods to us. There may not be much time so you must hurry.

Be safe my girl.

All my love, Father.

He passed the note to the other guard who inspected it further.

'I've arranged for my cousin to meet me beyond the walls. Please, my family needs me and I don't have much time,' Allura said, her eyes gleaming with false tears.

The guards nodded to one another and after a few 'be carefuls' and 'all the bests', she was on the other side. It was hard to believe that she had fooled them so easily, but as the gate closed, she thought she could hear a faint snickering behind her.

Must've been my imagination, she told herself as she moved along the edge of the castle walls.

Beams of light radiating from the castle as well as the occasional flash of lightning guided her through the night until eventually, she saw an orange glow through a thicket of nearby trees.

Only then did it dawn on her that if she wanted to reach the doorway, she would have to go directly through the woods.

Weighing up her options, she considered forgetting the entire excursion and returning to the castle with her tail between her legs. It was the safer option, the smarter one too, but Allura was rarely deterred by a little danger.

Entering through a gap in the dense collection of trees, she felt the damp grass transform into a thick mud that squished and squelched at her touch. Rain continued to fall fast and heavy, combining with the forest's smell of vegetation and spores to form a pungent yet oddly refreshing odour. She waded through the paste-like soil until the lights grew brighter and she passed into a clearing.

Then she heard the cracking of splintering wood somewhere amongst the trees.

'Is someone there?' she called out.

A poorly concealed giggle from somewhere in the dark answered her.

'Show yourself!' Allura demanded.

From behind a nearby oak tree, another giggle was followed by the appearance of a flying creature, no bigger than Allura's hand. It was humanoid in appearance, other than its wings and the tiny scales covering its entire body.

'What are you?' the creature asked in a playful tone and Allura took a few steps back as it fluttered towards her.

'I'm Allura. What are you?' she replied with a flicker of fear in her voice.

'Me? I'm a fairy. A lyte to be exact. And I didn't ask who you are silly, I asked what you are. I can smell that you're an embodiment, but what is it that you embody?' the lyte asked, hovering closer.

'Oh… hope. At least that's what Cognitius told me.'

'Oo-oo-oo, that's fun. So fun. How perfect,' the lyte said in delight, flying a few feet in front of her.

'Perfect for what?' Allura asked, taking another step back.

'For something I like to show embodiments like you. So pretty and a friend of Cognitius too? So wonderful. Would you like to see?' it asked enthusiastically.

'Okay,' Allura replied cautiously, taking a quick

reassuring look at the glow of the tower as the lyte let out an excitable 'WHEE!'

It flew upwards in a gleeful dance, flipping and weaving through the air as one of its scales began to shine an opalescent green. It continued to flip and twirl above her.

Then one by one, the rest of its scales also lit up in reds, blues, oranges, yellows and indigos. Allura's eyes struggled to keep up as it spun around the forest canopy, becoming a luminescent blur of shimmering lights, until eventually, it stopped to once again hover in front of her.

'What did you think?' it asked with a big smile across its tiny face.

'I've never seen anything quite like that,' Allura replied, feeling as though she had been infected by the lyte's intense optimism.

'SHE LIKED IT,' the lyte yelled out then whistled sharply.

With a cheer, seemingly a hundred more lytes emerged from every tree and bush around her, igniting in a similar performance of tantalising colours. They spun in a large circle above her, moving so quickly and smoothly that they became a single colourful ring, lighting up the night sky.

Allura no longer felt the rain or the cold as she became transfixed by the multicoloured performance, entirely unaware as the first lyte broke from the pack and eagerly watched her eyes widen in sheer astonishment.

The lyte continued to focus on her as she moved into the centre of the spinning circle, throwing back her hood to get a better view.

It's the most beautiful thing I've ever seen, Allura thought as the lyte licked its lips and its charming smile dropped into a sharp, toothy grin.

'SHE'S READY!' it screeched.

Suddenly, the circling lyte's descended, letting out churlish laughter as they bombed towards her.

'What are you doing?' Allura yelled as one of the creatures nipped at her hand.

She swiped it away with a cry and bolted towards the tower, weaving through the trees with the horde of diving lytes close behind her.

'I CAN SMELL THE JOY IN HER VEINS!'

'DELICIOUS JOY!'

'HER BLOOD WILL TASTE SO SWEET!'

The trees disappeared and Allura could see the remains of the tower in the centre of a field as another lyte stabbed its pointed teeth into her shoulder.

She brushed it away, only to immediately feel a similar pain in her thigh, her arms, and her leg. More and more lyte's dug into her flesh, each aching bite draining her of her will to go on.

Nearly there, she told herself. *Just a little further.*

Pushing on, she kicked and whacked at each horrible winged monster that tried to sink its teeth into her. Yet, every time she removed one, two more seemed to appear, equally eager to suck the blood from her.

If she could just reach the door, then she'd be safe. She could go back to Earth and forget all about this awful place.

With that thought in mind, she grabbed a large

stick from the ground and used it to swat at the creatures, swinging wildly around her as she continued on towards the tower.

A dozen more lytes clung to her as she approached the door, but still, she had made it. Allura grasped the handle and pushed with all her might.

But it didn't budge.

Pulling instead, she felt as though the tower had betrayed her as the door still refused to move an inch and more tiny teeth pierced her skin. Allura crumpled into a ball at the foot on the door, weakly banging against it, but there was no one inside.

There was no one to save her.

For all she knew, there wasn't even a 'doorway' in the first place.

So close. I was so close, she thought as her vision was overwhelmed by the lyte's shimmering colours and a quiet voice whispered in her ear:

'Don't worry little hope-girl, we'll send your bones to Cognitius.'

Then, in an instant, the vast spectrum of colours burnt away and Allura felt as though a wave of hands had pushed against her all at once. Shoving her and the lytes up against the door, a powerful voice bellowed:

'HALT!'

The lytes froze, some of them still recovering from the drastic blast of energy while others were simply overwhelmed with fear. A dense smoke encased the edge of the woods and a particularly brave lyte built up the courage to yell into it.

'YOU HAVE NO RIGHT TO COMMAND US

HERE!'

From the fog, Cognitius emerged with a crystal orb in her hand.

'I HAVE THE ONLY RIGHT! I RULE OVER ALL OF THE BLISS, NOT JUST THE GROUNDS OF MY CASTLE! THAT INCLUDES THESE WOODS AND THAT INCLUDES YOU! NOW LEAVE HERE AT ONCE!'

The lytes hovered awkwardly, muttering amongst one another, each looking for someone to stand up for them, but none did.

'NOW!' Cognitius commanded, and with that, they vanished into the woods. Weak and woozy, Allura tried to get to her feet, but she had been sapped of all her strength. Her body was full of pain and teeth marks as Cognitius scooped her off the ground and looked to the door.

'Homebound,' was all Cognitius had to say to trigger the shifting locks and twisting mechanisms, until at long last, the door swung on its hinges.

Couldn't have mentioned the password earlier? Allura thought as she was carried inside.

Although there were lit torches covering the place, the interior of the tower resembled an entrance hall that had long since fallen into disarray. The walls were made of cracked stone and the room was cluttered with relics of its past.

There was an overturned table, a collapsed chandelier, shattered goblets and a torn portrait of a young prince, but all of that paled in comparison to what sat in the middle of the room.

It was an enormous frame made of ancient glass

with a thin layer of some unknown turquoise liquid flowing at its centre.

The Doorway.

Cognitius tentatively placed Allura onto a large chunk of collapsed rock and pulled out a handkerchief that gleamed with a strange ointment. The old woman patted at the streaks of blood that dripped from Allura's many tiny wounds.

'I'm okay. Honestly you don't have to do that,' Allura murmured, even though the stinging was subsiding with each dab of the cloth. Thankfully, Cognitius ignored her and continued to wipe at the punctures in her skin until the hurting and even the marks themselves had disappeared entirely.

'How did you know I'd come here?' Allura asked as she sat up.

'I didn't. I just know that when you're scared you have a tendency to run away.'

'You don't know me.'

'I know you better than you might care to admit.'

There was a sharp edge to Cognitius' voice as she said those words and Allura realised that she didn't have the will to argue with her.

'Those things, they were going to kill me.'

'Oh most certainly. Lytes feast on the blood of the joyful until there is nothing left. We were fortunate there was any power left in the Eye of the Dundredge,' Cognitius said as the crystal weapon she had used turned to ash in her hand. 'But they wouldn't have had the chance to feed on you if you hadn't left your room in the first place.'

'Look, I don't belong here, okay? I don't need this

place and it certainly doesn't need me,' Allura said as her head dropped low.

With a sigh, Cognitius sat beside her.

'Then be my guest and step through the doorway. It'll take you anywhere on Earth you wish to go, you need only picture it in your mind. So, why don't you tell me, where will you go? Where is it exactly that you think you belong? Back with Mrs. Olderman? Or the Williams? Or the Graymonds?'

'No, they were all horrible.'

'On that we are agreed, but what about the Lawsons? Or the Eastgards? Or all the other perfectly fine families you ran from or pushed away?'

'Well, maybe I don't belong anywhere then,' Allura replied solemnly.

'Or maybe you belong here,' Cognitius said, offering an entirely different handkerchief to dry her eyes with. Allura gazed at the doorway, thinking about the families that hadn't loved her back and the ones she hadn't even given a chance.

'One week,' she said finally. 'I'll give this place one week, but then I'm gone.'

Cognitius agreed to her terms and they shook hands on the arrangement, but Allura had a sneaking suspicious that Cognitius had somehow got exactly what she had wanted.

*

Having spent quite some time drying herself off in her chambers, Allura slipped into a comfy set of pyjamas and sunk into the humongous bed.

54

Staring up at the skylight, she gazed at the churning clouds and listened to the pattering of thick raindrops against the glass. It calmed her racing mind and she enjoyed watching as the lightning tore the sky apart.

However, she couldn't shake the feeling that there was something off about it. Something that she wasn't able to put her finger on.

Then suddenly it hit her!

The thunder comes before the lightning here, she realised. Like a deep and rumbling warning that something terrible was on its way.

4

The boy, the girl and the marlee

That night Allura dreamt of the basement. At least it felt like the basement. She was trapped in an irrefutable blackness with no up or down, no floor or ceiling. Just her, alone in the dark.

Until suddenly, a strange rectangle of blinding light swung open, like a door burning through the void, with the vague outline of a person stood at its centre.

It was all so hazy that Allura couldn't quite make out who it was, but she had some idea.

I was so stupid to think I could ever get away, she thought, certain that Mrs. Olderman had come to teach her a lesson for thinking otherwise.

The figure held their hand out towards her, silently beckoning for her to come closer as she fought to escape, but it was no use. It felt as though she were trying to run through quicksand as some unseen force lulled her towards the light. The last thing she remembered was screaming as she plunged helplessly through the doorframe.

Then she awoke with a start, bolting upright in bed.

Her heart was racing and beads of sweat ran down her forehead as she realised that it hadn't been real. It couldn't have been, after all, none of it had made any sense.

Then she remembered where she actually was.

Orterra? Embodiments? Lytes? Wood gnells? I must still be dreaming.

A few sharp pinches to her skin later and she was forced to admit that as strange and foreign as this place may have seemed, it was undeniably real.

Dawn had come to Cambium, as it so often tended to do. Trading rain and lightning for a clear cerulean sky, beams of sunlight entered through the windows and shimmered off the golds and silvers of the room.

Allura was used to woodworm infested wardrobes and fractured mirrors, yet now she found herself in a chamber fit for royalty. After a few more minutes of savouring the softness of the mattress, she got out of bed and glanced out the window, noting that unlike the moon, the Orterran sun seemed to be equal in size to Earth's.

Rifling through the grand cupboard, she found a soft dressing gown to throw over her pyjamas and headed out into the corridor where she immediately heard the distant sounds of yelling.

The voices were muffled, but it was clear that they were screaming at one another and Allura quickened her pace as she started to make out snippets of the conversation.

'...no way...' the voice that sounded like a girl said.

'...skittering furball...' replied the voice that

sounded like a boy.

Allura continued to chase the yelling until she found herself in a rectangular room with a small banquet table at its centre and beautifully displayed tapestries lining the walls.

On one side of the table sat a boy, roughly the same age as Allura, with short black hair and thin, round glasses. Opposite him was a girl, also no older than twelve, with a sun-kissed face covered in freckles as well as long blonde hair that tucked into the various pockets of her light-blue overalls.

'YOU BETTER LEARN TO KEEP THAT THING UNDER CONTROL!' yelled the boy.

'HE'S NOT THE ONE THAT NEEDS TO LEARN HIS MANNERS!' the girl screamed back as Allura took a seat at the head of the table.

The squeaking of her chair caught their attention and they stared at her in an immediate curious silence.

'Hello,' said the girl, her voice cracking nervously.

'Yes, hello,' echoed the boy.

'Hi,' Allura said with a tentative wave of her hand.

'You're the new girl, right? Cognitius asked us to tell her when you were up,' the girl said, raising her eyebrows at the boy who looked back at her vacantly. She nodded her head towards the door and eventually he got the hint.

'Fine. I'll go get her, but everything-' he said, waving his hands over his plate, '-better still be here when I get back.'

With that, he stormed out the room.

'Why does he think you'll eat his food?' Allura asked, noting that the girl's breakfast consisted solely of brightly coloured fruit.

'Oh, he doesn't. He knows I'm not like that and besides I would never eat meat,' she said with an amused smile. Allura considered her words very carefully.

'*I'm* not going to eat it!' she said, insulted that he would even suggest such a thing.

'He wasn't talking about you either,' the girl said as she reached into one of her many pockets to pull out a ball of fuzz. Stroking it in her cupped hands, she spoke in a voice that flowed like honey: 'I don't know if you heard, but he was convinced that TibbidyBoo stole a sausage from his plate.'

'TibbidyBoo?' Allura asked as the girl opened her hands wider to show that the fluff ball had started to writhe and wriggle.

Eventually it uncurled fully, revealing itself to be a small creature with big round cheeks, four stumpy little legs, large eyes, a tiny black nose and a thin swishing tail.

'He's a marlee. I got him from Forevermores. They're cute, but they'll eat just about anything,' she said, running her hand along its hazel brown fur. It made a sweet chirping sound as she stroked it before suddenly leaping out of her grasp and darting towards the boy's unguarded plate. There was nothing the girls could do, but giggle as the creature gnawed into a piece of toast.

'I'm Ofelia, by the way, Ofelia Donnelly,' she said awkwardly, before snapping her fingers at the marlee which chirped back at her defiantly.

'I'm Allura.'

'Aalllluurraa,' Ofelia said slowly, as though she were testing how the sound felt in her mouth. 'That's a good name.'

'Thanks, and what about him?' Allura asked, gesturing towards the vacant seat where TibbidyBoo was now devouring an entire boiled egg.

'That's Noah. He's not usually quite so grumpy, he just isn't great with animals. And I think he's still a little shaken up from travelling in the storm last night.'

'Why were you travelling?'

'Apparently Cognitius needed to talk with my parents, but they wouldn't tell me what about, and Noah's parents take any excuse to visit Cambium.'

'So, you don't live here?'

'Oh no, we're from Endwood. It's still in The Bliss, but it's a good few hours ride from here. We'll be heading back later today.'

Allura felt a twinge of disappointment that they would be leaving her alone in this place with only an old woman, a walking wall of muscles, a pair of co-dependent twins and worst of all, Raven, for company.

Distracting herself from that fact, Allura decided to focus on something Ofelia had said that had captured her curiosity.

'What is 'The Bliss'?' she asked which made Ofelia's eyes go wide

'I completely forgot, you've only just got here, haven't you? Has no one shown you a map yet?' she asked as she reached into her bag to pull out a sketchpad and pencil. Shuffling closer, Ofelia turned to a blank page so Allura could see the paper as she started to draw.

The map began as two imperfect circles with one inside of the other, then Ofelia divided the inner circle into six pieces, giving each one a different label:

The Line
The Cycle
The Divide
The Bliss
The Balance
The Duality

'Each region is ruled by two counterbalances like Love and Hate, Life and Death, Faith and Doubt, Good and Evil. We're in The Bliss, so our leaders are the Embodiments of Knowledge and Ignorance, although no one has really heard from Ignorance in a long time,' she said as she filled the map with details, covering The Bliss in tiny trees and The Balance in pointed triangles.

Ignorance is bliss, Allura thought to herself as she tried to make sense of all of this before remembering that she had already met the Embodiment of Knowledge.

'Wait so Cognitius is the queen of The Bliss?'

'In a sense. Well, she's one of them at least.'

Allura played it cool and nodded her head casually, as though this were not her first time meeting royalty.

'And what's that?' she asked, pointing to the

outermost circle.

'That's the Border Ring. There are no rulers there. Ma says it's full of people with nowhere else to go.'

'So, what's beyond that?'

'Nothing but the sea. The Endless Sea.'

Allura sat back in her chair and scoffed.

'Are you alright?' Ofelia asked.

'Yeah, I'm okay, it's just that I've never even left England before, let alone Earth. This is all a bit much,' Allura explained, but she was certain that Ofelia couldn't possibly understand how she felt.

'Y'know, I've been here since I was three, but when I was old enough my parents told me that I used to live somewhere else. Some place called 'Cornwall'.'

Allura couldn't believe it.

'You're from Earth too?'

'Oh yeah, I had a whole little life there. At least that's what Cognitius told me. Apparently my birth parents and I would go to the beach all the time and watch the waves crash for hours and hours. Then I would fall asleep on my pa's shoulder to the sound of the tide coming in.'

'But if that's true, why are you here?' Allura asked, worried about the answer.

'There was an accident, or so I'm told, in one of those motorised carriages Earth people seem to love so much. It left me all alone, but then I was chosen to come here and taken in by my mum and ma.'

'I'm sorry,' Allura said solemnly.

'Don't be. I mean sometimes I wonder where I would be if I hadn't been chosen to come here.

Maybe I'd still be watching those waves, who knows? But I certainly wouldn't be here and that means I wouldn't know anything about my parents or my brother or my sister. I guess my point is, this place can seem big and scary at first, but if you give it a chance, it can feel like home.'

Allura smiled at her, feeling oddly comforted by the knowledge that they had both found their way to this place completely by accident.

She was about to thank Ofelia for telling her, but was interrupted by the sounds of approaching footsteps and TibbidyBoo scurried back into his owner's pocket as Noah re-entered the room.

'Cognitius is still talking with your parents,' he said in a huff to Ofelia, 'but she said she'll come find you when they're finished,' he addressed Allura in a much nicer tone as he sat back in his place and noticed his empty plate.

'Ofelia, where is that lovely little pet of yours?' he asked, his calm demeanour betrayed by the angry twitch in his eyes.

'Haven't a clue, but I do know that marlees love small, damp spaces so maybe you should check the dungeons,' Ofelia replied with a shrug.

Allura let out a little giggle and Noah glared at her.

'Something funny?'

'Not at all,' Allura said as Ofelia also started to laugh.

'Great, here I am starving while you two laugh your heads off,' he said, sulking into his chair. Then a thought crossed Allura's mind, the sort of thought that Mrs. Olderman would usually have discouraged and called her a 'little nuisance' for having.

But she isn't here, is she?

'No need to be so dramatic, I think I know where we can get all the food we want. It just depends on one thing,' she said.

'What's that?' asked Noah, and Allura gave a mischievous smirk.

'Whether or not you two know where the kitchens are.'

*

Ofelia must have said 'oops wrong way' at least a dozen times as she led them through the castle. They had poked their heads into three different studies, an armoury, two more libraries, an office covered in maps and charters, four bedrooms, a washroom and a room oddly filled to the brim with statues, before finally arriving at their destination.

'I knew it was somewhere around here,' said Ofelia as they entered the kitchen.

'Your memory continues to impress,' remarked Noah, 'but we really shouldn't be here. No one's meant to be in the kitchen but the chefs. If we get caught-'

'We won't,' Allura interrupted, certain that one of the bedrooms they had peered into had been occupied by a bundle of sleeping wood gnells.

The kitchen itself was enormous, with countless stoves and open fires built into the sides. Pots and pans hung from the ceiling and silver cooking utensils spilled from every drawer.

Ingredients for any meal imaginable were dotted

all around the place, but thankfully, what they were looking for was right by the door. Atop a countertop, which stretched so far into the distance that they couldn't even see the other end, sat a golden tray.

Neatly stacked on it was a tall pile of cookies, cupcakes and other chocolate covered pastries, which Allura and Ofelia immediately tucked into. TibbidyBoo picked at any crumbs they dropped and after a moment of hesitation, Noah too began to dig in.

'Fine, maybe this wasn't such a bad idea,' he admitted after his third bite of sponge cake.

'See what happens when you live a little,' Ofelia replied with a smug grin that quickly vanished as the door handle rattled.

'Someone's coming!' Noah said in a hushed panic.

'HIDE!'

Noah and Ofelia crammed themselves into two empty cabinets, shutting the doors behind them, while Allura ducked under the counter and held her breath.

The door opened and she heard two sets of footsteps against the hard-stone. One was light, as though hardly touching the floor at all, while the other was loud and heavy.

'Close it,' said the man who she immediately recognised as Raven, and the door clicked shut.

'I fear he's grown suspicious of me. There are eyes watching every move I make. I think he may know what I am... what I've done. I know he was your friend and you may have reservations, but I need your support on this.'

Who is he talking to?

'Remember, no one else can know. Not until the moment is right and all is certain. I simply need a little more time,' Raven continued.

They lingered in the room for a while longer before opening the door to leave. Crawling on her hands and knees, Allura moved to the corner of the counter and popped her head around to catch a feint glimpse of a large pair of scuffed leather boots with a gold lining along the seam.

She could not see who they belonged to, but the ragged state of them told her they were definitely not Raven's. Then the door slammed shut behind them and her new companions emerged from their hiding spots.

'Did you hear that?' Allura whispered.

'I didn't hear anything,' Noah said shakily.

'We all heard it,' Ofelia replied, giving him a nudge.

'Fine, but it's really none of our business,' Noah admitted.

'That depends on what it was about.'

'Whatever it was, I don't think Raven would like that we heard it,' suggested Ofelia.

Suddenly, a shared gasp escaped them as the handle rattled again. Scrambling to get back into the cabinet, Noah was only halfway inside when the door swung open. Allura and Ofelia were frozen with fear, but released a sigh of relief as Cognitius entered, looking not the least bit surprised to see them.

'Your majesty,' Ofelia said with an imperfect curtsy.

Was I supposed to do that too?

'There's no need for that,' Cognitius said before turning her attention to Allura. 'Apologies for my lateness, my business with Ofelia's parents went on a little longer than planned.'

She eyed the tray of baked goods on the counter and said:

'Once you've finished with that, why don't you meet me on the balcony? It's down the corridor and to the left.' Turning to leave, she stopped mid-way and looked back. 'Oh, and Master Tanden, I believe your father is searching for you.'

'Thank you, ma'am,' Noah said, his voice echoing inside the cabinet.

He backed out of his wooden confines after Cognitius left, his face blushed with embarrassment as he climbed to his feet.

'I wasn't going to say anything before but, a private audience with Cognitius? You must be special,' he said.

'What do you think it's about?' Ofelia asked, shoving a croissant into her mouth. Allura wasn't sure, but she was too focused on Raven's suspicious conversation to think about it.

All she knew for certain was that she had lost her appetite.

*

'That was fun,' Ofelia said as they escorted Allura down the hall.

'Even if we did nearly get into trouble,' added Noah.

'That's why it was fun,' Ofelia laughed, but Allura stayed quiet.

Say something, she told herself, finding it impossible to find the right words.

'Anyway, you should come visit Endwood some time,' Ofelia continued with Noah nodding in agreement.

'No, I mean yes,' Allura stammered. 'I mean I'm going home in a week so-'

'A week? That's ages,' Ofelia said enthusiastically.

Don't get too attached, Allura reminded herself as she told them she would be far too busy to come and visit.

'Oh, well it was really nice meeting you anyway,' said Ofelia with a disappointed lull in her voice. With that, they walked away, leaving Allura at the doors of the balcony.

She would have much preferred to have spent the rest of the day exploring the castle's many rooms and secrets with them. But instead, she simply allowed them to vanish down a stairwell without telling them how much she had enjoyed their company.

Once they were gone, she walked out onto the wide balcony and found Cognitius stood against the railing, holding a silver spyglass up to one eye. Allura moved slowly, stealthily, trying to stay as quiet as possible so as to have the element of surprise for once.

'What do you see?' Cognitius asked, as though

already mid-conversation.

Really? How did she do that?

Abandoning her shallow breaths and light footsteps, Allura moved to the railing and took in the view with the crisp clarity that comes when the sun shines after rainfall.

The woodlands seemingly stretched on forever with ancient trees standing tall on the rolling hills that warped the horizon, like brigades of dutiful sentinels grazing the rising sun.

'I just see trees,' Allura replied, simply and plainly.

'Is that all?' Cognitius asked, offering her the spyglass. Allura peered through it, at first seeing nothing but black smudges before realising she had accidentally covered the other end with her hand.

Looking again, she focused on the woods and spotted something big and furry darting from tree to tree. She wondered what it could be as Cognitius adjusted the magnifier with her hand.

'A bit to the left, my dear,' Cognitius said, correcting her course. When she stopped, Allura could see a winding dirt road that stretched from the very top of the woods, all the way down to the castle gates.

'That path runs through the entirety of this region to every town and village in The Bliss, including the place your predecessor lived,' Cognitius explained as Allura removed the spyglass and looked up at her inquisitively.

'Predecessor?'

'The Embodiment of Hope before you. His name

was Horas. He was a good man, but he left no heir. No living spouse or children and no will to dictate who he wanted his belongings to go to. As such, our traditions demand that all that was his, is now yours.'

Allura's heart raced once more. Everything she had ever owned had belonged to someone else, but never quite like this.

'Horas had a house in a town a few hours from here and if you wish, I can have my outer-guard, Abraham, escort you there. I trust him with my life and he would ensure you arrive safely. I know you like to think you can look after yourself, but I would have him stay in town until the end of your visit. Then, in six days he will return you here as per our agreement.' Cognitius said as she gently placed her hand on Allura's shoulder.

'However, I want you to know, that you also have the option of remaining here. The room you stayed in last night can be yours, permanently, if you would like.'

Allura considered her options.

While one held the opportunity of freedom, it also came without the guarantee of safety, and having just experienced the most perfectly pleasant morning of her life, Allura felt a strong pull towards Cognitius' offer of staying put.

Then a crucial question popped into her head.

'Where is this house?'

'As I said, it's a small town a few hours from here.'

'But what's it called?'

'Endwood,' Cognitius replied and with that,

Allura had made her choice.

*

She hadn't thought it would take long to pack her things, given the underwhelming lack of them however, Cognitius had insisted that Allura was supplied with the absolute essentials.

Her case was filled to the brim with clothes pulled from the wardrobes of the guest room as well as a comb, a toothbrush, plenty of snacks, a small lantern and some silver coins which Allura assumed were money (although she was told that she had not inherited a lot of it).

In the courtyard sat three horse-led carriages, one for her and one each for Ofelia and Noah's families. Dragging her absurdly heavy suitcase across the cobblestones of the busy courtyard, Allura started to take notice of the bizarre clothes everyone was wearing.

It was as though she had stepped back through time into some alternate past. Ofelia's overalls and Cognitius' robes had been one thing, but the casual way people wore colourful flowing capes and tight leather tunics was something else to behold entirely.

Distracted by the sight of them, Allura almost didn't notice as the gargantuan man she had seen the night before approached her.

The Embodiment of Strength, she reminded herself as she looked up at him.

Blocking her path to the carriages, he silently held out one of his hands to her, but she was mesmerised by his sheer enormity and continued to stare up at him absentmindedly.

'Um, hello? You're Abraham, right?' she asked nervously, but he didn't reply.

Racked with uncertainty, she offered him the handle of the suitcase and he took it from her, lifting it as though it were filled with feathers. Effortlessly, he placed it on the back of her carriage, then squeezed into the front, tucking a tall object concealed in brown cloth beside him. He then leant forwards and softly stroked the horse's manes.

Odd guy, she thought as familiar voices called from behind her:

'ALLURA! ALLURA!'

She turned to see Noah and Ofelia sprinting over.

'We spoke to our parents and they said we can ride with you to Endwood,' Ofelia said enthusiastically.

'If that's okay with you?' Noah interjected, but Allura was quiet, trying to hide her excitement.

'Of course,' she said flippantly, leaning against the carriage in a very cool and unbothered kind of way. The pair piled into the carriage excitedly and immediately started arguing about something or other, although Allura was too distracted speaking to Cognitius to pay any attention.

'Should you change your mind, Abraham can bring you straight back here.'

'I know.'

'Good. It's important you understand Allura, that whatever happens next is entirely up to you.'

Unsure what to say, Allura reached into her pocket and pulled out the spyglass.

'Sorry, I meant to give this back to you.'

'You keep it. Use it to remind yourself that wherever you are, there is always more to be seen.'

'Thank you,' Allura said, returning the device into her pocket.

'Safe travels Allura Saint-May, I will see you soon.'

'Goodbye Cognitius,' she replied, placing one foot onto the step of the carriage as a flutter in her heart and a churning in her gut told her that she was making a terrible mistake.

Maybe I should stay, she started to think when Cognitius grasped her hand.

'Allura,' the kindly old woman said with a serious expression. 'Hope is not important because it is easy. It is hope's endurance in the hardest of times that gives it power.'

Allura nodded, pretending she understood why she had told her that before entering the carriage and closing the door behind her.

Then, coach by coach, they left the courtyard with Allura, Noah, Ofelia and Abraham at the back of the convoy. As they passed through the gates, Allura took one last look at the castle, admiring the long-running walls and spiralling towers.

As she did, she noticed a small, dark shape stood on one of the bridges. It was a figure she recognised immediately. Pulling out the spyglass, she pointed it in his direction and expected to see Raven's obnoxious face glaring back at her.

But when she peered through the lens, there was nothing to see but an empty bridge and a remnant of black smoke hanging in the air.

5

The road to Endwood

The

route

through

the

woods

was

filled

with

constant

turns…

…but it was during one of the brief moments in which the path remained unwound that the trio in the back coach came up with a little game. It required each player to name an animal that began with the same letter and it had three simple rules:

1. Do NOT repeat another player's answer.
2. You MUST name an animal before the coach has fully turned the next bend.
3. NO MADE UP ANIMALS!

However, by the letter 'C' Allura had realised the game's fatal flaw; almost all of Ofelia and Noah's answers sounded made up to her.

'Chicken,' said Allura.

'Crawlion,' said Ofelia.

'Caprimagus,' said Noah, seconds before the carriage twisted around a bend.

'Camel.'

'Clawing kross.'

'Choi-' Noah started to say all too late as they completed the next turn. The girls burst into laughter while Noah folded his arms up to his chest in a great big strop, something he would do many more times before the game's end.

'That's not fair, I was just about to say 'choir whale',' he complained.

'Oh cheer up, you might win the next one,' Ofelia said, grinning from ear to ear.

'What's a choir whale?' Allura asked.

'They're these huge creatures that reshape lakes with their songs,' Ofelia explained eagerly. 'Some people reckon they're the reason The Divide has so many lakes to begin with.'

'Oh right,' Allura said, struggling to even imagine how big those lakes would have to be.

'Now I have a question for you,' Ofelia said, leaning forwards so that Allura had no other option but to gaze directly into the girl's bright blue eyes as she said in a cold and serious tone:

'What is a camel?'

*

They continued to play for a few miles of the journey, until eventually Noah and Allura had named nearly every animal they could think of (although Ofelia seemed more than ready for another round). The game was imperfect and not particularly exciting, but Allura enjoyed it nonetheless.

As it came to an end, Ofelia began to wriggle uncomfortably.

'My legs are killing me,' she said, 'it's so cramped in here.'

'Just do what I'm doing,' Allura replied, lying on her seat and allowing her legs to hang out the open window. Ofelia tried mimicking her, but didn't seem to take Noah into account.

'Sure, don't mind me,' he said, pushing her back into her spot.

'*Fine.* I'm going to ask Abraham if he would stop for a minute so we can stretch our legs,' Ofelia said before crawling towards the hatch that opened into the driver's seat.

'So, *you* can stretch *your* legs I think you mean,'

Noah said with a shake of his head.

'Don't you want a bit of fresh air?' Allura asked him.

'Fresh air? I don't mind. The outdoors? I don't mind. But the woods? No, thank you. Have you seen the things that are out there? At school, Mrs. Duke always says that there's nothing but trouble waiting in those woods.'

She might have a point, Allura thought, remembering her encounter with the lytes the night before.

'Doesn't it get boring though, living so safely?' she asked and Noah tutted, not realising that she was genuinely asking.

'I don't need adventure during the day, I get my fill when I'm asleep,' he replied.

'What do you mean?'

'Did Ofelia not tell you? I'm the Embodiment of Dreams.'

'You are?' she asked with a shocked rise in her tone.

'You don't have to be quite so surprised about it.'

'Oh no, I only meant, why you?'

'My mum embodies slumber and my dad embodies imagination, so I guess it made sense really.'

More sense than bravery at least, Allura thought before asking:

'Does that mean you have a power then? Like Arnold and Raven?'

'Erm, sort of.'

'Can I see it?' she asked with the urgency of

someone who couldn't believe that he hadn't mentioned this at the start of the trip.

'It's not really something I can show off,' he replied nervously, pushing up his glasses.

'Oh,' Allura sighed, terribly disappointed as she slumped back into her seat and looked out at the lightly frosted trees, wondering if she had a power as well.

Maybe I can breathe fire or walk through walls or talk to animals?

But before she allowed herself to get carried away, she brushed those thoughts aside, certain that anything special that came with being the Embodiment of Hope would never present itself to her. After all, she was still entirely convinced that this whole thing was some sort of cosmic misunderstanding.

'So, does this happen a lot?' she asked Noah. 'The wrong person getting picked.'

'Who told you you're the wrong person? There must be something pretty special about you to get all this attention from Cognitius,' he replied earnestly while Ofelia's head joined the rest of her body back inside the carriage.

'He says we can stop at the next straight bit of road,' she reported back.

'He talks?' Allura asked.

'In a way. What were you two chatting about?'

'Noah was just telling me what he embodies.'

'He hasn't been going on about the 'Subconscia' again, has he?'

Noah opened his mouth to bite back, but Allura

was quick to cut the impending argument off at the legs.

'What about you Ofelia? You said you were brought here from Earth like me, so you must embody something too, right?'

'Yes, I'm the Embodiment of Forgetfulness, which is pretty funny I think because I actually have quite a good memory,' she said, her elbow slipping as she tried to lean against the open window. 'When it comes to certain things at least,' she added.

They came to a stop a few minutes later and stepped out to see Abraham giving a special signal to the other drivers, telling them that all was well and that they would catch up later.

The rest of the carriages continued onwards. Although they were too far away for Allura to get a good look at any of them, she watched as Noah's father and mother poked their heads out of the front carriage to tell them to stay safe. Meanwhile, two women blew kisses to Ofelia from the carriage behind.

Once they had disappeared around a bend, Abraham dropped from the driver's seat and held out five fingers.

A countdown.

They all nodded and Abraham went to tend the horses.

'There aren't any lytes around here, right?' Allura asked, her skin still sore from the night before.

'During the day? No chance,' Ofelia replied.

'Alright then, shall we have a look around?'

'No. I think we should stay right here,' Noah said

sharply.

'Okay then, we'll be back in five minutes,' Ofelia replied, pulling Allura away from the carriage.

'Fine,' he grumbled stubbornly.

Allura was unsure if it was just the time of day or the distance from the castle, but she noticed a cold chill had seeped in, turning the fallen leaves hard and crisp. With crunches and crackles, the girls ran through piles of them before stopping at a spot just out of sight of the carriage. Ofelia began pushing the leaves together into a tall stack at the base of a tree then climbed up and perched herself on the thickest branch.

'Watch this,' she said as she reached into her pocket and pulled out TibbidyBoo. The sleeping marlee's eyes flickered open as Ofelia placed him on the branch beside her.

Dazed and confused, he took in his new surroundings and his ears pricked up as he spotted the pile of leaves below. Then an excitable chirp shot through the woods as he dived off the branch. Allura instinctively reached out to catch him, but she was too slow and the leaves shot up into the air as TibbidyBoo disappeared into the muck.

A terrible moment of uncertainty passed, but soon the leaves started to shake and the funny little creature emerged from the pile and scuttered back up the tree trunk, only to jump once again.

Then again and again and again.

The girls applauded and giggled at his acrobatic dives, until eventually Ofelia scooped him back into her arms.

'Very impressive,' Allura said, checking over her shoulders to make sure that no one was eavesdropping as she leant closer to the tree and spoke in a quiet tone.

'I know Noah asked us not to bring it up, but what do *you* think Raven was talking about back in Cambium?'

'You're still thinking about that?'

'I can't *stop* thinking about it.'

'Why?' Ofelia asked as she descended from the tree.

'Because, when people have secret little meetings like that it's usually not a good thing and I already didn't trust Raven.'

'Nobody trusts Raven, he's the Embodiment of Deception for Seldar's sake! That's why Cognitius practically had to force the regent of The Balance to make him his conferant.'

'Conferant?' Allura asked.

'His second in command.'

'Why would Cognitius do that?'

'Nobody knows, but they say Orville really wasn't happy about it.'

'What else do they say about Raven?'

'Not much. He's a pretty secretive guy, but there is a rumour that he fought for Malvus during the war. I mean that happened way before I was even born, but I still hear people talking about it now.'

What war? Allura wanted to ask, but before she had the chance, the hairs on her arm stood up and a dreadful shiver shot across her spine.

From somewhere in the distance, a loud roar tore

through the woods.

TibbidyBoo shrieked, hopping out of Ofelia's hands and rushing back up the tree.

'That didn't sound good,' Allura remarked, trying not to let Ofelia hear the fear in her voice.

'It was probably just a scribblefly. They make sounds like that to scare off predators, but they're no bigger than a button and just as harmless,' Ofelia said dismissively, snapping her fingers at TibbidyBoo.

Then they heard another roar, louder than the first. Closer.

'TIB! GET DOWN RIGHT NOW! I'M NOT KIDDING!' Ofelia demanded.

We need to go, Allura thought as Ofelia grasped her hand:

'What do we do?'

She sounded terrified as the thumps of footsteps beat in the distance. Allura glanced in the direction they had come, certain that if she ran now, she would make it back to the carriage in time.

Then she looked at Ofelia, recognising the helpless fear in her eyes.

'Just be ready to run,' Allura replied as she rolled up her sleeves. Digging her nails into the rough bark, she climbed the tree with urgency. Boosting herself higher and higher, she quickly reached the branch that TibbidyBoo was perched on and started to crawl along it. She was only a few feet from the frightened marlee when she accidentally looked down.

It didn't look this high up from the down there, she thought as her body turned rigid in the grips of the same fear she had felt on the bridge the night before.

Clinging to the branch for dear life, Allura shut her eyes tight and focused on what she knew she had to do. Inch by inch, she shuffled further along the branch and stopped at a point where it became too thin to support her.

Then, blindly reaching in the direction of TibbidyBoo's chirping, Allura stretched her arm out until she felt the marlee's fur brushing against her fingers, but still just out of her reach.

'Here boy. HERE BOY!'

'MIND OUT THAT HE DOESN'T SPARK!' Ofelia shouted from below.

'WHAT?' Allura called back, but it was already too late.

TibbidyBoo let out another small chirp and a tiny snap of electricity sparked at the tip of one his ears. From there it bounced from one ear to the other and before Allura could blink, it had ran down the rest of the marlee's body like a rolling wave.

In an instant, its velvety fur turned rigid with static energy. Allura tried to grab him, but the prickling fur made it feel as though she were grasping a cactus.

Oh forget this, she thought, quickly changing tactics.

'I'm going to shake him loose and when he falls, you catch him,' she said, peeking out of one eye as she started to pull the branch up and down, up and down, up and down.

TibbidyBoo's tiny claws dug into the wood, but he soon found that his resolve was not nearly as strong as Allura's.

Finally, his grip loosened and he was catapulted

from the branch.

Helplessly falling through the air end over end, the wind rushed against his fur, flattening his prickly hair as Ofelia jumped into action. But he was moving too fast, hurtling towards the ground at such a speed that there was no time for her to do anything but watch in horror.

'NO!' they both screamed.

Suddenly, a pair of hands wrapped around the marlee, scooping him out of the air.

Confused and bewildered, Noah Tanden stared at the wind-swept furball he had caught. With no idea what was going on, Noah burst into laughter at the sight of the funny little creature and its matted hair.

Then he looked up.

Allura watched a paleness engulf him as a low growling sound rose from behind her. She turned her head very slowly to see the cause of his peaky complexion.

The beast that stood before them shook violently, filled with unbridled rage like a nightmare made real, with two blood-red pupils filling each of its eyes. It was the shape of a monstrous wolf, but the size of a lion, with sharp tusks jutting from its mouth, horrible mangled ears and a snout that drooped, as though it was barely clinging onto the rest of its disfigured face.

'Nobody move,' Ofelia said sharply, 'it's a tearer.'

The beast began to prowl, rubbing its nose against trees and bushes.

'Shouldn'twerun?' Allura asked from her perch, barely moving her lips.

'No. They can't see very well in daylight and judging by the state of this one's snout, I doubt it can smell us. If we stay still, it might not even know we're here.'

And so, they stood, still as statues while the tearer prowled around them, not quite able to see them or catch their scent. Then, from her position in the trees, Allura felt a bead of sweat trickle down her forehead.

She held out her hand to catch the droplet, but it slipped through her fingertips, falling into a puddle on the floor with a splash.

The tearer sprinted towards the sound, snarling and clawing in a mad frenzy and when it stopped, it turned its head to look directly at Noah, or more specifically, at the wriggling creature in his hand.

'Stop,' Noah whispered to the marlee in a desperate voice, but it only seemed to squirm even more in his palm. The beast slowly crept towards them, dropping low on its haunches as it approached.

Allura didn't know a lot about animals, especially ones from other worlds, but even she could tell it was preparing to pounce.

This is a really stupid idea, she thought.

'HEY, OVER HERE!' she yelled, waving her arms wildly until she had drawn the tearer's full attention.

The creature lunged furiously at Allura's dangling legs and she scrunched them close to her chest as its razor-sharp claw slashed against the soles of her shoes. In its frustration, the tearer let out another deafening roar and the next thing Allura knew it was at the trunk of the tree, sinking its claws into the bark and shimmying its way up towards her. Allura moved further along the branch, only to hear the cracking of wood beneath her.

Then, with a swoosh of air, she tumbled to the ground, hitting the forest floor hard and fast.

Allura was stunned for a moment and found herself glaring up at the tangled web of tree branches along the forest canopy until her senses returned to her and she rolled onto her front.

Crawling frantically through the dirt and leaves, she failed to find her footing against the slippery mud as she heard a sickening thud behind her. She flipped once again onto her back, only to see an array of jagged teeth and saliva approaching her.

I should've gone back to Earth when I had the chance, she thought, but it was too late for that. Much too late.

There wasn't even time for her to scream before it leapt at her. And then...

Crack!

The beast collapsed against a tree.

Allura sat frozen in terror, uncertain of what had just happened.

Then in clearer focus, she saw Abraham wielding a long war hammer. The handle was composed of a dark wood while the head was made of some rusted metal and Abraham held it as though it were an extension of his own being.

On weakened legs, the tearer rose to its feet and glared at the man through one hanging eye. It roared once again, except now with a hoarse throat that sounded like it was gargling nails. The sound frightened Allura to her core, yet Abraham stood unshaken.

Calmly and purposefully, he pounded the hammer against the ground, once, twice, three times.

The ugly creature flinched with each thwack of the weapon, its patchy fur standing on end as it motionlessly watched him.

Then, with a fourth and final crack of Abraham's hammer, the tearer mewled softly and retreated into the forest. Large hands wrapped around Allura's body as she was scooped off the ground and planted back onto her feet.

'Th-Thank you,' she managed to say, but Abraham simply lifted his hand to show a single remaining outstretched finger.

One minute left.

Without another word between them, he walked off to the carriage as Allura spotted Noah and Ofelia stood amongst the trees, equally as shocked as her. She noticed that Noah had a steely look in his eyes.

I can't blame him if he's angry, it was my stupid idea to go into the woods in the first place, she thought as he strode towards her with a worrying determination.

Allura looked to Ofelia for any clue of what was about to happen, but there was nothing either of them could do to stop him as he opened his arms wide and wrapped them around her in a strong embrace.

'Thank you,' he whispered, 'I thought I was done for. You saved my life.'

Huh, she realised. *I guess I did.*

Allura had never really enjoyed school. In her experience the lessons were boring, the teachers were strict and the other kids were cruel, but even she found Ofelia's lecture on tearers to be genuinely interesting.

According to her, it was very rare for tearers to be found in those woods as their usual home was deep in the caves of The Balance.

'Then why was that one all the way out here?' Allura asked.

'I can only guess that something happened to its den, forcing it out,' Ofelia explained. Which of course rose the question:

What is out there that could possibly scare a creature like that?

They didn't say anything for a while, each of them picturing monsters bigger and meaner than the one they had just encountered.

'I bet you two wish you'd never got in this stupid carriage with me,' Allura said.

'Maybe a little,' Ofelia joked with a wry smile.

'Not at all, although I certainly wish *someone* hadn't insisted on stretching their legs,' Noah replied. As he and Ofelia pulled ghoulish faces at one another, Allura recalled a question she had wanted to ask them before all the excitement.

Now felt as good a time as any.

'Why did you want to come with me?' she asked, trying to make it seem as though the thought had only just occurred to her.

'Because you seemed like you could do with some friends,' Ofelia admitted.

'And we know the feeling,' Noah added, their answer lifting a great weight off Allura's chest. 'And for the record, I actually don't regret getting out of the carriage. Don't get me wrong it was terrifying and I never want to do it again, but seeing you and Abraham take that thing on was pretty amazing.'

'Don't forget when you caught TibbidyBoo,' Allura added.

'That reminds me, where is he?' asked Ofelia.

'He's here,' Noah said sheepishly, as he revealed the sleeping marlee tucked snugly in his arms.

'Would you look at that, you two made peace,' Allura said, mockingly.

'Hardly,' he replied as he passed TibbidyBoo to Ofelia. 'Don't forget, he did nearly get us all killed.'

'For which I really am very sorry,' Ofelia repeated for the umpteenth time.

'Don't worry, it's only the third time I've nearly died in the last two days,' Allura said, only half-joking.

'Maybe we need a pact then, just for the week that you're here,' Noah said.

'A pact?' Allura and Ofelia asked simultaneously.

'You know, like a promise we all make to look out for each other.'

'That's actually a very good idea,' Ofelia said enthusiastically as Allura continued to think it over.

'Great,' said Noah, sticking his arm into the centre of the coach and promising to look out for his friends. Ofelia then also promised to do the same as she added her hand on top of his.

Allura hesitated for a moment before softly sighing to herself.

Oh, why not? It's only for a few days.

'I promise,' she said, placing her hand onto the top of the pile and unknowingly sealing their fates.

6

Remains of the dead

By the time Allura, Noah and Ofelia's carriage caught up with the others, they were passing through an archway of tangled branches with the word 'Endwood' spelled out in flowers across it.

One the coaches parked in the stables and its horses were released out into the paddock, while the other stopped on the road. Its door swung open and a tall woman with heavy eyes and messy auburn bed-head stepped out. She stumbled for a moment, like a fawn taking its first steps, then stretched upwards and let out a long, drawn-out yawn.

Following her was a man dressed in smart clothes with a big round face, who was sketching furiously into a book. Allura was sure that there was something familiar about him, but she couldn't quite place it.

Hastily throwing his drawing pad back into the carriage, the man then ran towards Noah with a bellowing laugh and hoisted him into the air in a bear-hug.

'Alright then my boy, this is your stop. I'll be seeing you in a couple of days, okay? You look after your mother for me,' he said.

'I will,' Noah responded as his feet returned to the ground, feeling very self-conscious in front of his new friend. Only then, as the two stood side by side, did Allura realise why she had recognised the man.

He was, in almost every way, an older double of the boy she had just spent the last three hours with. As fathers and sons went these two could not have been more alike, sharing the same shade of dark brown eyes, the same big ears, the same thin glasses and the exact same short black hair.

However, the most obvious difference between them was their height and size, and whilst Mr. Tanden was hardly a tall man, he was a far sight wider than his son.

'Where's your dad going?' Allura asked as Mr. Tanden walked back towards his carriage.

'He's been helping plan the wedding for Lord Rutherford and Lady Dormé up in Highdenhome. Apparently, they wanted a 'touch of imagination' for the big day,' Noah replied, still overcome with embarrassment.

'Can't say I blame them, Elliott did such a wonderful job at our ceremony,' said one of the women emerging from the other coach.

She was a particularly petite woman with ivory skin, prominent cheekbones and beautiful brown hair which was tied neatly into a braid with violet ribbons.

'It was an incredible day, as I'm sure Darnigold and Orville's will be. Although, I wouldn't be surprised if theirs was a tad more extravagant,' the woman said in an Irish lilt.

Introducing herself as Ofelia's mother, Lydia Donnelly shook Allura's hand while Ofelia jumped out of the carriage and bolted towards them.

'Ma, you'll never guess what happened!' she exclaimed.

Please don't tell her, Allura wanted to say.

'After you and mum rode off, we went into the woods...'

Just stop there.

'...and we ran into a tearer!'

Now you've done it.

'WHAT?' Lydia's small lips dropped into a dreadful frown.

'It was unbelievable. It tried to eat Noah, but then Allura distracted it,' Ofelia said, not noticing the growing concern on her mother's face.

'And where was Abraham during all this excitement?' Lydia asked, trying to spot him amongst the coaches. The features of her face seemed to become more than just defined, but angular, as though pointed and sharp.

Ofelia would have unwittingly continued to condemn Abraham with her story if Allura had not quickly interrupted.

'He was the one who scared it off actually. I wouldn't like to think what would have happened if he hadn't been with us the whole time,' she said, nudging Ofelia.

'Oh, well thank the gods he was there then,' Lydia said, releasing her tension in a single breath as she held Ofelia tight.

Moments later, they were all waving goodbye as

the last carriage rolled down the road. Although Noah pretended not to care, Allura noticed his grip tightening around his mother's hand. Once the coach was nothing more than a dot in the distance, Ofelia started looking around, searching for something or someone.

'Where's Mum?' she asked Lydia.

'She went straight to the house with Cam and Abby to get lunch started,' her mother replied, before turning her attention to the rest of them. 'You're welcome to join us if you'd like?'

It took Allura a second to realise that the invitation had been extended to her as well as Noah and his mother.

'I erm-' Allura muttered uncertainly.

'Oh, you have to come,' Ofelia pleaded.

Well, I can't seem to spot Abraham anyway, she thought, only then realising that he and her suitcase had seemingly vanished.

'If you're sure you wouldn't mind,' Allura said.

'Not at all,' Lydia replied as she looked to Noah, only to see his mother still staring absentmindedly down the road. 'Patricia? Can I tempt you with some tea?'

The question hung in the air with no answer to meet it.

'Mum!' Noah said sharply, snapping his mother back into the moment.

'I'm so sorry, what was that?' Patricia asked with a rattle of her head.

'Tea, Mum. They invited you for some tea.'

'Oh! Better not I think. I might go have a little lie

down actually. Those trips always take it out of me, but thank you anyway,' Patricia replied before walking off wearily towards town.

'I ought to go with her, she can get into all sorts of trouble when she drifts around like that,' Noah said before rushing to be by his mother's side. Meanwhile, Allura followed Ofelia and Lydia to their house.

The walk from the stables was short, but Ofelia still found time to identify at least a half-dozen different birdcalls on the way. However, when they did arrive, Allura had to take a moment to marvel at the sight before her.

They had made their home in an old windmill, with a smaller rectangular building covered in lightly chipped blue paint and streams of dark green ivy attached to it.

A brick chimney spat out smoke from the building's tiled roof, while the countless windows ensured every room remained light and airy at all times.

Ofelia pointed to a small oval window that sat above the spinning slatted blades at the very top of the house.

'That's my room. Come on, I'll show you,' she said and Allura followed her inside, noticing as they ran in that the hall was drowning in deep green garlands, bowls of red berries, high hung wreathes, wintery paintings and many other festive-looking ornaments.

I guess they have Christmas here too, she figured as they arrived in the kitchen where a woman in a puff-sleeved blouse and a long skirt leant against the worktop.

Her face was much softer than Lydia's and Allura admired her hair, similar to her own in terms of its curls and volume, but much more shaped and styled.

Rays of light cascaded into the room, shining against the ruby gem that hung from a thin chain around her neck and giving her bronze skin a glowing radiance.

'There you are,' she said with a broad and beautiful smile, her voice somewhere between a cheerful sing-song and a gentle lullaby.

'Mum, we saw a tearer,' Ofelia repeated and Allura wanted to forcibly clamp her mouth shut, but Faye didn't seem to share Lydia's concern. In fact, she seemed to be the exact opposite of concerned.

'You did? A fully grown one? Did it have all four pupils yet?' she asked, her smoky grey eyes alight with curiosity.

'I'd imagine they didn't have time to count while running away from the monster, my love,' Lydia answered sternly from the doorway.

'Of course, yes, because everything that lives in the woods is a monster,' she replied, winking at the two girls.

'Not everything, just the ones that try to eat our daughter,' Lydia said in annoyance, as though she were talking to a mischievous child.

'Well can you blame them,' Faye said with a cheeky smile.

'Never mind that, where's my journal? I need to fill it in while it's all still fresh in my head,' Ofelia said pressingly, but neither Faye nor Lydia knew the answer.

She rushed through the kitchen and up a set of spiralling metal stairs. This left Allura to awkwardly follow after her, stopping at the foot of the steps to clear her throat.

'I like your hair,' she told Faye.

'I was about to say the same thing,' she replied and Allura smiled shyly before hurrying up the staircase, stopping in her tracks halfway up as she heard the mention of her name in the kitchen below.

'So that's her? The one we were warned about?' Faye asked.

'Yes,' Lydia replied.

'What do you think?'

'She seems like a sweet girl and I think Ofelia's rather fond of her.'

There was a lull in their conversation after that, a point at which an invisible tide of tension rolled in. Allura continued to wait silently, until finally, Faye could not stop herself from saying:

'You know, I'd be lying if I said I wasn't worried about her in that place all on her own.'

'Abraham will keep an eye on her.'

'I know, but perhaps we could ask her if she'd prefer to-'

'Cognitius made it very clear that this is the way it has to be. We're not even supposed to be talking to her,' Lydia said pointedly and Allura could picture the cold edge returning to her face.

'That doesn't mean I have to like it,' replied Faye.

Allura wanted to stay and hear more when a

squeaky voice called out from the top of the steps.

'Who you?'

Looking up, she saw that the voice belonged to a small girl in blue pyjamas clutching what looked to be a toy pig with a single horn jutting out of its head.

Carefully, so as to not make too much noise and reveal that she had been listening the whole time, Allura climbed the steps to meet the girl at the landing.

'Who you?' she repeated.

'I'm Allura. Ofelia's friend.'

'Why?'

I don't know, she thought, still not entirely sure how she had ended up here.

But before she could answer, the thumping of Ofelia's feet rattled another set of steps above her.

'Abigail, what're you doing? You're meant to be napping,' Ofelia said as she ran down before picking the little girl up and returning her to her bed.

'Sorry about that,' Ofelia said to Allura as she closed the door to her sister's bedroom. 'I hope she didn't bother you too much. When my parents told me they were adopting the Embodiment of Curiosity, I was expecting a few questions here and there, but it is literally all the time with her.'

'So, your whole family are embodiments?' Allura asked as they hurried up the next set of stairs.

'Only me and my siblings. It's how we all ended up together. Each of us were brought here from Earth without homes or people to care for us. So Mum and Ma took us in and made us a family,' Ofelia explained as they entered her bedroom.

It was a spacious circular room with rustic oak floorboards, although they were hard to notice amongst the piles of half-legible notes and incomplete parchment scattered around everywhere.

Drawings and sketches were plastered along the curving walls, while origami butterflies and paper snowflakes dangled overhead. They hung from zig-zagging beams across the ceiling, the tops of which had been made into a nest of pillows and twinkling lights.

Opposite the stairs sat a thin wardrobe beside a four-poster bed with colourful flowers wrapped around its frame. Allura snuck a peek inside the open cupboard and saw at least three more pairs of overalls and dozens of shirts, each of which appeared to have been hand-sewn together from her mothers' discarded outfits.

There were also several cages dotted around the place for TibbidyBoo to play in, connected by transparent tubes barely big enough for the plump marlee to squeeze through.

Four oval windows were built into the walls with one looking towards the town of Endwood, one occasionally blocked by the blades of the windmill, another offering a view of the rectangular building attached to the mill, and finally, one overseeing the back garden.

'Where is it? Where is it?' Ofelia asked over and over again as she searched through the drawers of her desk when a fraction of sunlight caught her eye, triggering an idea. She clambered onto her bed, opened one of the windows and started throwing handfuls of balled paper down onto the skylight below.

'CAM! CAMERON!' she yelled until the shutters opened to reveal an older boy in mismatched clothes with a book in his hand. He moved to the window with a slouch as his eyes struggled for a moment to adjust to the harsh light (the result of hours upon hours of reading by candlelight).

'WHAT?' the older boy shouted up at her with a sharp tone.

'Did you take my journal?'

'No, I haven't even seen your dumb book,' he said, squinting further as he spotted Allura behind her. 'Who's that?'

'My friend.'

'Your what?' he asked as though certain he had misheard her.

'Forget it, just crawl back into your cave,' she said, slamming her window shut while Allura spotted a thick brown book with a metal clasp tucked beneath the bed.

'That it?' she asked.

'Oh well done,' Ofelia said, freeing the book and sitting at her desk with Allura watching over her shoulder as she flicked through it.

The first half seemed to be an ordinary diary, cataloguing everything Ofelia had done each and every day of the year, although from what Allura could see it didn't look like she had filled it in very much.

'I like to jot stuff down, you know, just in case I...'

Ofelia trailed off.

'Forget?' Allura said, finishing her thought for her.

'That's right, but if you ask me all this writing's a bit boring, it's back here where things really get interesting,' Ofelia said as she flipped to the second half of the book.

Each page was dedicated to a different creature with names, facts and figures written in meticulous detail. The curious thing about this section of the book was that only some of the pages had drawings while others had been left blank.

'So, you only draw the ones that you've actually seen in real life?'

'Exactly,' Ofelia said, etching out a drawing on an otherwise blank page with 'TEARER' written neatly at the top. As she did, Allura peered out one of the windows to see several black birds swooping across a small field full of drooping plants and wilting crops.

'Is that garden all yours?' she asked.

'Yeah. My ma says it's all done for the winter, but Mum reckons the squilms are just about to bloom. I hope she's right because otherwise I'm watering them in the middle of the night for nothing,' she said whilst shading in the creature's jagged teeth.

Based on the state of the field, Allura felt inclined to agree with Lydia.

It was long dead.

'So, what do you think?' Ofelia asked, spinning in her chair to reveal her finished drawing. The open page showed the monster drawn with immaculate precision and Allura was stunned by Ofelia's attention to detail down to the smallest intricacy.

She had perfectly captured the beast from the way each of its claws twisted in different directions to its misshapen snout.

'It's beautiful,' she said. 'Terrifying, but beautiful.'

*

Soon after the girls finished their lunch, Abraham arrived on the doorstep, and although she didn't really want to leave, Allura knew that it was time.

She offered her hand out to Ofelia to shake as she had seen one of her old foster fathers do with his friends on their way out.

But Ofelia wasn't one for such formalities.

Embracing her in a big hug, she trapped Allura's outstretched arm between them.

'I can pop by later to check on you if you'd like?'

'Don't worry, I'll be fine on my own,' Allura replied.

'Well if you change your mind, you're always welcome here,' Faye said, but Lydia was quick to sternly interject:

'I'm sure she'll be just fine.'

Yes, I'm sure I will, Allura thought, suddenly feeling rather unwelcome as Ofelia and her mothers waved her off.

Together, she and Abraham rounded a corner onto the main dirt track and silently followed the path. After a few minutes of walking, they crossed over the river Pale on an oak bridge, decorated with lamps and potted flowers, and into the lively heart of Endwood.

The main street was wide and busy with smaller alleys and pathways branching off of it. From end to end the entire place was alive with the smells of fresh fruit and slabs of cooked meat, as well as the sounds of passers-by, jingling coins and the occasional snort from livestock tucked away behind the houses.

Twisted trees stuck out of the street, as though they had sprouted through the very cobblestones themselves and each one was adorned with twinkling lights and sparkling decorations, while overhead streams of shining crystals stretched from rooftop to rooftop.

Along the main road there were ordinary-enough butchers, grocers and cobblers intertwined with tilted, bowed and warped buildings like Bread and Bark (the wood gnell bakery), Carrian's Cloaks, Forevermore Pet Shop ('For Radar Cats, Unidogs and Other Exotic Creatures') and countless other bizarre and wholly unique businesses.

They offered everything and anything, from floating gold charms to stuffed centaur hooves, but even they were nothing compared to the things being sold by the many bustling market stalls that seemed to fill any bit of available space.

Allura found them to be comfortingly familiar havens of haggling and she finally felt in her element as she listened to the sweet sounds of furious negotiations:

'Fifteen! Fifteen!'

'You've got to be joking me!'

'Final offer. Take it or don't, just get out of my face.'

As they made their way through, Abraham offered Allura his arm, wordlessly directing her to grab onto it and not let go, lest she be lost to the crowds. Despite the surrounding chaos, they managed to stick together, flowing seamlessly along the street and stopping at a stall offering an assortment of colourful fish and strange seafood.

There, the vendor in a red raincoat with a pipe in his mouth looked up at Abraham in surprise.

'By the gods! Abe? Is that you? We ain't seen you round here in years.'

Abraham remained quiet but smiled amiably at the man.

'Oh mate, we heard what happened to Horas. I'm sorry, he was a good man. No one here ever had a bad word to say about him.'

Abraham nodded appreciatively, then pointed at a pink scaly fish and held up three fingers.

Three?

'You got it,' he said, looking at Allura as he filled a paper bag. 'You his new ward or something?'

'No,' Allura replied, trying to think of a good way of phrasing what she wanted to say next, but only coming up with: 'I'm sort of Horas' replacement.'

'Well I'll be. You're our new Embodiment of Hope, huh? Hey, best of luck to you, those are some mighty big shoes to fill,' he said, handing the bag over in exchange for two silver coins.

'Thanks,' she replied.

As if I didn't feel enough pressure already.

Under Abraham's guidance, they went on to visit six more stalls, The Singing Sol tavern and a bakery as they filled their wicker basket to its absolute maximum with a larder's worth of food.

It would have been far too much for any regular person to carry all at once, but Abraham did it without even breaking a sweat.

Their final stop was Potions & Poisons where Abraham left Allura to wait outside as the light of the sun began to fade.

There, as she watched the people passing by, her eyes were drawn to a boy and a girl leaning against the walls of The Graver's Mark butcher shop across the street.

They were clearly siblings, both of them looking like the other one in a wig and pulling the same sneering expression at anyone who got too close to them.

Both had pointed noses and jet-black hair, although the boy wore his unkempt and short while his sister's was long and wild. Even their clothes were similar, wrapped in black cloaks that hung heavy over them, giving them the appearance of two conspiring bats.

Allura watched them curiously, mostly because they seemed to be doing absolutely nothing at all. Occasionally, the boy would point at some poor soul and whisper something to the girl that would make her let out a laugh like a pig's squeal, but other than that they didn't appear to be up to much of anything.

That was until a middle-aged man in a tweed jacket and shiny leather shoes exited a shop further up the road.

Their eyes glistened as he headed towards them with a bouquet of fresh flowers clutched in his hands. Neither of them moved an inch from the wall as the man drew ever closer. Until suddenly, the boy stuck his leg out into the street, tripping the man face first into the mud.

The girl rushed to help him up, but 'accidentally' trampled his bouquet as she did. More importantly however, Allura noticed the boy reach into his pocket and swipe a few coins as his sister supported him, only to swiftly allow him to topple over once again.

It's none of my business, Allura told herself as the mud-sodden man, red with embarrassment, crawled back to his feet and made off with what remained of his floral arrangement.

In her years of bouncing from home to home, Allura had learnt the importance of picking her battles, and the most important rule of all when it came to battle-picking was to never fight someone else's.

Yes, when it really came down to it, her belief was that we are all on our own, or at least that's what she'd always told herself.

And so, with that in mind, she tried not to focus on the terrible siblings, looking further up the road instead as a wrinkled old man came shuffling down. He moved slow and steady, each step a milestone, with only a long cane to support him.

An ideal target if ever there was one.

Allura glared through the crowds and carriages to

once again see the pair preparing to spring their trap.

It's none of my business, she repeatedly told herself as the man drew nearer and the boy readied himself. They were only a few feet away from striking when Allura couldn't help herself but call out:

'OI!'

The siblings snapped their attention from the old man and leered at her as she shot daggers back at them.

Completely unaware of the tension that had formed around him, the old man slowly walked on by as the two troublemakers looked ready to bite Allura's head clean off.

Clenching her fists, she watched as they stormed across the road towards her and knew that if she was going to make a break for it, now was the time.

The thought of her school bully, Mabel, and the memory of her foot against her stomach was almost enough to make Allura turn and run, but she pushed past it and stood strong.

They were only moments from collision with the boy clicking his knuckles in anticipation and the girl grinding her teeth together with an uncomfortable crunch, when an immense shadow shrouded Allura.

Before she knew it, the pair were almost tripping over one another to duck into a nearby alley.

That was lucky, she thought, feeling a hundred feet tall as she turned around to see what had blocked out the light.

Behind her, closing the rotting door of Potions and Poisons as gently as he could, was Abraham.

Completely unaware of what was going on, he tucked a small blue vial into his pocket and raised an eyebrow as if to ask if everything was alright. Allura nodded, keeping what had happened (or had almost happened) to herself.

With that, he led her back through the town teeming with trade and over the bridge which was now basking in the warm glow of lamplight.

On the other side, they stopped at a junction in the road which offered only two routes. To the right was a thin path still waterlogged from the night before, while to the left was the main road which would take them back towards the Donnelly's home.

Allura imagined Ofelia would be practicing her animal calls or showing Faye and Lydia her sketches, but she would never know as Abraham chose the trail on the right, causing her heart to sink just a little.

They followed the path for a few minutes before stopping at a gate in a small brick wall with a metal plaque that read 'Horas M-'. Whatever else the sign had once said had been weathered away, but beneath it, Allura's travel case sat at the foot of the wall.

Just past the gate, the house sat in full view, although much like the Donnelly's, it wasn't really a house at all. Instead, it was a large log cabin with a shed stuck onto its side.

The strangest thing about the cabin was that it looked neither old nor new, its wood neither rotten nor pristine. Instead, it stood with a perfect sense of belonging, as though it were as much a part of the woods as the hills that loomed behind it or the trees that swayed in the wind beside it.

Allura stared in wonderment at the structure from behind the wall, ready to hurry inside when she noticed that Abraham was overcome with a visible uneasiness. He pulled at his shirt collar as if it were choking him.

'Are you okay?' she asked, unlocking the gate latch for him.

He looked at her for a moment, a sad fog in his eyes, then he quickly recollected his composure and walked through.

What was that all about?

With a loud creak, the cabin door opened into a snug living room. There was an unlit brick fireplace nestled into the wall between two sofas that sat facing one another, and beyond them, a rustic kitchen area lay in the far corner with a pile of pots and pans still splayed out on the drying rack.

As the natural light of day dimmed, Abraham lit the various candles and lanterns dotted about the place, while Allura poked her head into the three doors spread around the room.

The first led to a bedroom, while the second opened into a bathroom. The third door however, which stood taller than the others, refused to budge no matter how hard Allura pushed or how vigorously she twisted the handle.

After a few failed attempts at prying it open and an unimpressed glance from Abraham, she accepted defeat.

Probably just leads to the shed anyway.

Instead, she decided to investigate the bedroom further whilst Abraham worked on the fireplace, but as she entered, she noticed that the room felt draughtier than the others, as though it had suffered the most from the loss of its occupant.

Sitting on the bed, she found herself transfixed by a watercolour painting of a bear on the wall in a flowery meadow. It was comforting to see an animal she recognised and it reminded her of the one she had seen hanging from the Christmas tree in London, which already felt like a lifetime ago.

Lying down and running her hands across the rest of the bed, she noticed a dip in the mattress. A sudden discomfort ran through her as she pulled away the covers to reveal a person shaped indent, as though the fibres themselves remembered the man who had once laid there.

Then and there she decided that she would not be sleeping in a dead man's bed.

The sofa will have to do.

Returning to the main room, she felt a wave of heat emanating from the fireplace that spat tiny embers as she basked in its warmth. Meanwhile, Abraham expertly removed the head, scales and bones of two fish in one precise flick of his wrist, then placed the third fish into a metal box filled with ice.

Allura was so used to doing all the cooking that it felt oddly unnerving to see someone else do it for her.

The least I could do is try to talk to him.

'This place is nice,' she said.

'Hmmm,' he replied.

'The people seem nice too, well most of them.'

With a familiarity, he moved about the kitchen as

though it were his own, not stopping for a moment to look for any tools or utensils.

'Did you use to live in Endwood?' she asked and Abraham nodded.

'Why did you leave?'

There was no answer and although she wanted to give up trying, there was a suspicion that she needed to confirm.

'He was your friend, wasn't he? Horas, I mean.'

Abraham stopped on the spot and turned to look at her. Calmly, he dropped the pot he was holding onto the countertop and moved towards her. With each step he took, the sounds of the fire seemingly grew louder and louder, until it was roaring as he stood over her.

Then he reached into his pocket, pulled out a folded piece of paper and handed it to her. Sitting on the sofa opposite, he watched as she opened it to reveal a faded, but detailed drawing of three people.

Although he was considerably younger and had a beaming smile across his face, Allura eventually recognised the tall, dark-skinned man in the middle of the sketch as Abraham.

The other two however were a total mystery to her until she spotted the caption at the bottom which read:

'Rutherford, Abraham and I.'

'Which one is Horas?' Allura asked and Abraham gestured to the man on the right. That section of the paper was particularly sun-damaged, but from what she could tell he had warm brown skin, a short beard, curly hair, wiry glasses and clusters of freckles across his cheeks.

She felt as though she was looking into the face of a ghost and couldn't help but feel haunted by him.

'And Rutherford? Is that Orville Rutherford?' she asked, pointing to the man on the left. 'The same Orville that's getting married? That Noah's dad and Raven are working for?'

Abraham nodded again.

'So, you were all friends?' she asked, delicately handing the paper back to him as he got up to return to the kitchen.

She took his faint smile as a yes.

'Are you and Orville not still friends?' she pressed further.

Staring at the drawing, Abraham seemed as though he was about to say something, but instead he picked up the pot and got back to cooking.

*

With a full belly, Abraham left soon after the iridescent light of the giant moon rose behind the clouds. Before he went, he showed Allura where the key to the shed was hidden and gave her the written address of an inn at the centre of town, suggesting that it was where she could find him if she needed to.

Finally alone, Allura sprawled out over one of the big squishy sofas, only to feel something hard pushing into her back. Rooting through the cushions, she pried the object loose and held it into the light.

Upon examination she saw that it was a small, music box.

Turning the metal crank, she was disappointed to

find that where she had expected a spinning ballerina or at least some angelic melody, there was nothing.

Must be broken, she thought, discarding the box onto the table, only for it to start vibrating gently as faint sounds emanated from inside. The noises grew louder and louder as it shook and shuddered until, one by one, the sides of the box unfolded to reveal five tiny wooden figurines.

There was a drummer, a guitarist, a pianist, a trumpeter and even a singer, but for a while they just stood there, tuning their individual instruments until eventually the frontman took to the microphone.

'HELLO LADIES AND GENTLEMEN! WE ARE THE BOX OF MISFITS!'

The drummer tapped his sticks together.

'ONE! TWO! ONE, TWO, THREE, FOUR!'

With that, the miniature musicians produced a noise as loud and lively as any concert. They played nothing that Allura recognised, but it was catchy nevertheless and her foot began to tap along as she succumbed to the infectious rhythm of their songs.

She was really beginning to enjoy it when a loud scratching sound caused them all to stop.

Where did that come from?

BANG!

The wall shook as something heavy crashed against the locked door that she had failed to open earlier.

'THANK YOU! YOU'VE BEEN A WONDERFUL AUDIENCE!' the lead singer said, while rest of the band packed up their instruments.

There were more sounds of wood being torn from

the door and another bang against the wall as the panels of the music box folded and clicked back into place.

'Wait, please don't go!' she said, spinning the crank to no avail. Then another thud from behind the mysterious door made her wish that she could join them in their little box.

Tossing on her shoes, Allura hurried to escape out the front door when the crashing and tearing seemingly stopped and was replaced by a solemn whimpering.

Sounds like whatever is in there might be hurt.

Grabbing the key from the mantelpiece, Allura crept towards the door with the knife Abraham had used to gut the fish in hand. The key slipped perfectly into the lock and she held her breath as she turned it in place.

Twisting the handle, she felt a waft of stale air release from the room. It stank like a warm rot and she had to take one last breath of fresh air before entering.

The inside was dark, lit only by the open door and a single ray of moonlight that snuck in from a crack in the ceiling. Shakily holding the knife out in front of her, she took one tentative step after another.

Until suddenly, her foot collided with a metallic tray that clanged loudly as it skidded along the ground like a dinner bell being rung.

Allura's whole body went rigid.

Misty breath emanated from the blackness and a mountainous figure rose slowly in the corner of the room. It clambered on all fours towards her, before staggering onto two feet as a rumbling sound grew in the back of its throat.

Allura backed away as it approached, but tripped on a pile of ropes and buckets. Tangled in the clutter, she watched helplessly as the shadow moved into the moonlight to reveal itself.

The next thing Allura knew, she was face to face with a colossal brown bear.

7

Angelursi

Sharp chestnut eyes looked at her with a vested curiosity as Allura shivered on the cold stone floor.

She held out the knife, swinging wildly at the air, but with one swipe of the bear's paw, the blade was knocked from her hand. Then all she could feel was hot breath and drops of saliva as the enormous beast pressed its face against hers.

What's the trick with bears? Are you supposed to make yourself look really big or really small?

She couldn't remember which it was, but she certainly felt very small.

Pinned under the weight of the creature, she watched as it sniffed around her, the rough and wet texture of its nose leaving an imprint on her cheek. Then, as though she weren't even there, the bear pounced towards the knife, licking it clean of any trace of fish guts that had clung to it.

While it was distracted, Allura scurried along the floor and back into the kitchen, quickly but quietly closing the door behind her. She managed to scramble to her feet and grabbed the iron rod from the fireplace, arming herself as she hid behind the sofa and prepared for the door to be reduced to splinters.

There, she waited for what seemed like a lifetime and it was only when the antique clock by the door chimed nine times that Allura realised the bear hadn't made any sound in quite some time.

The danger had passed, for now at least, but in its place came an unusual predicament.

What to do about the bear in the shed?

Plucking the note Abraham had left her from the table, she ran out into the night, a part of her praying for the animal to not even be there by the time she returned. However, as she made her way to the bridge into town, an idea struck her and the next thing she knew, she had turned and ran in the complete opposite direction to Abraham's address.

Ignoring the little voice in her head telling her that this was a bad idea, she approached her destination and snuck through some bushes into the back garden.

Uneven dirt and dried vegetation snapped underfoot as she stumbled across the farm, stopping at the sight of a solitary lantern, swinging at its keeper's waist side. It was too dark to see who was holding it, but Allura knew it could only be one person.

Ofelia Donnelly, out tending the squilms.

'Now, I don't want you to feel any pressure, but Mum and I have been watering you every night for the last three months. So, we would really appreciate any sign that you're actually growing down there,' Ofelia said to the dirt.

'Pssssst,' Allura called out to her from the dark.

'Hello?' she asked in a startled cry. 'Who's there?'

'Shush, it's me,' Allura replied, moving into the lamplight.

'What are you doing here?'

'I could really use your help with something at the cabin.'

'Oh no, I'm not supposed to leave the garden this late,' Ofelia said apprehensively.

'Please, I need you.'

'Well... what is it?'

Allura gave a nervous smile, the ridiculous nature of the situation only then dawning on her.

'How much do you know about bears?'

*

They rushed back to the cabin with no more talk of broken curfews or worried parents. Instead, Ofelia was abuzz with questions about the bear's age, weight, size and colour. None of which Allura could answer with much certainty.

'All I know is it's a bear. Or at least I'm pretty sure it's a bear. It's big and furry and walks on four legs,' Allura said as they approached the gate and as soon as they entered the cabin, Ofelia darted towards the shed door.

'WOAH! What are you doing?' Allura asked.

'It's in here, right?' Ofelia checked, her hand grasping the doorknob.

'Yeah, but don't you want something to defend yourself?'

She was taken aback, as though the thought hadn't

even occurred to her.

'Did it attack you?'

'No,' Allura admitted.

'Then why would I need to defend myself?'

And with that, she cracked the door open.

'WAIT!' Allura said, picking up the fire iron once again and taking the lead.

As they crept in, the only sound was the echo of water dripping through the hole in the ceiling, leading Allura to wonder if the bear really was gone. Then the creature stirred, unfurling itself from its curled-up ball in the corner.

The girls jumped and Allura was moments from turning heel and locking the door behind them when she noticed something in the light of the lantern. Although the bear was truly enormous, it had a thin, malnourished frame, with its chest reduced to a tight collection of bones and skin.

Something about its weak state caused Allura to lower the metal stick without even realising.

'What was Horas doing with this thing?' Allura asked.

'It looks like he was letting her use this place as a den,' Ofelia replied, inspecting the deep claw marks in the brick and the bedding of sticks and shredded bark in the corner.

'Her? How do you know?'

'The eyes. You can tell by the colour,' Ofelia replied, leaning in closer than perhaps was wise.

'Well, I suppose she couldn't have broken in,' Allura said as she pushed against the shed's double doors and realised that the lock was still intact. 'So, if Horas was letting her live here, why wasn't he feeding her?'

'I'm not sure, but she's definitely hungry,' Ofelia said.

'So, do we feed her?' Allura proposed, as insane as it sounded.

'Do you have anything?'

'Like what?'

'Nuts, beans, fish-'

Allura clicked her fingers and scurried into the kitchen, pulling the fish from the ice-filled box and slapping it onto a metal tray along with a large bowl of water. Ofelia followed her out of the shed and noticed something sat on the table.

'Where did you get this?' she asked grabbing the mysterious blue vial from the countertop.

'Abraham bought it from that shop, Potions and something,' Allura explained, only just realising that he had left it behind.

Ofelia asked her if she knew what it was, but Allura shook her head and so, without further explanation she poured a few drops onto the fish and they returned to the shed.

Allura crouched down low, ready to push the tray towards the sleeping beast.

'Are you really sure this is a good idea?' Allura asked.

'Yeah. Maybe. Probably.'

That'll have to do I suppose.

The bear's eyes opened as the tray scraped along the floor, and after a very brief moment of uncertainty, it sunk its head into the bowl. There it lapped and slurped and swallowed until there was no water left. Then it turned its attention to the food and after a few ravenous bites, not a trace of the fish remained either.

'I think she liked it,' Ofelia whispered.

'Let's just hope it didn't give her an appetite,' Allura replied as a powerful rumble erupted from the bear's stomach and it rose onto its paws once again.

Within moments, its shallow breathing turned heavier and with each breath more flesh and muscle formed around its frail frame. Until all too quickly, as though time had reversed, the bear looked strong and new.

'What was that blue stuff?' Allura asked in disbelief.

'It's Abundantil, it can make one meal feel like ten,' Ofelia explained.

As incredible as it was, Allura's dread worsened into a cold, foreboding terror. Faster than she could raise the iron rod to protect herself, the bear sprinted in her direction, knocking her to the floor.

'Please don't eat me!' she cried out helplessly before suddenly bursting into fits of inexplicable laughter.

A bright pink tongue licked at her face with a coarse but slimy touch, like sandpaper wrapped in a disgusting layer of slobber. The sensation against her skin was bizarre, sapping Allura of her fear with every lick. Meanwhile, Ofelia took a closer look at the bear.

'By the gods,' she uttered to herself.

'What is it?' Allura asked, catching her breath as

the playful creature finally set her free.

'She's an angelursi! I couldn't see it earlier, but she is! I can't believe it! That explains why she was so hungry!'

'A what?'

Ofelia went to repeat herself, but was interrupted by another chime of the clock.

'Oh no, is that the time? I've got to get back. Mum and Ma will have realised I'm missing by now,' she said, taking one last look at the incredible creature before dashing for the door.

'But what do I do?' Allura asked.

'Don't worry, she'll be exhausted after that. Should be fast asleep soon and then we'll take her out tomorrow.'

'Take her out?'

'She's going to need some fresh air after being cooped up in there.'

'She's not a dog Ofelia, we can't just take her for a walk. I know this place is different to where I'm from, but I imagine people would still be freaked out by a massive bear strolling down the road.'

Ofelia thought for a second then pointed towards a cluster of trees and said:

'There's a lake a little bit beyond those trees, we'll take her there at first light tomorrow.'

Allura gave an unconvinced glare, but Ofelia assured her it would all be fine.

'Alright, tomorrow morning. But you better be here first thing!' Allura shouted down the path.

'I won't forget!' Ofelia replied as she disappeared into the wooded trail.

Once she was gone, Allura shut the door and popped back into the shed as the bear returned to its curled-up position in the corner with a happy purring sound.

Leaving it to sleep, she turned her attention to the bookshelf by the fireplace and started surveying its contents carefully.

After a thorough search, she stopped on the spine of a book entitled *The Wilderlife: A Comprehensive Guide to Animals of The Bliss by Armandia Jackel*. Fervently flicking through it, she found what she was looking for on page 172 in the 'Rarest of Rare' section.

There it was: 'The Angelursi'.

She examined the passage, discovering factoid after factoid, but not quite finding anything that would have stirred such a reaction from Ofelia.

Did you know that an angelursi's body deteriorates faster than any other mammal if they don't eat for more than 24 hours?

Did you know that like most Orterran bears, all male angelursi have blue eyes while all females have brown eyes?

Did you know that although the angelursi was once featured on the banners of The Bliss, the species is actually native to the island of Tar-Mori?

Then Allura's heart started to pound as she read about what specifically made the angelursi quite so unique.

No wonder Ofelia was excited.

Throwing the book aside, she ran into the other room and stealthily approached the slumbering bear.

Now up-close, she noticed the abnormality in the creature's fur across its back.

How did I not see it before?

Lightly brushing her hand against it, she felt that the odd section wasn't made of fur at all, but feathers. Then suddenly, Allura was tossed across the room as the area she had been touching unfurled itself.

Stretching out from the bear's back, like those of a giant hawk, were a pair of wings that shook and flapped in its sleep

Where in the world did Horas get you? Allura wondered in astonishment, thinking back to the book she had just read:

Angelursi, otherwise known as the angel bear.

8

The party

The wind was still and a thin veil of mist hung in the air as the morning light peeked over the horizon. Allura had risen with the sun and waited eagerly for Ofelia as every tick of the clock taunted her.

Tick. *Where is she?*

Tick. *Did she forget?*

Tick. *What if she was lying?*

Tick. *Why did I believe her?*

After half an hour, Allura decided she'd had enough of waiting and headed into the shed where the angel bear was still fast asleep.

If I'm going to take her out, I need some way of stopping her from running off.

As quietly as she could, Allura searched the small room until she found a long length of rope on top of an old barrel.

She took it in hand and approached the dozing bear with light steps, her bare feet tensing against the stone floor's freezing touch. The creature's snores were loud and guttural as Allura gingerly tried to wrap the rope around its neck like a dog's leash, but its eyes burst open all too quickly.

Panicked and confused, the bear pushed Allura away with a snarl and bared its teeth as it rose onto two legs, bumping its head against the roof.

'Woah, woah, woah, calm down! It's alright!' she said, holding up the rope into clear view. After a moment of examining it, the angel bear dropped onto all-fours and apologetically nuzzled into Allura's chest.

'Big drama queen,' Allura said as the bear stood still long enough for her to tie the rope in a loose knot around its neck.

Throwing on a sturdy pair of boots and unlocking the shed's double doors, Allura tugged at the rope and smiled to herself as the great big bear followed her outside.

She guided it across Horas' garden and through a conveniently bear-sized gap in the stone wall that led to the edge of the woods. There the bear stopped in its tracks, unwilling to take another step further.

'What is it?' Allura asked, but the bear timidly placed a single paw onto the woodland muck and let out a curious growl at its cold damp touch.

Then another paw extended beyond the treeline, claws sinking into the mud as she sniffed the fresh air.

Weary from an unsettled night's sleep, Allura thought that this was the perfect opportunity to rest her tired eyes, if only for a moment. However, when she opened them, she caught only a brief glimpse of the bear running off into the trees and felt the rope tighten in her hands.

Clinging to the makeshift leash and trying desperately to slow the bear down by digging her heels into the ground, she succeeded only in being pulled face first into the muck.

Her grip loosened as she fell and the rope flailed about wildly before vanishing from view.

As failures go, that one was pretty bad.

'HEY!' she called after the bear before covering her mouth, only then remembering that she needed to keep quiet so as to not wake the rest of the town.

Racing past snapped branches and trampled bushes, Allura followed the paw prints through the woods, her heart pounding in her chest until she came upon the lake Ofelia had described.

The pool of crystal blue water was serenely still, like a liquid mirror of the sky with a pebbled shore around its edge and an ominous wall of spiked rocks on the opposite side. Allura gazed at the lake's beauty when, without warning, the reflected image was broken by the ripples of something lapping at the water.

Further along the bank, she spied the angel bear dipping its pink tongue into the water and Allura raced over, her fear disguising itself as anger.

'You can't do that!' she said furiously, causing the bear to look up at her, its mouth dripping with water and its tongue lolling to the side.

'What were you thinking? Do you have any idea how much danger you could be in? If you run off like that again, I won't be able to let you out anymore! Do you understand me?'

Big, unblinking eyes looked back at her like a

scolded child frozen with fear at the sound of their parent's raised voice.

'Do you understand?' she reiterated, but the bear simply nuzzled into her again, pressing its face against her stomach and imprinting a big wet patch across her shirt.

Allura's arms dropped slowly, until they were holding onto as much of the bear as possible and just like that, her rage dissipated. She sunk her head into its soft warm fur, closing her eyes with a deep sigh.

'I'm sorry, I know you were thirsty and excited. You just scared me is all,' she said and after a while, she released her grip to sit on the pebbles while the bear gleefully splashed her paws in the water.

As she watched, Allura found it harder and harder to remember why she was ever mad in the first place, especially since she knew better than anyone what it was like to want to be free.

With a part of her thinking of her past, Allura decided to look to the future instead, to plan what she would do when she got back to Earth. Cognitius had told her that the doorway was capable of sending her wherever she wanted, but the furthest she had ever strayed from London was a few school trips to neighbouring counties.

While returning to Mrs. Olderman was certainly not an option, Allura knew she could never bring herself to leave the city altogether. Although no house or family had ever quite felt like home, the city itself had given her the closest thing she had ever felt to a sense of belonging.

Even when everyone else had rejected her, she

always had London. Which was exactly why she knew she would have to leave this strange world behind.

If I stayed it would only be a matter of time before they realise there's no place here for someone like me. Especially not as the Embodiment of Hope of all things.

As she thought of her home city, her eye was drawn back to the bear and she was struck by an idea.

'I should probably give you a name if we're going to be spending the rest of the week together,' she said, struggling to pull the carefree bear's attention away from the tree trunk it was rubbing its back against.

'How about... London?' Allura suggested, receiving as close to an approving look as one can get from a bear.

'Alright then, London it is.'

*

Allura sat happily by the lake for an hour, lazily listening to the whistling of the wind through the trees until the mist had disappeared entirely in the light of the fully-risen sun. Yet still there was no sign of Ofelia.

I really thought she would come.

Feeling downhearted, Allura was swiftly pulled away from her self-pitying as she heard the cracking of twigs from beyond the trees surrounding the shore. She jumped to her feet whilst London continued to scratch herself on a tree, entirely unfazed by the noise.

Then there was another snap from behind a nearby bush which rustled and shook at the force of something pushing through. Finally, the bush spat out a small boy wrapped in thick leather padding, like something Allura had seen cricket players wear.

This was finally enough to catch London's attention and she sauntered over to pick the mysterious, leather-clad figure up by the collar of his jacket like a lioness carrying her cub in her teeth. He let out a terrified squeal and only then did Allura recognise him.

'Put him down,' Allura demanded, waving her arms about until the bear released the boy.

'Allura?' Noah asked, poking his head out of the bindings like a frightened tortoise.

'Noah? What are you doing here?' she asked, helping him to his feet.

His face was protected by a wiry helmet and his body was wrapped in an undersized jacket that restricted his movement to a funny little waddle. Still terrified, he dusted himself off as the answer to her question called out from the woodlands.

'NOAH? WHERE ARE YOU?' Ofelia said before stepping into view from the trees and wagging her finger like a displeased schoolteacher. 'Noah Tanden, you stupid boy. The one thing I said, the ONE thing, was that you had to stay close, and what do you do?'

'Well, it's a good thing I did, because look, I found her,' he replied.

London quickly grew bored of their bickering and decided to take a dip in the lake, and she wasn't the only one to have lost interest in their arguing either.

'No offence Noah, but what *are* you doing here?' Allura asked bluntly.

'I saw Ofelia buying some fish in the market, but I know she doesn't eat that sort of thing so I asked who it was for,' he explained.

'And you just told him?' she asked Ofelia.

'I'm so sorry, my parents made me go Atrilarium shopping, so I thought while I was out, I might as well get the bear some food, but then he caught me off guard and it all sort of slipped out.'

Allura wanted to be angry, but in truth she was grateful to learn that Ofelia had not abandoned her after all.

'I'm sorry Allura. Really, I am. I just... forgot it was a secret.'

Allura rolled her eyes.

Embodiment of Forgetfulness indeed.

'But why did you come? I thought you hated the woods?' Allura asked Noah.

'Normally, yes. I avoid them at all costs, especially when there's something like that roaming around,' he said, pointing with a shaking finger at London. 'But I suppose that's also why I had to come. You're up to something dangerous and I made a promise that I would do whatever I could to help you.'

Not quite as cowardly as I thought, Allura told herself as London let out a playful growl and Noah tightened the strap of his helmet.

Never mind.

'Well... thank you. I'm glad you're here, both of

you,' she said.

'I told him he didn't need the outfit,' Ofelia remarked as they moved to the edge of the lake and watched the bear paddling blissfully through the water.

'I can't believe it. A real angelursi, I thought the only ones left were on Tar-Mori,' Noah said in amazement.

'Her name's London.'

'Since when?' Ofelia asked in surprise.

'About an hour ago.'

As London dipped and dived beneath the water, checking that they were still there every time she resurfaced, Ofelia laid out a picnic blanket and unpacked some food for them.

Leaving six fish and a bowlful of berries by the water, they tucked into a basket of sandwiches, fruits and sweets so packed with sugar Allura could taste it before it had even touched her tongue.

With every passing minute, Noah removed another clunky piece of his heavy protective gear, until finally, he was as defenceless as the rest of them.

'At least now you'll be comfortable when she eats you,' Allura joked.

'Him, comfortable? I can't even imagine what that looks like. He's not comfortable in his own house,' laughed Ofelia.

'You try living on the high street at the busiest time of the year and tell me how relaxed you feel. I can barely step out my door without getting trampled.'

'Oh, chin up, it's almost Atrilarium Day,' Ofelia replied with a smirk.

'Don't remind me,' Noah shuddered.

This was not the first time Allura had heard of Atrilarium. She recalled sellers in Endwood's market stalls mentioning it as they peddled decorations and last-minute gifts.

It was however the first time she had thought to ask:

'What is Atrilamarium?'

'Atrilarium,' Noah corrected her.

'You don't have that on Earth?' Ofelia asked in surprise.

'Don't you pay attention to anything in Earth History, Ofelia?' Noah scoffed. 'They have different holidays for all their different religions, just like us. Atrilarium Day happens to be around the same time as a magical festival known as Christ-Mass there.'

'What's that?'

Before Allura could answer, Noah started to explain it with a confidence that she could tell was rare for him.

'An annual ritual where they feed sweet treats to a winter spirit called Sander Clause in exchange for presents.'

'Is that true?' Ofelia asked Allura in wonderment.

'It's pronounced 'Christmas', but sure, everything else was spot on,' Allura said with a giggle.

'I wish we had a Sander Clause,' Ofelia mumbled as Allura learnt about the origins of Orterra's most-celebrated holiday.

Atrilarium Day, as Noah explained it, was the

celebration of the defeat of a great dragon named Aterosk. According to legend, the monster had terrorised Orterra for years with no one, not even the giants, being able to stop it.

It was only when the town of Trunkton was reduced to ruins that a band of heroes finally came together and slayed the beast. After so much devastation and terror, the anniversary of its death was remembered each year with gift-giving, festivities and merriment.

'Sounds nice, when exactly is it?' Allura asked.

'It's um- a few days from now,' Noah said as an uncomfortable look fell upon his and Ofelia's faces.

'Oh, I see,' Allura replied, realising why they were uneasy. 'I'm leaving on Atrilarium Day aren't I?'

'You don't have to,' Ofelia said swiftly, but before Allura could respond, London approached them inquisitively. Noah squirmed as she plodded towards him, then let out a laugh as she shook herself dry, soaking the two girls.

They both yelped, but were quickly quiet when the bear extended her wings, glossy and gleaming in the sunlight, and started to flap them dry.

'Wow, she really is magnificent,' Noah said, astounded.

'Yeah, she is,' Allura agreed breathlessly.

'I think she wants to fly,' Ofelia said as London continued to flap her wings while turning her eyes towards the sky.

'No. No way, anything could happen to her if we let her fly off,' Allura replied, hastily pushing on her wings to return them to their holstered position.

London let out a sorrowful groan as a small flock of pidgpodges passed overhead and Allura looked up at them, then back at the mewling bear.

'Alright girl, but I can't let you go on your own,' she said. Noah and Ofelia watched in confusion as Allura undid the rope and retied it around London's chest. She then tied the other end around her own waist. London seemed confused for a moment as well, then leant forwards, inviting Allura to climb onto her back.

'Please tell me you aren't doing what it looks like you're doing,' said Noah.

'Please tell me you are!' said Ofelia.

'What do you think, will this work?' Allura asked with a tremble in her voice.

'Definitely. An angel bear of this size could take all three of us easily,' Ofelia replied.

'You volunteering?' Allura asked, but Noah was quick to interrupt.

'No way, if this goes wrong, I'm going to need someone to help get you to a healer.'

He had made an annoyingly good point. If she was going to do this, she would have to do it alone.

'I could go instead,' Ofelia offered.

Undeniably tempting. But what if it went wrong?

'No. I'll do it. I trust her,' Allura replied, scrambling onto London's back and sinking her fingers into her fur as she whispered in her ear: 'Not too high, okay?'

'Good luck,' Noah said, his peaky complexion creeping back in.

'Just remember,' said Ofelia, 'whatever you do,

don't -'

Whoosh!

They set off down the shore, losing Ofelia's words of advice to the wind as they tried to gain enough speed to take off.

Don't what? Allura wondered as London's paws thumped against the pebbles with her wings outstretched.

They had started with the wall of spiked stone behind them, but as the lake became a blur and London's panting grew harder, the circular shape of the shore became their undoing.

Allura glanced up to see that they had almost completed a lap of the lake and were fast approaching the wall of rocks.

We need to get into the air, she realised as London started to slow, her nerves getting the better of her, but there was no time to stop.

'COME ON GIRL! YOU CAN DO IT!' Allura yelled as she tugged at the rope and London turned her wings to the wind.

With a powerful flap they lifted off the ground and the sharp sound of claws against stone rung out as they left the ground behind them.

'WOOOO!' Allura screamed in delight as they rose into the air.

She heard the cheers of her friends down below as she flew in circles around the lake, holding out one of her hands to feel the wind slipping through her fingers. With every lap of the water, they rose a little higher, the air becoming colder and colder with each elevation.

Then she had to shut her eyes tight and hold on for dear life as London pointed her snout to the sky and flew them directly upwards.

Allura refused to open them again until they had levelled out, but once they did, she saw that the view was as stunningly beautiful as the one from Cognitius' balcony.

Countless trees with their leaves turned brown by the autumn filled the landscape, while the thatched and tiled rooftops of small cottages and giant manor houses perched on distant hills pumped out smoke from their chimneys.

Up in the freezing sky, Allura wished she could bathe in the warmth they exuded and so, to distract herself from the cold and the terror of falling, she tried to spot Endwood. Her eyes darted around for a while before finding the town next to a truly enormous tree stump amongst the patchwork pallet of reds and browns.

The town looked like a miniature model of itself from up there, and she imagined how small she would have looked to any market traders who happened to look up from the main street.

We're probably just two tiny specks all the way up here.

But that thought served only to remind her of just how dreadfully high up they really were.

Ignoring the voice that pleaded with her not to look directly down, her eyes almost popped out of her head as she stared at the lake, now no bigger than a puddle.

A low-lying cloud passed below them and the

immense height of it all began to overwhelm her.

'Down,' Allura squeaked. 'DOWN! WE NEED TO GO DOWN!'

Pushing manically at the bear's fur, she found that they were suddenly free falling towards the ground. Her legs dangled in the air as they fell and her cries were drowned out by the screaming wind.

She pulled harshly at the creature's fur, trying desperately to regain control, but instead caused the bear to lose focus and spin wildly.

Their trajectory led them away from the lake, with Noah and Ofelia running between the trees beneath them. The features of the land grew increasingly larger as they spiralled towards the surface.

Crack!

They tore through a row of thin trees and bushes before colliding with the marshy ground. Allura was thrown from London's back, the rope snapping as she catapulted through the air.

Tumbling and turning, she saw nothing but a blur of motion before landing in a pile of leaves and mud that cushioned her fall.

'Are you okay?' Noah asked, rushing over to help her up.

'What happened?' asked Ofelia.

'I don't know,' Allura replied as she hurried towards London who was sprawled out, motionless. 'London? I'm so sorry. It was an accident. Are you okay?'

Urgently shaking the bear, she prayed for a response, while Ofelia rested her head on London's stomach and listened closely. She was still breathing, although in a shallow sort of way.

Judging by the creased look on Ofelia's face, Allura could tell that they needed to wake her up to really know if she was alright.

What have I done?

Ofelia looked at Noah with a tilt of her head.

'What?' he asked.

'Do that thing you do.'

'I've only ever done that to people and even then, I can't properly control it.'

'Well then, maybe it's easier with an animal,' she suggested, but Noah just scoffed.

'I don't know what you two are talking about, but Noah if you might be able to help her then you have to do it. Please!' Allura begged.

Noah looked at her, then Ofelia and finally down at London. She was the most peaceful thing in that chaotic bit of forest and he knew she needed his help.

'Fine,' he said, rubbing the back of his neck before kneeling beside Allura and placing a single hand on London's head.

He pushed up his glasses then shut his eyes.

After a moment, his eyelids fluttered and after another moment, so did London's. A gentle breeze flowed through as both of their bodies started to shake and Allura watched in terror as they lurched and rattled.

Then Noah crumpled to the floor, writhing for a moment longer before lying as still as the bear.

'Did we just kill Noah?' Allura asked in horror as the pair continued to lie as lifeless as two discarded dolls.

Suddenly, he burst awake with a funny little 'paaaaah' sound.

'Did it work?' Ofelia asked, but he was too dazed to answer as London's eyes snapped open as well.

'You're awake!' Allura yelled, wrapping her arms around the confused bear's neck. 'I'm so sorry girl,' she said as London nuzzled into her again, which Allura took to mean that all was forgiven.

'What was that?' Allura asked Noah.

'Embodiment of Dreams, remember?' he replied as he lifted himself off the dirt. 'I popped in and told her to wake up.'

'So, you *can* go into animals' dreams. That is so cool! What was it like?' Ofelia asked as she had London's eyes follow her finger before checking the bear for any broken bones or abrasions.

'It was weird. Foggy I guess, but from what I could make out I think she was flying through the pouring rain,' he said struggling to recall the fleeting details.

'But it wasn't normal rain…' he chuckled to himself, the one thing he could remember coming into clear focus.

'It was raining fish.'

*

After giving London enough time to recover, the three children worked together to heave the great bear onto her paws. Having decided that there had been enough excitement for one day, they started to make their way back through the woods towards the cabin.

They were trudging through piles of mushy leaves and over moss covered stumps when the conversation turned to a subject that Allura had been trying to avoid.

'Why do you want to go back to Earth?' Ofelia asked.

Because I don't belong here.

Because it's only a matter of time before you won't want me around anymore.

Because I always find a way to mess things up.

Any of those would have been far more truthful answers than the one she gave.

'Orterra. Embodiments. Flying bears. It's all just a bit too weird for me,' she replied and Noah let out a hearty laugh reminiscent of his father's.

Ofelia meanwhile remained very quiet.

Before Allura could better explain herself, voices began echoing around them. They were too faint to make out the words, but Allura was certain that she recognised their snide tones. Climbing up a nearby mound, she confirmed her suspicions.

'They're coming this way,' she said.

'Who are?' asked Noah.

'Some horrible kids I saw in town yesterday tripping people over and nicking stuff from their pockets.'

Ofelia and Noah's faces dropped.

'That'll be the Kraws,' Noah said.

'You know them?' Allura asked.

'Know them? We hate them. Everybody does. Raiph and Cinder Kraw are the most horrible people in Endwood, other than their dad that is,' Ofelia answered.

'Well that's not great because their coming this way.'

'We have to hide London,' Noah realised as he and Ofelia tried to push the bear in the opposite direction.

Allura however, continued to watch the horrid pair over the mound as they threw rocks and sticks at a small bird's nests until it dropped to the forest floor. She was familiar with bullies like them and knew that in her experience, running and hiding rarely solved anything.

'What if we don't hide her?' she suggested.

'We have to, she'll scare them to Yragshall and back,' Noah replied.

'Exactly,' Allura said joyfully, although she wasn't entirely sure what that meant.

Ofelia looked at her with shock.

'She could seriously hurt them. Then everyone in Endwood would know about her. They'd never stop hunting her.'

Allura's desire to see the panic on Raiph and Cinder's faces was overruled by the thought of London being turned into a fur-skin rug by the fire.

'Alright fine,' she conceded, picking berries from a bush and using them to coax London into following her as she ducked into the mouth of a cave. The spot acted as the perfect hiding place with its many boulders and fallen rocks.

'Keep her quiet, I'll try to lure them away from here,' she said.

'I'm coming with you,' Ofelia insisted.

'Hang on, you're just going to leave me alone with her?' Noah asked, pointing at London.

'It's her or them.'

'Point taken.'

Leaving Noah and London behind, the two girls climbed over the mound and almost immediately bumped into the troublesome siblings.

'Thought we heard voices,' Raiph said, arms folded.

'What're you two doing out here?' Ofelia asked accusingly.

'Whatever we like,' Cinder replied, circling them like a shark.

'Who's your friend, Ofelia?' asked Raiph.

'She hasn't got any friends,' his sister snickered, pulling a coin from Ofelia's pocket, but Allura firmly grabbed her by the wrist.

'Wait a minute. I recognise you, you cost us that mark the other day. Was hoping to see you again,' Cinder said.

The next thing Allura knew, they were wrestling over the coin, with Cinder lifting it up high so she couldn't reach. Instead, Allura tackled her into a tree, sending the coin tumbling to the forest floor.

Scrambling to pick it up before Cinder could recover, Allura stood up proud with the coin in hand.

'You shouldn't have done that,' Cinder said through heavy breaths.

'Why not?' Allura asked. 'What're you going to-'

Boom!

An invisible blast of power shot out from Cinder, pushing Allura and Ofelia onto the dirt. They rose slowly to their feet, their legs still shaking from the impact as Allura pulled Ofelia by the arm into a dead sprint.

'You could've mentioned she was an embodiment!' Allura scolded Ofelia as they ran through the woods. The sounds of Raiph and Cinder's feet trampled behind them as they hopped over fallen trees and murky puddles.

They were approaching the edge of town, the warm glow of the street within sight beyond the river when Ofelia's foot snagged on a log. She came crashing to the ground and Allura turned to help when another wave of unseen energy slammed into her.

'Gotcha,' Cinder gloated.

'Okay, we give up,' Allura surrendered from the forest floor before grasping a small stone and tossing it at Cinder.

It was a cheap move. One which she wasn't particularly proud of, but then again it wasn't exactly an even fight. The rock hurtled towards her attacker, but stopped inches from her shoulder and dropped dead out of the air.

Only then did Allura notice the shimmering aura in front of them, a protective force-field radiating from Raiph.

'How stupid do you have to be to pick a fight with the Embodiments of Attack and Defence?' Cinder chortled.

'That was a good try though, to be fair,' said Raiph.

'Not good enough,' Cinder replied as she prepared

another assault, but as she did, Allura felt something that she had only ever experienced when the essence of hope had first struck her.

It was an all-consuming calmness, except now it surged inside of her, rushing through her body to become something indescribable. Something that yearned to manifest itself.

She raised her hands, channelling that feeling and directing it towards Raiph and Cinder. Closing her eyes, she allowed it to flow through her, building and building, until she was ready to let it go all at once.

And then there was…

Nothing.

Well now, that is disappointing, Allura thought as she readied herself for the beating that was surely coming.

Suddenly, Cinder fell backwards as Ofelia swiped her legs out from under her and they tussled on the ground.

Taking advantage of Raiph's confusion, Allura charged into him, knocking him over.

'Gonna really hurt you for that,' Cinder screamed, wildly swinging her fists. Meanwhile, Raiph overpowered Allura and grabbed a large stick off the ground.

He raised it above his head, ready to swing down, when a roar crackled through the woods like thunder.

The branch tumbled to the ground as Raiph quaked with terror.

'What was that?'

'Sounded like a tearer to me,' Ofelia said, winking at Allura as London let out another far-away growl.

'I think it's coming this way,' added Allura

'Come on let's get out of here,' Raiph said, pulling his sister off of Ofelia.

'But I was just about to make her cry,' Cinder argued.

'LET'S GO!' he barked before running away.

'This isn't over!' Cinder warned as she chased after her brother.

Even after they were gone, Allura and Ofelia continued to lie on the forest floor with twigs and leaves in their hair as they slowly caught their breath. Allura looked over at Ofelia, her ridiculously long hair now looking like a puddle of gold around her head.

'Are you two okay?' Noah asked as he and London appeared from over the mound.

'Yeah, we won. Can't you tell?' Allura joked.

'Good thinking getting her to roar like that,' Ofelia said.

'All her idea,' he replied as Allura patted Ofelia on the back and slapped the coin back into her hand.

'You did good,' she said.

But you should've just let me use the bear from the beginning.

*

Allura didn't pay attention for most of the walk back to the cabin, her mind distracted by what she had experienced during the fight.

It had been as though pure power was raging inside of her, like electricity had been coursing through her veins. But it was something she chose to keep to herself as nothing had come of it in the end.

They had only just returned London to the shed (where she promptly fell asleep) when Noah caught a glimpse of the clock on the wall.

'I should probably get going. I told Mum I'd wake her up from her midday nap before the markets shut.'

'Me too, I promised I'd help my parents set up the house for the party tonight,' said Ofelia.

'Party?' asked Allura.

'Did I forget to say? My parents are having a celebration for the big wedding tomorrow. You two have to come,' she insisted.

I've never been to a party, Allura thought, trying to imagine what exactly she would do at one.

'Allura?'

'I'll have to see. I don't know if London will need me,' she said.

Disappointment washed over Ofelia and there was a noticeable deflation in her peppy demeanour. They said goodbye and left with Noah reassuring Allura that they would look after London once she was gone.

It was the strangest thing, but in the excitement of the flight and the fight, Allura had completely forgotten that all of this was temporary. That she would soon forget this place and these people she had come to think of as....

No! *Don't get attached! It's what's best for everyone*, she told herself.

Isn't it?

*

Abraham returned that night with a large shank of meat slung over his shoulder. Despite his mimed objections, Allura helped him turn it into a flavoursome stew and they enjoyed it in silence, interrupted only by the occasional slurp or the gnawing of teeth against bone.

Once their bowls were empty, they sat by the fire and Abraham sipped at his flagon of blood-red wine.

'Are you going to the Donnelly's party?' she asked and he shook his head.

'Why not? It's to celebrate Orville's wedding. I'm guessing that's a big deal here?'

He nodded.

'I'm pretty sure you can talk. Can't you give me a little more than just nodding and shaking your head?'

Taking a swig of his wine, he offered her a thumbs down and with that Allura dropped her inquiry, deciding instead to simply listen to the crackling of the fire. But as she did, a curiosity grew in her like an itch that had once felt too dangerous to scratch, but now was too powerful to ignore.

'Do you-', she stumbled on her words. 'Do you know how Horas died?'

A solemn look ran across Abraham's face.

I shouldn't have asked that, she thought, but eventually he replied with a shake of his head, taking care not to look her in the eyes as he did.

He was lying, she was certain of that, but before she could ask him anymore questions, he downed his drink and left.

What are you hiding? she wondered as he vanished into the darkness.

Carrying what remained of the meal into the shed, she placed it in front of London who inspected it with her wet snout.

'It might be lamb, or maybe pig. I don't even know if you have those here,' Allura said, but before long, the food was gone and London quickly fell back to sleep, leaving Allura to crash onto one of the sofas.

From there she stared out the open window and noticed a distant rhythmic tune being carried on the wind. The sounds of Ofelia's party, no doubt.

What would I even do there anyway? she asked herself, remembering the gatherings that Mrs. Olderman used to host.

From what she had glimpsed of them from upstairs, her parties were certainly no fun at all. Just a bunch of boring old gossips gibbering on and on about this and that, and badly singing along to songs they clearly didn't know the lyrics to.

I really shouldn't go, I won't even remember any of this in a few days.

She mulled over that thought and others like it for some time, until the image of Ofelia's disappointed face caused her to extinguish the fire, grab her coat and make for the door.

In and out, I'll be five minutes at most, she reassured herself as she felt the shifting of gravel beneath her boots.

On the way she saw enormous fireworks leave a trail of smoke from the Donnelly's garden and light up the night sky with multicoloured magic. The embers of the magnificent explosions caught on nearby clouds, spreading across them until they too had turned yellow or green or red.

The display had only just ended when Allura approached the Donnelly's house, where music blared and shadows danced along the curtains. Despite her anxious mind begging her not to, she knocked on the door.

Almost immediately, it swung open and there stood Faye with a wide smile and open arms.

'Allura! How wonderful to see you!' she said, ushering her inside while guests danced and chattered loudly amongst themselves.

Banners hung from every doorway, balloons filled every room and colourful glitter covered every surface. It was an unusual mix of party decorations intermingled with the Atrilarium Day tinsel and garlands. The centrepiece being a dark green tree standing proudly in the sitting room (a tradition Allura assumed Orterra had borrowed from Earth).

Atop the fireplace, a music-box-band played as Faye led Allura through the house, passing people she recognised from town, each one with a giddy smile on their face.

She waved to Lydia who either didn't see her or chose to ignore her as she hurried around to freshen drinks and plump pillows. All the while, Ofelia's little sister chased after her.

'Who they? What that? Where Ma?' Abigail rattled off question after question until Lydia finally had enough and passed her to Cameron who was sat in solitude in one of the corners of the lounge reading a book, completely unimpressed by the whole affair.

Faye guided Allura to the opposite corner of the room where Ofelia and Noah had thrown together a bundle of pillows to sit on.

'Look who's here,' Faye said, presenting Allura to them like some grand prize.

'Told you she'd come,' Ofelia said to Noah as she pulled Allura down onto the pillows. 'I'm so happy you're here.'

'To be clear, I never said you wouldn't show up,' Noah clarified, giving Ofelia an unpleasant glare.

'London didn't really seem to need me, so I thought I'd pop by,' she explained.

I've shown my face. Now, I'll hang around for ten minutes then slip out before I have the chance to ruin it, she decided.

But an hour soon whizzed by and the three continued to discuss everything and anything from Ofelia's plans to become a zoologist to Allura's near-death experiences to Noah's irrational fear of balloons.

Faye even returned to their corner a few times to answer Allura's questions about the party, explaining that tomorrow's ceremony was not just any old wedding, but something very special that hadn't happened in centuries.

A coupling of two rulers from different domains, forming an unbreakable union between The Balance and The Cycle.

'As for why we're celebrating, well who needs a reason to have a good time,' Faye said before joining the tail of a conga line as it snaked past her.

The party had kicked into full swing and the three

friends watched as Lydia frantically tried to keep the house in order.

'Does your mum even know how to relax?' Noah asked.

'I'm not sure, maybe I should ask your mum to teach her,' Ofelia replied, pointing to Patricia who was half-asleep on one of the sofas.

'Fair enough.'

'He does have a point though,' Allura said, unable to think of a moment that she had seen Lydia do anything except fuss and scowl all night.

'Hmmm,' Ofelia said, her nose twitching irritably. Then she hopped up and hurried out of the room.

'Did I upset her?' Allura asked.

'Coming from someone who actively tries to rile her up, I really don't know,' Noah replied.

I knew I shouldn't have come. This was a huge mistake.

Allura's breath drew fast and she got ready to leave when Ofelia burst back into the room, followed by both of her mothers. Lydia stood in the centre of the party and Faye whispered to the tiny musicians who promptly put down their instruments.

'If I could steal the spotlight for a moment, it's been brought to my attention that I have been a little preoccupied all night,' Lydia said, making Allura feel sick.

She already had a sense that Lydia didn't care for her and now Ofelia had told her what she had said. In that moment Allura wanted nothing more than for London to burst through the wall and swallow her whole.

Instead, all she could do was watch as Lydia continued to talk softly to the room. Then her eyes met Allura's directly as she said:

'For that I am very sorry. An unwelcoming host makes for an unwelcoming home, and so, with that in mind, I hope this can start to make things right.'

Ofelia returned to the pile of pillows as Lydia cleared her throat and began to do the last thing that Allura had expected.

She started to sing.

I've seen lakes that shine and shimmer,
A beauty beyond compare,
I've felt snow fresh from the heavens,
Amongst the mountain air.
I've seen cities born of magic,
Magic people I have known.
I've stepped along the wastelands,
Where new life has never grown.
I've seen fields of crimson flowers,
It's the place that pixies roam.
Yet through all my travels one fact remains,
The Bliss is still my home.

The song got faster as one by one; people started to join in. First Faye, then Ofelia, until the whole room had erupted in song as the music-box-band kicked back into full swing.

So, you can keep your monsters of the lake,
And your frigid mountains too.
Cities are too cramped anyway,

And the wasteland? No thank you.
Oh, the fields and hills are fine and all,
But I'll have to give it a miss.
See there is no place I'd rather be,
Than the forests of The Bliss.

Verse after verse, the song grew louder and the singers grew rowdier until it became like a sea shanty that pirates would bellow on their adventures.

Everyone was on their feet, and even Allura, who if asked would say she hated dancing, couldn't resist. She joined the rest of them as they locked arms and spun in a circle starting with Ofelia, then Noah, then Faye and then Lydia, each one laughing joyously as they skipped along.

They sang and danced until even the little wooden musicians were tired and at that point, Allura finally had to admit that she was very glad she had come.

*

As the party began to wind down and guests filtered out, Allura, Noah and Ofelia crashed back onto their den of pillows in exhaustion.

'Do you think she'll be there?' Ofelia asked.

'No way. Not by invitation at least,' Noah responded.

'Who are you talking about?'

'Evelyn Dormé,' Lydia said, joining them on the pillows.

'Who?'

'The mother of the bride. No matter how much Darnigold may wish she wasn't,' she explained.

'Why wouldn't Darnigold want her mother there?'

'What you have to understand is that Darnigold is the Embodiment of Life, and Evelyn is her counterbalance, the Embodiment of Death. They both came into the roles at the same time, decades ago, but when Darnigold discovered what her mother represented, she saw an opportunity.'

Allura found herself leaning in closer as Lydia spun her a tale of heartbreak and betrayal. As the story went, Darnigold Dormé valued life above all else and came up with a plot to rid Earth of death.

Using the resources of The Cycle, she had created a device. An object so powerful and terrible that it was capable of not only destroying an embodiment, but the very essence of what they embodied as well. A bomb that could eviscerate anything caught in its blast, even death itself.

The weapon was destruction incarnated and had been given a name to reflect that:

The Eviscero Charge.

Although the name meant nothing to Allura, she could have sworn she felt a cold shiver run down her spine at the very mention of it.

With the weapon in hand, Darnigold had begged Evelyn to allow her to extract the essence of death from her so that they could destroy it once and for all, freeing Earth from its influence. However, no matter how hard Darnigold pleaded with her, Evelyn refused.

If Darnigold wanted to destroy death, she would have to destroy her own mother as well.

Of course, Darnigold could not bring herself to do

such a thing and so the Eviscero Charge was disassembled and its schematics were locked away in the deepest vaults of The Cycle. But while the bomb had never been used, the relationship between mother and daughter had been fractured forever.

By the story's end, Allura was seething, with her fists clenched so tightly that her nails had dug marks into her skin.

'Are you okay Allura?' Noah asked, noticing the rage in her.

'She could have stopped everyone from dying, but chose not to? How could she be so selfish? How could they all be so selfish? Death, deception, misery. We don't need those. Earth doesn't need any of these negative embodiments,' she said.

'Even forgetfulness?' Ofelia asked with a hurt tone and Allura's exhausting anger quickly subsided into a mellow sadness.

'No, I- I didn't mean that. It's only that, if she hadn't been so selfish, I might still have a family.'

She could tell Noah and Ofelia were surprised by that and Lydia took Allura's hand in her own.

'Evelyn had her reasons for doing what she did, but there is a purpose to everything that happens. You being here with us now is all the proof you need of that, because if you weren't here then we wouldn't be able to bring you to the wedding tomorrow.'

'Really?' she asked, hardly believing what she was hearing.

'If you want to come that is,' Ofelia added.

Allura's eyes lit up as an uncontrollable smile stretched across her face.

Almost exactly as she had planned, Allura spent the night on a sofa, it just wasn't Horas'. Instead, this one belonged to the Donnelly's who had offered her and Noah the chance to sleepover.

There, in Faye and Lydia's vacant sitting room, Allura slept on a beige sofa opposite Ofelia with TibbidyBoo tucked between her arms (as it turned out he was a bit of a snorer). Noah meanwhile had transformed the pillow fort into a makeshift mattress and was resting soundly on the floor.

Despite her cosy surroundings, Allura found herself caught in a nightmare, as her dreams quickly returned to the basement once again. Exactly like last time, it was a never-ending twilight until a single figure emerged from the doorway of light.

It reached for her, grasping desperately at the air as Allura fought with every muscle in her body to escape.

'What are you doing?' a familiar voice asked.

It was Noah, but there was something different about him. As though in that sea of hazy darkness he was the only thing she could see clearly. He stepped out of the dark and looked around curiously, wandering closer to the light with every step.

Allura tried to speak, to warn him to stay away from it, but she couldn't. When finally Noah noticed the horror on her face, it was already too late as the figure in the doorway placed a single hand on his shoulder.

'Allura, what do you think this is?' he asked in a

misty voice.

Then with a gasp, her eyes sprung open and she almost let out the screams that she had been denied in the dream. It took her a moment to recover and another moment more to notice that Noah was awake as well.

'I'm sorry,' he whispered. 'I can't always help it.'

'So that was- I mean, you were really there?'

'I honestly didn't mean to intrude. Sometimes dreams pull me in whether I like it or not.'

'I think you're confusing dreams for nightmares.'

'What makes you say that?' he asked.

'Please,' she said holding up a hand to stop him, 'I don't want to talk about it. Just go back to sleep.'

'Okay, I'm sorry,' he said, rolling onto his side and shutting his eyes to allow one solitary moment of pure silence to pass before he whispered:

'Allura?'

'Yeah?'

'I'm sorry about your parents. We didn't know if they were dead.'

Allura didn't reply for a while, a part of her wishing she hadn't said anything about them in the first place. But she could tell he was being sincere and didn't want him to think she hadn't appreciated him saying it.

'It's okay. I don't really know for sure either.'

'Then why'd you say it?'

'I guess it's just easier.'

'Easier?'

'Than thinking they didn't want me.'

Another silence set in and Allura thought he had

gone back to sleep when he said:

'For whatever it's worth, I'm really glad you're here.'

She didn't know what to say and so she simply said nothing, allowing him to believe that she had fallen back to sleep. After a while longer, snow began to fall outside and once she was certain that Noah had drifted off, Allura moved to the window to watch it.

With each gentle snowflake that drifted past, she thought, as she so often did, of her parents whose names she would never know and whose faces she had never even seen.

9

A day to remember

'Eat up everyone! We need to be dressed and on the road in twenty minutes,' said Faye as they all tucked into breakfast.

The Donnelly's kitchen table was small and round, but somehow, they had all managed to squeeze in. Allura was enjoying a conversation with Lydia about her work as an eldrologist (investigator of magic phenomenon) at the town's local Hest, when she could have sworn she heard someone say the word 'dresses'.

A concern rose in her, like a wave yet to crash as she took stock of her own outfit. She was still wearing the same clothes that she had arrived to the party in, a buttonless cotton shirt and brown trousers, heavily stained with grass marks from the day before.

From across the table, she managed to catch Noah's eye.

'Dresses?' she mouthed.

'What?' he mouthed back.

'Dresses?' she repeated silently. He thought for a moment, gazing off as he tried to decipher her words, then he simply shrugged.

This is getting me nowhere.

'Don't worry,' Ofelia whispered, 'you can wear one of mine.'

'Great,' she said, feigning excitement.

There is no way I am wearing a dress.

*

The dress was dark green and sleeveless with a ruffled collar and embroidered patterns running down it like the roots of a tree. Allura didn't know a lot about dresses and so she genuinely wondered if they were all *this* uncomfortable. She had only agreed to wear it because everyone else had dressed up so nicely.

Ofelia for example was nearly drowning in the material of her deep blue dress - like the clear sky over the ocean - while Noah was adorned in a creaseless buttoned-up shirt and black pleated trousers.

Allura had even gone as far as to allow Ofelia's mother to attempt to detangle her hair and let her natural curls flow. She found Faye's gentle and patient hands to be preferable to Mrs. Olderman's 'chop and be done with it' solution.

But still, her dress was not all bad, its best feature being a large pocket sown into the side in which she could fit the looking glass Cognitius had gifted her.

She had managed to grab it in the earliest hours of the morning whilst sneaking out to feed London and wrap her in a warm blanket. Although, part of her now felt like she should offer it to Noah's mother as a thank you for letting her and Ofelia ride with them to Highdenhome.

Not that Patricia seemed to mind having them along, partly because the carriage Elliott had sent for them was twice as big as the one Allura had rode in from Cambium.

As they rolled through the main street of Endwood, she admired the ornately decorated trees which looked all the more festive in the white blanket that had encased the town. Despite the cold, the street was still littered with people getting ready for Atrilarium Day, slipping and struggling through the thick snow with arms full of gifts and firewood.

The carriage was somewhere in-between Danderstorm's Haberdashery and Flickshaw's Flying Rickshaws when Allura thought she spotted Abraham amongst the crowds.

A part of her wanted to call out the window to him, to tell him where they were going, but something in his steely expression when she had asked him about Orville told her that he probably wouldn't approve of her going.

After all, why wouldn't he be going to the wedding himself? she wondered before deciding to keep her mouth shut.

However, by the time they crossed over another bridge and out into the surrounding woodland, she had convinced herself that she really should have said something.

*

An hour ticked by and Noah's mother was

predictably fast asleep, a light snore purring from her while outside the snow had kicked up into a dense white fog.

'I meant to ask you-' Ofelia said, stopping mid-sentence to double check that Patricia really was asleep. A thin line of drool rolling down her chin confirmed it.

'When you and London were flying, what really happened?'

'What do you mean? I already told you, she freaked out for some reason,' Allura replied, but Noah and Ofelia both looked at her with raised eyebrows.

'Alright, fine *I* freaked out. We were so high up and all I remember is thinking that we were definitely going to die if we didn't get back on the ground. Then the next thing I knew we were crashing.'

'I KNEW IT!' Ofelia blurted out.

'Shush,' Noah said as Patricia stirred in her sleep.

'I knew it,' she repeated quietly, 'you're afraid of heights.'

'Well, I wouldn't say afraid exactly,' Allura said, embarrassed by the accusation. 'It was just that when I looked down, everything started spinning. Like I had no control over anything. I was certain I was going to fall.'

'Maybe that's exactly the problem, you looked down,' Ofelia said with a grin.

'Easy for you to say with your feet on the ground.'

'Believe me, when I fly, I'm going to do it with purpose. Landing will be the last thing on my mind.'

'But it's not the flying that will kill you. It's the falling,' said Allura.

'So don't fall.'

'Now why didn't I think of that?' Allura asked with as much sarcasm as humanly possible.

'I think you're both crazy if that's any help,' Noah interjected.

'Yeah maybe,' Allura chuckled, drawing a bear with wings on the fogged-up window.

As she did, the falling snow began to slow, becoming gentler and gentler until the endless whiteness that surrounded them dissipated. Where Allura had expected to see trees and an expanse of snow-covered woods, there was only a large wall of rocks and boulders.

'Oh, wow,' Ofelia gasped.

'What?' asked Allura, turning to the other window.

Then she saw it.

A valley of snow-kissed mountains with their peaks disappearing into fluffy clouds while foaming rivers gushed at their bases. Giant birds circled the colossal towers of pointed stone and Allura could make out the vague outlines of small huts and villages built into the side of the mountain itself.

'I hadn't realised we were in The Balance already,' Noah said breathlessly and Allura thought back to the map Ofelia had drawn for her at Cambium. Remembering the small triangles she had added to The Balance, only now did she understand what they had represented.

'We'll be at Highdenhome soon,' Patricia said

unexpectedly, causing everyone to jump out of their seats.

Not too soon hopefully, Allura thought, enjoying the view.

*

The route through The Balance took them around the sides of the mountains and across treacherously narrow pathways with the wheels of the carriage grazing the edges of the steep cliff faces.

Eventually, through bated breath and clenched teeth, Allura heard the crunch of snow beneath the horse's hooves give way to a sturdier clip-clopping noise as the coach found firmer terrain.

Other than the mountains behind them, all they could see in every direction was flat grey stone with vibrant plants and trees growing from the many cracks in its surface. The snow meanwhile had stopped entirely and the clouds had seemingly vanished with the mountains to give way to a bright and clear sky.

'They say that Orville himself raised the ground beneath his castle you know?' said Noah, relishing in the chance to show off his history knowledge.

'He can lift rocks?' Allura asked.

'He can do more than that. He's the Embodiment of Order. He can connect with the inherent chaos of nature, then mould it according to his design,' Patricia explained.

'But yeah, basically he can move rocks,' Ofelia nodded as the carriage slowed to a walking pace, before coming to a complete stop as it joined a queue of other travellers.

There were golden carriages adorned with diamonds the size of fists, lone riders on trusted steeds, coaches led by enormous boars and winged horses whizzing by overhead with their riders waving smugly at the people below.

Allura watched with jaw-dropping awe as they approached Highdenhome and she saw that it was exactly as Noah had described. The castle sat at the top of a giant circle of raised stone that loomed taller than the trees. The only way in or out was a single steep road that stretched all the way up to the gated entrance.

Highdenhome itself was a vast collection of towers carefully stacked together, some were short and stocky while others spiralled into the sky, as tall as the mountains themselves.

'Each one has a specific purpose,' Patricia said, pointing at different towers as she spoke. 'That one is the armoury and that one is where the servants sleep, oh and that is the infirmary.'

'Do you suppose they have a different tower for every meal of the day? Like a breakfast, lunch and dinner tower?' Ofelia joked and although Allura laughed, a little part of her was curious if there was any truth to it.

One by one, coach by coach they made their way up the stone road. The sounds of cheering and celebratory music accompanied the sweet smells of cinnamon and freshly baked pastries that wafted down from the castle.

Once at the top, they rolled through the gates and

exited the carriage, leaving it and their driver in a courtyard full of other carriages and drivers.

Allura stumbled at first, the restrictions of her ill-fitting dress nearly tripping her as she hopped out. Ofelia helped her find her feet and together, the four of them made their way towards the main courtyard.

There were at least twenty armour-plated guards in the first area alone and despite the fact that Allura knew they were there to keep the guests safe, she couldn't help but feel a little uncomfortable around them.

Calm down, she told herself, struggling to put her mind at ease which was only made worse when a giant rock golem stomped past.

With each pound of its heavy feet, the ground shook and Allura froze at the sight of the creature, craning her neck just to look at it. The golem was five times her size and made entirely of cracked stone, sounding like a landslide with every movement.

'Don't worry, Orville created them to keep watch, but they would never hurt anyone, not unless he commanded them to,' Patricia said as she pulled Allura away. Her words were a comfort, yet when Allura glanced back at the golem, just for a moment, its vacant eyes seemed to stare back.

Pushing it out of her mind, Allura took in the main courtyard as they entered through a tall archway. It was enormous, and once the rest of the Donnelly clan arrived, the place began to fill up with people from every region, all sporting elegant gowns and sharp suits.

Although she hated to admit it, Allura was glad they had made her wear the stupid dress.

From there, the day exceeded her wildest expectations, overflowing with merriment and raucous laughter while good food and sweet tasting drinks were carried around on floating trays.

Entertainers performed on a stage in the middle of the courtyard, each one delivering a thrilling display only to be upstaged by the following act. There were sword swallowers, fire eaters, ribbon dancers and world-class singers in the first hour alone. The crowd watched each one in absolute wonderment, although Noah seemed to flinch quite a lot during the more dangerous performances.

The audience itself did not rely on the arranged entertainment to have fun however, as despite their fancy dresses and clean-cut jackets, Allura was surprised to find that they were actually quite a rowdy bunch. Every time a guest of high esteem arrived, a little man with an unusually loud voice would blow on a horn and announce them to the crowd.

Naturally, as the day went on, the audience had made a game of the whole affair, purposefully cheering louder and louder for each new guest that entered.

'PRESENTING, LADY SYDNEY HARROW – CO-RULER OF THE DUALITY!'

The crowd erupted into applause.

'PRESENTING, LORD MARR SHAW – CO-RULER OF THE LINE!'

The crowd went wild, sprinkling cheers and

whistles in amongst their claps.

'PRESENTING, LORD RAVEN SOLMEN – CONFERANT TO HIS LORD RUTHERFORD!'

Highdenhome was deafened by applause, as though everyone had forgotten who they were actually clapping for. Allura however, had suddenly lost all interest in the game.

'I didn't know Raven would be here,' she said.

'Ignore him,' Ofelia advised, only half paying attention as a small pixie covered her in colourful face paint.

Raven waved as he entered, wearing an elegant black coat with a high collar and gold sequins, while the twins from Cambium followed close behind. They moved like a pair of shadows cascading from a single person as he swiftly crossed the courtyard.

Allura maintained a watchful eye as he dipped into a stone corridor that ran along one of the courtyard's edges, leaving the twins outside to keep guard.

Curious, Allura held up the looking glass and peered into the corridor. She couldn't see anything at first, but after a few minutes Raven reappeared and gestured for the twins to follow him towards one of the towers.

She fought the urge to keep watching Raven and instead focused further on the corridor, until finally, a woman's face poked out from one of the arched windows. She had long grey hair, craggily umber skin, and heavy bags under her eyes which were fixed on the marble balcony overlooking all of Highdenhome.

Suddenly, her gaze dropped and Allura found

herself staring eye to eye with the mysterious woman. Flinching from the spyglass, she quickly held it up to her eye again only to find that there was no trace of her.

'Allura,' a stern voice called from behind, making her jump yet again.

'What are you doing here?' Raven asked.

Oh great.

'Ofelia's parents invited me,' she said, gesturing to the group around her who were distractedly watching a dancing wood gnell on stage.

'I'm glad to see you've found new people to latch onto,' he said snidely.

'At least they're *good* people,' she replied with defensively gritted teeth.

'I'll take your word for it. How are you finding Orterra? Still thinking of cutting your visit short?'

'I'm making do, although I am surprised to see you here. All these people having fun, doesn't seem like your sort of thing.'

'I am Orville's conferant, where else would I be?' he said coldly before reaching into one of his pockets to pull out an envelope. 'It's fortuitous that you should be here actually. Cognitius asked me to stop by Endwood and give you this, but now I suppose you've saved me the trouble.'

'Is she not here then?' Allura asked, reaching for the letter.

'She's tending to matters in Giant's Peak I'm afraid, being one of The Bliss' regents keeps her very busy,' he said, raising the envelope out of her reach.

'And you're not I suppose,' she said, causing him

to lean towards her.

'Careful now, you have no idea the things I am up to,' he said with a harsh inflection as the black vortex in his eyes flared up.

'What's going on?' Ofelia asked as she finally noticed what was happening and linked arms with Allura.

A snicker escaped Raven's thin lips as Ofelia's face had been painted in the red and black stripes of some Orterran creature, but Allura appreciated her support nonetheless.

'I was simply delivering a message,' he said, innocently handing over the letter. 'I better get going, wouldn't want to miss what comes next.'

Keeping her eyes trained on him as he and the twins walked off into one of the towers, Allura only allowed herself to shudder after he had vanished from sight.

'That man makes my skin crawl,' she said as she tucked the sealed envelope into her pocket.

'Lucky he left because I had no idea what I was going to say next,' Ofelia admitted, but before Allura could tell Ofelia about Raven's clandestine meeting, horns blared from the main tower.

All eyes turned upwards as the small announcer approached the edge of the balcony with a red scroll in his hand.

'PRESENTING, HIS EXCELLENCY, THE EMBODIMENT OF ORDER, CO-RULER OF THE BALANCE AND LORD OF HIGHDENHOME; SIR ORVILLE RUTHERFORD!'

Allura watched through the spyglass as a well-groomed man in a blue overcoat adorned in medals stepped up to the front of the balcony. After everything she had heard about him, it was nice to finally see the man in person.

He looked just as he had in Abraham's drawing, except for a few more wrinkles across his face and streaks of grey in his hair. His eyes had a tired quality to them and his skin was a bit pale, although compared to Raven he looked decidedly tanned.

However, one thing was for certain, the crowd was thrilled to see him.

'My friends, my family, my people. I thank you for being here on this day and can only hope that I can repay the favour of your time and loyalty through my leadership,' he said in a bold and eloquent voice.

After the applause died down, the little man cleared his throat.

'AND NOW, HER EXCELLENCY, THE EMBODIMENT OF LIFE, CO-LEADER OF THE CYCLE AND KEEPER OF DORMÉ MANOR; LADY DARNIGOLD DORMÉ!'

The doors swung open once more and from them, exited Darnigold.

A vision of beauty in a flowing white dress, she had a crown of flowers over her gorgeous braided hair, with a handful of loose curls, and a smile that entrapped the hearts of all who saw it.

'People of The Balance, people of The Cycle and people of Orterra. Know that this union will strengthen the bond between us all. Our love for you is as true and unbreakable as our love for one another. Today I will not only be swearing my soul to Orville, but to all of you as well.'

Even Allura had to applaud, although she wasn't sure if she was clapping for the speech or for Darnigold herself. There was something enchanting about her, as though her words had a weight to them, an authentic sincerity.

Strange rituals and vows took up the next hour, culminating in the couple exchanging personal objects and swearing to place them on each other's graves when the time came. Allura had thought it was a little morbid, but she could see that there was a sweetness behind it.

More than anything she was surprised by how captivating the whole thing had been, finding herself disappointed when it eventually came to an end.

'Darnigold Dormé. How long do you wish to bind yourself to this man?' the minister asked.

'Forever,' she answered unwaveringly, as a bead of sweat ran down Orville's forehead.

'And you, Orville John Rutherford. How long do you wish to bind yourself to this woman?'

The crowd hung in suspense, hands ready to clap and throats prepared to cheer.

'I-um-' he muttered, choking on his words.

Cold feet? Allura and the rest of the onlookers wondered as he continued to stammer.

Then his face turned a sickly purple and he clutched at his collar, gasping for air.

'What's going on?'

'What's he doing?'

'Is he alright?'

He reached out to Darnigold, and she to him,

before dropping to the floor as the crowd's murmuring rose to a collective scream.

'HE'S DYING!' someone yelled as a stone golem came crashing through the wall to the west, while another collapsed the one to the east, each one sending fragments of stone sailing into the crowds.

With loud booms and thumps, the golems fell alongside their master, causing the crowd to erupt into chaos.

'COME ON KIDS!' Lydia shouted, holding Abigail close and making her way towards one of the corridors away from the crowds. They all grabbed hands, with Ofelia at the end of the chain and Allura trailing behind her.

'WAIT!' Allura called out, struggling to keep up.

Ofelia stretched her hand out to her as the gap between them shrunk. Allura reached for her in return. They were inches from each other's grasp when a panicked knight came charging through and collided with her, sending Allura toppling to the ground.

Ofelia called for her as she was dragged further and further away by the frenzied crowd. Allura tried to shout back, but finely polished shoes trampled around her and every time she tried to get back up someone's knee would crash into her back or a foot would trip over her ankle.

She decided to try to crawl to safety, but the world above had turned to mayhem as the stampede shook the very ground around her. Only making it a few feet forwards, she felt a thick boot slam down onto her hand.

The scream she released spooked a winged horse nearby and it reared its legs, ready to crush her with its hooves. Protectively holding her throbbing hand over her face, Allura prepared for the worst.

From somewhere in the chaos, an unseen figure tackled her out of the way as the creature came crashing to the floor. Colliding hard against the cobblestone, Allura felt a terrible pain quickly run from her head down to the rest of her body as her vision became blurry and the colours of the world instantly drained away.

Consciousness was escaping her, but in her final lucid moments she caught one last glimpse of the mysterious woman Raven had been speaking with, emerging from the corridor and slipping away into the crowd.

Then, all she could see was darkness.

10

There went the groom

'How is she?' a strained voice asked.
'There will be some aching and swelling, but she's going to be alright,' a silkier voice replied.

Sore and bloodshot, Allura's eyes flickered open and the first thing she saw was the very last thing she had expected. There, on the bed opposite her, was Orville Rutherford, the dead groom himself.

Except he wasn't dead.

His purple complexion had vanished entirely and he was sat straight up in his bed, somehow looking regal even then. She tried to sit up as well, but the strength to do so eluded her.

'Take it slowly. You took a nasty bump to the head,' the nurse said, although her towering height, opalescent skin and pointed antlers jutting from her head made her unlike any nurse Allura had ever seen before.

The woman stirred a cauldron in the corner of the room, releasing a gold mist that hung in the air and smelt like lilac. With a nod from Orville, the nurse left, closing the double doors behind her and Allura turned to look at him.

'From the expression on your face I would say that she is the first grail you've ever seen. They truly are a marvellous species. It's a shame so few of them ever leave that island of theirs,' Orville said softly.

Allura stared at him blankly for a moment, whether it was due to her injuries, the shock or just genuinely not understanding what he was talking about, she couldn't be certain.

But eventually, when she realised that staying silent had become the rudest thing she could do, she blurted out:

'So, you're not dead?'

'Either that, or we both are,' he said as he fiddled with something shiny in his hand.

Allura let out a small laugh as she looked around the circular room, seeing that it consisted of four beds with silver railings, some regal desks that were positioned against the walls, cabinets filled with shimmering and glowing vials, and beautiful stained-glass windows that looked out over the courtyard and filtered gleaming sunlight into the room.

As hospital rooms went, this one was clearly fit for a king.

'How did I get here?' she asked.

'When I awoke, they told me that a girl had almost been trampled to death in the courtyard, so I had them bring you here,' he explained.

Allura felt touched that someone like him, a total stranger (and a royal one no less), would have any concern for her. She thanked him as the mist that wafted from the cauldron caught her eye.

It shifted and formed together until a gold image

of the stampeding crowd appeared in the floating vapour. A sense of uneasiness washed over her as she watched the vision unfold and she wished it would go away.

Her discomfort must have been clear on her face as Orville got up and with a flick of his hand, he dispersed the image.

'My apologies,' he said, 'the memormist only shows what you're willing to let it. Try not to dwell on what happened and it shouldn't appear again.'

'Why is it here?'

'My conferant was hoping to find some clues towards the identity of my would-be assassin in my memories.'

'Any luck?'

'Afraid not.'

'And *how* is it that you're not dead?' she asked as he crossed the room, still holding the shining object as he picked up a little glass jar in his other hand. Holding it up to her, she saw that it was full of a thick yellow liquid that oozed and bubbled.

'It's called Ultima Oscula. The Final Kiss. A particularly poisonous type of flower. Thankfully they managed to draw it from my system before it could do any serious damage,' he explained.

'You ate that?' she asked in disgust.

'Well, it didn't exactly look like this when I ate it, but yes. Although in all fairness, you should have seen the feast we had before the vows. I ate a great many things that I had never even heard of before.'

Knock! Knock! Knock!

'Come in,' Orville ordered and when the door

opened, a familiar face poked his head in.

It was Noah's father, who entered with a jolliness about him, moving with an infectious spring in his step. He shook Orville's hand as though he would never let it go with a big grin across his face.

'So wonderful to see you're alright, sir. I wouldn't be able to forgive myself if you had...' he paused, unable to bring himself to finish the thought.

'I am fine Elliott, but it wouldn't be your fault if I wasn't. My personal safety is not a part of your responsibilities. It's only a pity that such a magnificent ceremony was interrupted,' Orville said graciously, making Elliott blush.

Then he spotted Allura and knelt beside her bed.

'You must be Noah's new friend, Allura?'

'Yes, that's me,' she replied with a nod, oddly relieved to hear that someone had described her as Noah's friend.

'He wanted to come and see you, Patricia and all the Donnellys did too, but I'm afraid the guards aren't letting anyone else in so, I told them I would come and see how you are on their behalf.'

'Me? Oh, never better,' she said, gesturing to the bandage around her head and he let out a deep chuckle before bombarding her with more questions:

'Can I get you anything? Do you need more pillows? Do you want some ice for your head? Would you like me to open a window?'

Allura struggled to sound more lucid than she was, her brain swirling and sloshing like soup inside her skull, but finally she managed to convince him that she really was alright.

'Wonderful, I'll let the others know,' he said, 'and don't worry, we won't be leaving without you.'

He squeezed her arm in a comforting way then spoke with Orville again before heading for the door.

'It really was an amazing day Mr. Tanden,' Allura said, deepening Elliott's blush as he left.

'Sounds like you have some good friends,' Orville said as he moved to stand at the end of her bed.

'I think so.'

'I had friends like that once,' he said with a noticeable crack in his voice.

'What happened?' she pried, pretending not to know who he could be talking about.

'Sadly we... drifted apart.'

He was being as withholding as Abraham had been and she didn't like it one bit. Whether it was the bump to the head or simply how at ease she felt in that warm and snug room, Allura decided to be bold.

'Was one of them named Horas?'

'How did you know that?' he asked, his demeanour changing very suddenly as though every muscle had clenched.

'Because I'm his replacement,' she said with a little flourish of her hands.

Almost as if his own legs couldn't support him anymore, Orville sat at the end of her bed, analysing her as though she were some incredible jewel he had found.

Then he held the metal trinket he had been playing with up to his mouth and she could tell that the cogs of his mind were whirring rapidly.

'I'm sorry what did you say your name was?' he

asked and Allura only then realised that they had yet
to be properly introduced.

'Allura. Allura Saint-May.'

He gazed at her, transfixed.

'And you are Horas' successor? The new
Embodiment of Hope?'

'Trust me no one is more upset about it than me.'

'No, not at all. Forgive me, I'm just a little
stunned. You have to understand that Horas and I,
we weren't simply friends. We were like brothers.
He helped me through some very trying times
indeed.'

With every kind word about Horas, Allura felt the
mountain of responsibility grow ever taller. She had
thought that leaving and letting someone else be
chosen was the best way to honour the man, but now
even that felt like it would be a disappointment.

'I don't think I could ever live up to him,' she said.

'What makes you say that?'

'For starters, I'm not sure I even really believe in
hope. I mean I know it exists, but I can't say I see the
point. All it ever seems to do trick people into
thinking everything's going to magically work out.
But more than that, it seems like everyone loved
Horas and from what I can tell, he always knew how
to help. I only ever seem to mess things up.'

'I'm sure that's not true.'

'Oh really?' she asked, pointing to her bandaged
head again.

He chuckled at first, then thought for a moment
before handing her the shiny object he had been
fiddling with. Turning it over in her hands, she

inspected it haphazardly before realising what it was.

Made of a sleek and polished silver, she recognised it as some type of war medal that hung from a red ribbon. She made sure to hold it with care after that, as though it were made of glass rather than solid metal. But what surprised her most about it was that it wasn't Orterran.

It was from Earth.

'You see before I came here, a very long time ago, I used to live in a place called Stockwell,' Orville said.

No way, she thought.

Eagerly, she explained to Orville that while her memories there were not exactly the fondest, she had also lived in Stockwell, if only for a few months during her time with the Trott family.

Orville peppered Allura with questions about what had changed or remained the same over the years since he had last been there, until eventually he returned to his original point.

'I lived there for almost thirty years and would have gladly spent the rest of my days there. But it wasn't to be. You see in 1939, I was enlisted in the army as an infantry soldier in a great battle that I suppose you would now know as the second of the world wars.'

As he spoke, Allura examined his face. There were a few noticeable wrinkles here and there, but he certainly didn't look anywhere near one hundred years old.

A perk of being an embodiment, she figured.

'It felt like the whole world was aflame, like chaos

itself had come to destroy us,' he continued and as he spoke the gold mist shifted behind him, taking the shape of planes, bullets and dying men.

Then the violent images faded away and the golden silhouettes of a woman and a little girl appeared at a train station alongside a younger Orville. His family waved as the train took him away and Allura was unsure if Orville was aware of how much he was revealing to her.

'By the time I was chosen as the Embodiment of Order, I had lost everything and everyone,' he explained as the image of his quaint little house in Stockwell manifested in the mist, now reduced to rubble.

'I was angry, scared and alone. Even this world and the immense power it gave me wasn't enough. I just didn't see the point of going on without the people I had lost,' he said, swinging his hand through the memormist and falling quiet.

After allowing him to sit in the silence, Allura felt she needed to know:

'So, what changed?'

'I met Horas...'

Exactly what I need, more pressure, she thought.

'...and he was a mess.'

Wait what?

'Horas had grown up here, but he wasn't chosen as an embodiment until later in life. When eventually he did become our Embodiment of Hope, he was overwhelmed with nerves and uncertainty and a sense of responsibility, until he became as lost as I was. But we found each other and together we made our way. He taught me to embrace my role here, while I helped him find his own path.'

Orville paused again, seemingly lost in his memories before snapping back to the present.

'I suppose what I'm trying to say is, things may seem out of place right now, but eventually, you will find your way as well.'

'Thank you,' she said sincerely. Although she was sceptical of what he said, she couldn't pretend his kind words hadn't meant anything to her. 'If you don't mind me asking, why did you and Horas stop being friends?'

Orville sighed and began to pace around the room.

'For the longest time I had viewed this place – this world - as a way of escaping the problems of Earth. I thought that I would never again have to take up arms against my fellow man in some pointless war, but I was wrong.'

The memormist sprung back into life as a tall and well-armoured figure came into view.

'You see about two decades ago a man named Malvus became convinced that there was no place for non-embodiments in positions of power. He valued strength above all things, believing that the weak and powerless belonged firmly under the heel of the 'mighty'. While I and the other key-embodiments rule the domains of this world, most of us would never dream of subjugating those who are not chosen, nor should we elevate those who are.'

As though through conscious effort, Orville closed his eyes and conjured an image of himself, Abraham and Horas together in the mist, battling against a gathering of Malvus' forces.

'And so, as Malvus' numbers grew, Cognitius raised an army to challenge him. We were all involved in one way or another. Not just the people of The Balance, but The Bliss, The Divide, The Duality, The Cycle and even what little remained of The Line had a role to play.'

Vague outlines of two enormous armies took shape, charging towards one another. Thousands upon thousands of soldiers surged onwards with swords and shields in hand.

Amongst the human figures were centaurs, giants, lytes and all manner of magical creatures that had been enlisted by both sides.

Eventually, the two forces collided in a puff of golden smoke.

'The war was long and arduous, with unimaginable losses on both sides, but eventually through blood and sacrifice, we prevailed,' Orville said as the gold image of Cognitius standing victorious amongst her army filled the room.

She hasn't aged a day, Allura thought.

'But that's good, isn't it?' she asked, blown away, but utterly confused. 'How could winning the war have driven you and Horas apart?'

Orville squirmed uncomfortably.

'The truth is, at the start of the war I was very hesitant to get involved. I felt I owed it to myself and the people of The Balance who look to me for guidance, to steer them away from what I had experienced on Earth. But Horas convinced me otherwise. He said that I had a duty to this world to stop tyranny in its infancy.'

Allura could see a powerful sense of unease overcome him as his eyes struggled to meet hers.

'Yes, we won the war but the damage that was done seemed irreparable. My faith in the goodness of Orterra was broken and I blamed Horas for convincing me to choose a side in the first place. Unfortunately, it took a few decades, and meeting Darnigold of course, for me to realise how foolish I had been.'

The memormist remained strangely still while he spoke, as though his guilt ran too deep to allow those memories to be exhibited.

'I owed Horas everything and I was deeply ashamed of the way things ended between us. Now all I can do is regret not being with him at the end.'

With him at the end, Allura thought, those words running around her head until suddenly it all clicked together, like a jigsaw she didn't even know she was solving.

She thought of how Horas had made no arrangements for London and remembered Abraham's reaction when she had asked him about his death.

'Horas was murdered, wasn't he?' she asked.

Orville sighed and she waited impatiently as he plucked up the courage to tell her the truth.

'Yes, we believe he was.'

If Allura hadn't already been lying down, she would have needed to.

'Who did it?' she asked with a quake in her voice.

'I'm afraid, at the moment, we do not know.'

A cold shiver shot down her spine. Horas had been killed and not only did they not know who was responsible, but no one had even wanted to tell her.

She wanted to ask who else knew, a little disturbed by the thought that everyone and anyone she had met over the last few days could have been keeping such a secret from her. However, Orville reassured her that Cognitius had selected a very small group of people to know the truth.

Although it did explain why he was in Cambium on the night she arrived, it did not fill Allura with confidence to learn that Raven was also included in Cognitius' secret council. He was the last person she wanted involved, especially when she recalled the conversation she had overheard in the kitchen.

'I think he may know what I've done, what I am,' she had heard him say.

At the time Allura had thought he sounded concerned, but now she could only think of him as boastful.

'I could help,' she found herself saying.

'How's that?'

'I'm living in Horas' house. Maybe he left a clue or something that could help us figure out who killed him.'

'You didn't even know him, why would you want to help?' he asked in surprise. Allura thought back to that night. To the sharp screech of the tyres as the bus skidded towards her. She could still feel that tightness in her chest, that sickly certainty that she was going to die.

If not for the essence of hope, she would have been

under those tyres.

If not for Horas, she would be dead.

'No reason, it was just an idea,' she said.

'Well regardless, Cognitius has left the search in my hands and I don't want you looking into this.'

'I wouldn't tell anyone if that's what you're worried about.'

'No, Allura.'

'But I can-'

'Just STOP!' he snapped, a sudden temper exploding from within him, one which she could tell he rarely let out.

Simmering his rage, she realised that he was worried, scared even. 'I don't want you getting involved and that is a direct order from a regent of The Balance'

Good thing Endwood isn't in The Balance, Allura thought as Orville continued to rant.

'It's too dangerous. Horas was last seen leaving Endwood a few days ago, rambling about some conspiracy he had uncovered and now he's dead. I had hoped that was the end of it, but what happened today has confirmed to me that his death was not a one-off attack. It was just the first in a series of assassinations targeting the embodiments of positive forces.'

'But why would anyone do that?'

Orville looked around the room suspiciously as though he felt he had already said too much, but he quickly composed himself and whispered to her:

'Everyone has their reasons. The truth is the negative embodiments: Death, Cruelty, Selfishness,

Deceit, pretty much everyone in the Counter Club really, are all obvious suspects. They can be resentful and vengeful towards those who contribute more good to Earth or Orterra than they do. By the gods, my own co-ruler served Malvus in the war. That should tell you all you need to know about his kind.'

Allura thought of what had happened with the Embodiments of Life and Death. How Darnigold had hoped to use the Eviscero Charge to destroy death itself, but Evelyn, her own mother, refused to give up that which made her powerful without a thought for the people of Earth.

It made Allura angry to think that there were more like Evelyn, people hoarding their power at the cost of innocent people.

'What's the Counter Club?' she asked.

'They like to think of themselves as a society, but in reality, they are nothing more than a hive of high-ranking counterbalances who get together and gossip about the state of things whenever there's a good enough reason for them to be in the same place.'

I'd bet my life that Raven is one of those counterbalances, Allura thought while Orville rifled through his bedside drawer, pulling out a thick dishevelled notepad.

'I'm confused, if you don't want me to help then why are you telling me all this?' Allura asked.

'Because this isn't over, if we are being targeted then I think the new Embodiment of Hope should be aware. I owe Horas that much at least,' he said as he tore a single piece of paper from the pad and handed it to her.

'This is murmur paper, should you run into trouble or find yourself in need, write on here and I'll get the message.'

Allura turned the page over in her hands, checking for any sign that it was anything more than an ordinary piece of paper, but finding none.

'Thanks, but I think I already have some of this,' she said innocently.

'I doubt that,' Orville said before grabbing a quill from one of the desks and scribbling 'hello' onto the notepad.

It sat on the page for a moment, then Orville held it up to his mouth, brought his lips together, and blew. Letter by letter, the words drifted off the page, fluttering in the air then reforming and gently drifting onto the sheet in her hand.

Allura looked in astonishment at the page, which now bore the same word in the same squiggly handwriting.

'Wherever you are, just write on the murmur paper and blow on the page. The words will find their way to me.'

'Huh, kind of like texting,' Allura noted to herself.

'Texting?' he asked.

Maybe he really is one hundred years old.

*

They talked for a while longer after that, with Orville wanting to know everything about Allura's time on Earth and her journey to Orterra. Although she wasn't usually the sharing type, she felt oddly at ease with him, and found herself divulging scarcely told stories of her life in the foster system.

Somehow he had even got her to discuss her parents, shaking his head solemnly as she explained just how little she knew of them.

'It's all so unnecessary, isn't it?' he said when she was done.

'What is?' she asked.

'Heartache.'

There were more things she had wanted to say and more questions she had wanted to ask, but numerous advisers, guards and governors came by all too soon with urgent business that demanded Orville's attention.

'It would seem that running a kingdom actually requires some work,' he said. 'Even on my wedding day.'

'Well, try not to eat anymore poisonous flowers,' Allura replied with a smile as a guard opened the doors. The chatter of a frenzied mob of lords and noblemen waited outside and Orville glanced at them with dread.

'I'm very glad we got a chance to meet Allura,' he said, shaking her hand.

'Me too,' she replied, his grip far stronger than she had expected.

As he approached the door to leave, Allura called out to him.

'It's not true, is it?'

'What's that?'

'That you lifted the whole castle off the ground. I know you probably have a power, but surely that can't be true, can it?'

A thin smile crossed his lips as he left and the doors closed behind him.

I'll take that as a no.

Suddenly, her bed was hoisted into the air as the very stone beneath it rose higher and higher. Allura laughed as she and her bed towered over the room and then, in a heartbeat, the ground returned to normal and her bed dropped with a clang.

The noise caught the nurse's attention and she came rushing in with a horrified look on her face, only to find the room unaltered and Allura sat giggling on her bed. The nurse simply tutted and slammed the doors.

As soon as she was alone, Allura sprung out of bed and grabbed the murmur paper. There was something important that she realised she had forgotten to mention. Something she had seen during the wedding.

Searching through the room's many drawers, she found a quill and some ink and started to write:

I'm sorry I didn't mention it before, but I saw something strange during your ceremony. There was a woman watching from the shadows. I don't think she wanted anyone to see her, but someone knew she was there, I saw them talking to each other...

Her hand stopped for a moment, uncertain if she should involve herself further in something that had already taken Horas' life and nearly cost Orville his.

But then she remembered the look of fire and rage in the eyes of a man who was supposed to be her guide that night on the bridge. That unearned fury had been burned into her mind and so, she took a deep breath and put pen to paper.

...it was Raven Solmen.

*

The journey back to Endwood was travelled in the dead of night and Allura remained silent for most of it, disappointed that she hadn't seen Orville again before leaving Highdenhome while the murmur paper remained frustratingly blank.

Her mood wasn't at all helped by the gentle hugs and soft voices from her coach-mates, as though they thought her bump on the head had turned her to glass.

Despite their carriage being uncomfortably small and worn down, with side panels decorated in peeling paint and windows covered in scratches, Allura appreciated the Donnelly's insistence that she ride with them on the way back.

Although I wouldn't have minded the extra legroom.

Worse than that however were Faye and Lydia, who found a different way of saying sorry for losing her in the madness every few minutes. That was why Allura had decided not to mention Horas' murder, convinced that if either of them knew there was a killer on the loose, they would never let her out of their sight again.

As they traversed their way down the mountainside, Allura started to rummage through her pockets and was surprised to pull out the letter from

Cognitius that Raven had given her.

I'd forgotten about you, she thought as she opened it up and tried to read with as much privacy as she could manage in such a small space:

Dear Allura,

As I write this, I believe you will have just arrived in Endwood for the very first time and although it may be presumptuous of me to say, I think you will like it there. I intend to give this letter to Raven and while I have not told him this, I suspect that he will run into you at Orville and Darnigold's wedding.

Allura almost dropped the letter out of sheer dumbfounded shock.

Call it intuition or fate, but something tells me you will be there. If so, I apologise that I was not able to attend as there is some business at Giant's Peak that requires my immediate attention.

The reason for my letter however, is that I have decided that on Atrilarium Day, I will be escorting you back to Cambium myself (the wood gnells can get rather erratic on the holidays anyway).

I hope you have started to find your feet here, but I fear I may have sent you out into this world unprepared. In truth this place has much to offer, not least of which includes the good people in it, but unfortunately, much like Earth, there is a capacity for great evil in Orterra.

Should you ever feel in danger, I implore you to

rely on those around you and to trust the people who want to help you.

I have hope that they won't let you down.

Kindest regards,
Cognitius

Allura slipped the letter back into her pocket as Ofelia stirred from her nap.

'Oh look,' she said as she yawned and gazed into the darkness, 'I think I just saw a blissul tree. We must almost be home.'

Yeah, Allura thought. *Almost.*

*

By the time the Tandens and the Donnellys arrived in Endwood, Allura's eyelids felt heavy and her movement was sluggish and slow which made it very hard to decline Ofelia's offer to stay another night.

'I should probably check on London and besides, after the day I've had, having an angel bear watch over me doesn't sound like such a bad idea,' she said quietly, before thanking Noah and Ofelia's parents for her mostly wonderful day.

It was tricky to convince them that she didn't need to be escorted back to the cabin, but when finally she did, she found that it was a long and challenging walk.

The torrent of snow beat against her, dimming the light of her lantern with every gust as she did her best to protect the flame with her hands, frightfully aware of the fact that without it, she would never find her way back in the whiteout.

The dress didn't help either with the tattered fabric constantly threatening to trip her up at every turn. However, through a mix of good memory and unusually good luck, Allura found her way back to the cabin.

She stumbled through the gate and along the front garden. Then, sliding the key into the lock, she noticed something unusual.

Before she could even turn it, the door popped open.

Did I forget to lock it?

She couldn't remember as she stepped inside where she could hardly see a thing as the light of the lantern had been reduced to an ember.

Using what little fire was left to ignite the numerous candles around the room, Allura felt a sickening horror rise in her as she gradually took in what she was seeing.

Books laid scattered across the floor with mantelpiece decorations smashed beside them while every cupboard and drawer hung open with their contents emptied, as though someone had been hurriedly looking for something.

The rest of the cabin had suffered a similar fate. Almost everything that wasn't nailed down had been either taken or destroyed. Shattered mirror glass and tattered bed sheets had been flung across every room and the soft feathers that had once sat so comfortably inside the cushions were now sprinkled over the sofas.

As she gazed at the mess, Allura felt numb when

a thought suddenly hit her:

LONDON!

Allura hurried towards the shed door and twisted the handle, barging against the wood with all her weight, but it would not budge.

'LONDON? LONDON CAN YOU HEAR ME? ARE YOU IN THERE?'

Allura screamed louder and louder, banging and kicking against the door. After an onslaught of pounding and knocking, she slumped down to the floor in defeated silence.

A cold and lonely moment passed.

Then she heard a groan, followed by shuffling from behind the door.

Springing to her feet, Allura turned the knob again only to find that this time it opened with ease. In the shed she was relieved beyond measure to see London, completely unharmed with her tongue sticking playfully out of her mouth.

Realising that she must have curled up against the door when the noises started outside, Allura burst into happy tears and wrapped her arms around the bear's neck.

'Good girl,' she said as she squeezed her tight.

After a while, she returned to the living room and felt a great sadness swell inside of her. The room that had once seemed so warm and lived in was now cold and unwelcoming.

Looking around, she tried to find anything that they might have left behind, but not even the music box had been spared.

Who would do this? she asked herself.

And why?

She was exhausted and had no answers, but did come to one concrete conclusion. Whatever this was, it was far from over.

11

Secrets and lies

Behind thick clouds, the sun rose slow and steady over the rooftops of Endwood, each one layered in sheets of snow with only their thick chimneys left uncovered, pumping out small puffs of smoke which drifted lazily into the sky.

Household by household, the tranquil town stirred awake in their warm beds and although the snowfall had stopped, the chill outside still remained. It was the type of cold that turned breath into mist and left thin layers of ice glistening over the river.

A perfect winter's morning and Allura hated every second of it.

She had suffered through many sleepless nights in her life, but this one was by far the worst. Every rustle of the trees and whistle of the wind had made her jitter, fearful that whoever had wrecked the cabin would return to finish the job.

However, with the breaking of dawn, her courage returned and so, adorned in her hooded cloak and muddy boots, she made her way into the sleepy town. Her first stop was the address Abraham had written for her: Crookstead Street.

Allura made her way down the narrow alleyway and stopped at a bottle green door matching Abraham's description on the note. She knocked once... twice... three times, but there was no answer.

Well, that's just great. No one's home.

Turning to plan B, she trudged off towards Noah's house. Although she hadn't wanted to involve him or Ofelia, she was feeling unbearably alone and with Abraham not around to help, it seemed she had no other option.

It took her a moment in her groggy state to remember which house on the main street Noah had pointed to on their way to Highdenhome, but eventually she found it. Predictably, Noah took the news poorly, his hands shaking as he swallowed shallow sips of tea with a loud slurping sound.

His breathing had only just returned to normal by the time they got to Ofelia's and he hadn't said a word since the kettle had finished boiling. Ofelia however had plenty to say.

'They took everything?'

'Everything they could carry.'

Slurp!

'And you think they were looking for something to do with Horas?'

'Well think about it. Horas is murdered, then someone tries to kill Orville and then the cabin gets robbed. They have to be related,' Allura insisted.

Slurp!

Ofelia gave her a quizzical look and Allura caught a glimpse of herself in a small mirror on the wall. Gazing back at her was a girl with manic hair and restless eyes who looked truly unhinged.

Slurp!

'You don't believe me,' she said accusingly.

'Of course I believe you,' Ofelia replied, remaining cool and collected. 'I'm just trying to think how it's all connected. I wish we had some real proof.'

'Proof?' Allura asked with a rising temper in her voice. 'What more proof do you need than me telling you what happened?'

'I'm sorry, I'm not trying to upset you,' Ofelia said softly.

'Well, you are!'

Slurp!

Allura didn't know if it was the lack of sleep or if they were both genuinely trying their hardest to get on her nerves, but Noah's tenth sip of tea was the final straw.

'SHUT UP!' she screamed, banging her fist hard against the kitchen table. Noah almost dropped his mug in surprise and neither he nor Ofelia dared say anything else as Allura examined the startled looks in their eyes.

This was a mistake, she thought.

'You know what, forget I said anything. I'll sort this out myself,' Allura said sorrowfully as she got up from the table and ran for the door.

The squeaks of Noah and Ofelia's chairs told her that they were giving chase and so she ducked behind a bush outside of the Donnelly's home. From there, she watched as the pair sprinted out the door after her and stopped in the middle of the dirt road. They looked up and down the path, but could find no trace of her.

'Cognitius warned us something like this could happen,' Noah said.

'It's not her fault.'

'I know, but what do we do now? Should we tell your parents?'

'No, we need to talk to Allura before telling anyone else.'

'Alright fine, what's the plan then?'

'I don't know,' Ofelia admitted. They talked a little while longer then agreed to split up to find her, with Noah checking the main street and Ofelia searching the cabin.

'This is not what I thought I would be doing today,' he complained before saying the one thing Allura had dreaded most. 'I swear, our lives were a lot quieter before she turned up. Maybe it would be better for her if she just… well you know.'

He stopped himself, catching his own hurtful words before they could come out of his mouth, but he had already said too much. It was only made worse when Ofelia responded with an undiscerning 'hmmm' as they both rushed off, leaving Allura to sit and wallow in her lonely hiding spot.

What was I thinking telling them? They don't need the trouble I bring.

Ten minutes of agonising self-blame passed before Allura made her way out of the thicket and back to the cabin, making sure to move stealthily through the trees to avoid bumping into Ofelia on the path.

When she arrived, she was sure to be in and out as quickly as she could, packing her looking glass and the murmur paper in a little brown rucksack.

If they don't want me, then I'm gone, she decided, pulling London out from the shed.

Together they traipsed through the woods until they arrived at the shores of the lake, its waters now frozen. Allura sat on a log while London carefully stepped onto the ice, her claws digging into it as she stared at the frozen water.

Crack!

She smashed through the ice, plunging into the cold. Allura bolted onto her feet and ran for the lake, unsure what exactly she would do when she got there. Thankfully, she wouldn't have to find out as London emerged from the hole in the ice with a large green fish flapping in her jaws.

'Whoever raided the cabin took the Abundantil so you better eat up. We've got a long journey ahead,' Allura said, as she skimmed a stone across the fractured ice.

London had barely finished swallowing the tail of the slimy fish when there was a snap in the woods and her ears pricked up in excited anticipation.

'It's not them. They're not coming. It's just us from now on.'

The bear looked at her with its big eyes and for a brief moment, Allura thought she could understand her sadness. Then with a groan London started to roll playfully in the freshly laid snow.

Maybe not then.

While London amused herself, Allura pulled out

the murmur paper. She had lost count of how many times she had checked it during the night and the lack of a reply to her message about Raven only confirmed what she had known all along.

Orville doesn't care. No one does.

They had all been pretending she belonged there and worse than that, she had started to believe them. But now she knew the truth. Even her so-called friends thought she should leave and without Abraham around, she had never felt quite so alone.

As the cool winter wind brushed against her skin, Allura realised that this place had done something that even Mrs. Olderman hadn't managed to accomplish.

It had broken her heart.

I don't need them, she told herself, her eyes burning with hot tears as London nuzzled up to her.

A part of her wanted to lie down on the rocks and sleep, but another part of her, the part that was stubborn, hurting and angry, was already trying to remember the route back to Cambium.

It was still early morning, leaving her the rest of the day to find her way back, but she knew it would be difficult to follow the road from the sky. However, if they stayed high up and quiet, she was certain that they could make it to the castle unseen.

Great, so all I have to do is get over my fear of heights. Nice and easy.

Although what she would do when she actually got to Cambium also presented its own problems. She would not only have to convince Cognitius to let her return to Earth earlier than promised, but she would also have to make arrangements for London after she was gone.

The longer she thought about it, the more her plan unravelled in her mind and so she decided to simply not think about it and get going before anything or anyone could try to stop her.

However, before she could put things into motion, she heard voices from the clearing, belonging to neither Noah nor Ofelia.

'Give it here,' one of them said.

'Leave it alone,' the other replied.

'See if they know Malvus' anthem, I love that one.'

'Would you shut up? It hasn't even started yet.'

'Well hurry up then.'

Allura left London by the water and crept into the woods towards the commotion, her stomach dropping as she spotted them; Raiph and Cinder. As obnoxiously loud and irritating as ever. They moved along the dirt path, getting closer to the lake.

They'll spot us if we try to run, Allura realised trying to formulate a plan when whatever they were fiddling with released a sudden ping.

'You got it working!' said Cinder.

'Told you, you were being too rough with it.'

Then a familiar voice announced: 'HELLO LADIES AND GENTLEMEN! WE ARE THE BOX OF MISFITS!'

Allura's jaw dropped.

She had been so concerned with being right, so convinced that the world was out to get her that she had completely missed what was right under her nose. Ofelia was right, the robbery wasn't related to Horas' murder, not unless those two idiots were the culprits.

Marching towards them, her anger only grew as they hurled abuse at the band.

'YOU!' Allura roared.

'Look it's the little Earth girl,' Cinder said with a snort.

'We were looking all over for you yesterday,' Raiph said.

'Where'd you get that?' Allura asked, ignoring their chides as best she could.

'We found it.'

'You're lying. It's mine. You stole it.'

'Woah, that's a very serious accusation. How about this? You give us a few bits of silver and in return we let you use it once a week,' Raiph said with a smarmy smile.

'I am warning you. Give it back,' Allura said sternly, but they continued to snigger.

Deciding enough was enough, she tried to snatch the box from him, but her hand slammed against an invisible wall of energy that sent a shooting pain up her arm.

'Oops, shouldn't have done that,' he said, and with a boom, Allura was thrown high and away from them, landing on her back on a prickly bush.

Ignoring the stinging in her spine and the fuzziness that clouded her vision, she got to her feet and ran back towards the lake, narrowly avoiding another blast of energy.

'Yeah, keep running,' Cinder taunted as they

chased after her, but before they could even reach the pebbled shore of the lake, something came charging towards them.

It was huge and furry, blotting out the sun as it stood up on two legs like a ten-foot wall of claws and malice. Its mouth opened wide to reveal a sea of sharp teeth and the Kraws quaked with fear.

All London had to do was let out one, half-hearted roar and they were shrieking and hollering as they sprinted back into town, tripping over one another and dropping the music box as they went. It might not have solved all of Allura's problems, but it felt undeniably good to see them run.

'AND DON'T YOU *EVER* STEAL FROM ME AGAIN!' Allura yelled after them.

Picking up the music box, she wiped it clean of the mud and their grubby fingerprints, then stroked London's fur as her snarling face returned to its usual soft features. Suddenly, a loud racket of murmuring and pounding feet emanated from the edge of town.

'THE KIDS SAID IT WAS OVER HERE!

'BE CAREFUL, THEY SAID IT WAS FIFTY FEET TALL!'

'I DON'T CARE HOW BIG IT IS, I'M GONNA KILL IT!'

At least a dozen burly farmers, blacksmiths and merchants brandishing axes, bronze swords and pitchforks flooded into the forest. London growled in alarm as the bloodthirsty masses headed in their direction.

'We've got to go,' Allura whispered, springing up onto the bear's back. With a tug of the rope, they scampered through the woods.

The sounds of angry townsfolk grew fainter and fainter behind them, but they both knew that they wouldn't be safe until they were miles from there. However, the further from town they ran, the thicker and more tangled the bushes and brambles became, preventing London from gaining enough speed to fly.

This left them only one option: the main road.

Leaping onto the pathway, they followed its twists and turns before coming to a long stretch of straight but narrow road, at the far end of which Allura noticed a figure moving towards them.

It was an old traveller pulling a small cart behind him and he was clearly startled by what he was seeing. Wiping his glasses, he seemed almost convinced that the enormous bear must have been some speck on the lens.

Come on, move out the way, she thought, trying and failing with all her might to direct London back into the trees.

Allura felt truly powerless as they bounded towards him. All she could do was watch as the elderly stranger reached into his cart and pulled something from it.

A bow and a quiver.

Only then did she notice the dead animal hanging from his cart.

A hunter, she thought. *My luck really is extraordinary.*

'We've got to fly girl!' Allura yelled, gripping the rope and pulling upwards, but London didn't listen and continued steadfast towards the man as he placed an arrow into the bow.

His shaking hands caused the first shot to succeed only in piercing a nearby tree.

'LONDON! WE HAVE TO FLY!'

Undeterred, the angel bear continued onwards at full speed as another arrow shot through the air, whizzing over Allura's head.

She ducked down and found herself glaring into London's fixed eyes.

She's afraid, she realised.

The idea of something as formidable as her being scared of anything had never even crossed Allura's mind and yet she could see it clear as day in the bear's dilated pupils. Grabbing London's ear, she spoke into it in a loud but calming voice.

'I know I messed up before, but we won't crash this time. I promise. Please, please, you have to trust me. You have to fly!'

London's eyes moved away from the man and up into the sky. With a growl, she opened her magnificent wings wide, brushing them against the trees as she ran.

'THAT'S IT! COME ON GIRL!'

But seeing London's wings only strengthened the hunter's resolve. A wicked grin stretched across his face as his frosted breath slowed and his eyes narrowed.

This time Allura was certain he would hit his mark.

Pulling his hardest on the bowstring until the feathered end of the arrowhead brushed against his cheek, he waited one moment more, then set the arrow loose. It twirled through the air with a whistle, spinning towards London's skull as a breathless moment passed.

The world seemed to move in slow motion, the arrow frozen mid-flight and London equally stuck in place. There was nothing Allura could do and yet something stirred inside of her, just as it had when they first fought the Kraws.

She couldn't tell what it was. Was it just a feeling? No, it was more than that. Much more. Like a certainty. Yes, an unshakeable belief that everything would be alright.

Then, in a flash of piercing light, the arrow dropped dead in the air.

A surging wind carried them upwards and London's dangling claws clipped the hunter's head as they floated over him at immense speed.

The glorious angel bear glided over the ground with Allura pumping her fists as they rose higher above the forest canopy, skimming along the treetops.

Allura's heart was beating so fast that she had forgotten to be afraid, only feeling pure joy as they ascended away from the danger.

But as the distance quickly grew between her and the ground, the paralysing fear took hold once more. Everything below turned into a whirling vortex, waiting to swallow her whole as shallow breaths barely filled her lungs.

Losing control of her own mind and body, her grip on the reins began to loosen.

Then she remembered what Ofelia had said about flying with purpose and she shut her eyes to the spinning world. Releasing the grasp that it had on her, she focused only on the cool air rushing against her skin, the thick fur pressing into her hands, the rumbling beneath her feet as London's wings rose and fell over and over again.

These were fantastic, incredible things. Things that she was privileged to experience and were most certainly not to be feared.

I promised her we wouldn't crash, she reminded herself as her eyes opened slowly.

Taking in the far expanse of trees glowing in the sunlight, Allura had never breathed air so clean nor seen a sight quite as beautiful. She saw it all from hundreds of feet above the ground and for the very first time, she wasn't the least bit afraid.

Taking control with the rope, she guided them higher and higher until they floated through the misty sky, tasting freshly fallen flecks of snow on her tongue.

In that moment, Allura wouldn't have wanted to be anywhere else, although she was still perplexed about how they had escaped the arrow's path.

What was that light? she wondered.

She tried listing the possibilities in her head, from a trick of the eye to a sunbeam reflecting off of the arrowhead, but in truth, there was no way of knowing.

Yet, Allura felt deep in her bones that there had been something more to it; something much, much more.

*

The road from Endwood to Cambium was flooded with searching townsfolk and midday travellers, leaving Allura and London with nothing to do but fly in a loop in the air far from town until the prying eyes on the road had given up and gone home.

Allura still intended on following the path all the way to Cambium, but for now at least she would simply have to wait and enjoy the ride.

They had been in the sky for at least an hour when London came in to land by a river a few miles from Endwood. The bear's stomach rumbled and Allura realised the reason for their stop.

'Alright girl,' Allura said, gesturing to an icy river into which London dived in search of food.

That bear is never not hungry.

'Now isn't that something,' a croaked voice said.

Allura spun on her heel, thinking that the sound had come from behind her, but there was no one there.

'Who said that?' she called out nervously.

'Me,' the voice whispered and Allura turned again to see someone sat on a rock by the riverbed. They were hunched over and adorned in a white hooded cloak with a long wooden staff in their hand.

'Who are you?' Allura asked as the figure pulled back their hood and she stepped back in shock, convinced that her eyes were deceiving her.

But there was no denying it.

It was her.

The old woman she had seen speaking with Raven

at Orville's wedding.

Running her fingers through her hair, which only seemed to make it messier than before, the woman cleared her throat with three little coughs and said:

'Nice to meet you. The name's Evelyn Dormé, but my friends call me Death.'

12

Death in the woods

Frightened and bewildered, Allura glared at the oddity perched peacefully atop a mossy rock in front of her, watching London with a keen interest.

It was easy to believe that she was who she claimed to be. After all, Evelyn Dormé was Darnigold's mother, and in certain angles she looked like the mirror image of her daughter.

That was except for a few added decades, several missing teeth, bonier fingers and much longer and greyer hair that stretched all the way down to her entirely bare feet.

'What do you want from me?' Allura asked whilst making sure to maintain the wide distance between them.

With a harsh crack of her neck, Evelyn turned to look at her with eyes that seemed strangely youthful and fuller of life than the rest of her withering features.

'Do I know you?' Evelyn asked.

What is she playing at?

'I'm Allura,' she said, but received no reaction from Evelyn, as though the name meant absolutely nothing to her. 'I'm the new Embodiment of Hope.'

The old woman continued to observe and analyse Allura's face before finally saying:

'Well good for you.'

'You really don't know who I am?'

'Sure, I do. You're Allura, the new Embodiment of Hope,' she said, shuffling off the rock and closer to the river.

'Don't get too close to her,' Allura warned, checking on London as she nipped at the water.

'Relax, she won't hurt me,' Evelyn reassured her, unaware that she wasn't the one Allura was worried about.

The playful bear stopped splashing for a moment and tilted her head as Evelyn plunged her hand into the surging river. For a few seconds, the entire wood fell silent and a small black cloud formed above Evelyn.

Suddenly, the noise of the world returned and the cloud dissipated as she pulled a fish from the water. It sat motionless in her hand while London stood in the river with her jaws wide, readily awaiting the tasty treat, but not before Evelyn had taken a bite herself.

Allura recoiled as the deranged woman swallowed the chunk of raw fish, then tossed the rest into London's mouth.

'Don't be scared,' she said, misinterpreting Allura's look of disgust as she sat back down. Allura moved closer, certain that if this woman wanted her dead then she already would be.

'I'm not scared. I've seen what embodiments can

do before,' Allura replied, more shocked by her eating the fish than having seen her kill it. Meanwhile, Evelyn continued to stare at London in amazement, not looking away for even a second.

'You say that like you ain't one of us.'

'I'm not. I was chosen by accident, I don't even have any powers.'

'They'll come, they always do. Besides, when you live as long as I have you learn that there ain't no such thing as an accident.'

She spoke very differently to the eloquent and precise way that her daughter did, and while Allura deeply wanted to believe that she was right, she would have preferred almost anyone but Evelyn to have been the one saying it.

'Hang on, if you don't know who I am then what are you doing here?'

'Not that it's any of your business, but I got a meeting at Tetricore tomorrow. A very special meeting.'

'The Counter Club?' Allura said aloud, recalling what Orville had told her about the group of negative embodiments. Evelyn's eyes remained fixed on London as she explained:

'That's the one. It's once in a blue moon that we get so many of us together at the same time, but almost everybody is in The Balance for my daughter's wedding so we're finally coming together at Tetricore. Only thing is there's this rule you see, can't go turning up empty handed. Gotta bring a gift, a doohickey to wow all the others so, I thought I'd pop down here to Endwood and get something special from the best merchant in all of Orterra.'

'Will Raven Solmen be at the meeting?' Allura asked.

'Well he better be, it was his idea we all get together in the first place.'

'I saw you two at the wedding,' Allura revealed nervously.

'Did you now? You know girly, you're quite nosy and very bold to be talking to a ruler of the realm of life and death like that.'

Allura tensed, looking up for any dark clouds that might have been rolling in overhead.

'Luckily for you, I'm nosy too,' the old woman cackled, still not looking at her.

'So why were you talking with him in secret?'

'Because he was the one what snuck me in, wasn't he.'

'Why would he do that?'

'Well I wasn't exactly welcome now was I? Although part of me wishes I hadn't gone to the damned thing. Terrible, wasn't it? I do hope Orville's alright. I've never particularly liked the fella, but I can't help respecting him. He's fought for two worlds and he seems to make Darnigold happy enough.'

'Are you saying you don't know who poisoned him?'

'Not a clue. Did you do it?'

Allura scoffed. Everything Evelyn said only reminded her of the choice she had made. Her selfish decision to allow the people of Earth to continue to die needlessly. And so every time she made a joke,

Allura imagined she was laughing at the people she had allowed to suffer.

'Why do you look at me like that?' Evelyn asked, as though she could see the spite in her face without even a glance in her direction.

Has she got a second pair of eyes or something? Allura wondered, noticing that the small owl carved into the head of her staff was pointed towards her.

'Like what?' Allura asked.

'Like you want me dead.'

'Because -' she hesitated, her rage now wavering at the old woman's confused tone. Taking a deep breath to compose herself, Allura gazed into the churning water and let her anger subside before calmly saying: 'I heard a story about you.'

'Oh you heard a story did you? A bedtime story, was it? One of those stories that make your hairs stand on end when you hear about how wicked I am.'

'Well, is it true? Did you choose to let people on Earth die?'

'I did.'

'Then how could you ask me why I would hate you,' Allura replied coldly.

With a small snort, Evelyn tightened her grip on the staff.

'That is not the reason.'

'Yes, it is,' Allura replied determinedly

'No, it's not,' Evelyn refuted.

'It really is.'

'Nope.'

'It is!' Allura said, raising her voice. 'Because if you hadn't done what you did then I would probably have a family!'

'There it is!' Evelyn said smugly. 'You don't hate me for letting strangers and people you'll never know die. You hate me because you think I'm someone you can blame for the way your life turned out.'

'That's not true.'

'Girly, do you even have the faintest idea how many people have called me a monster for the choice I made? Not because of how it affected Earth, but because of how it affected them specifically.'

Allura shifted uncomfortably. She had thought she'd had the right to be angry, but the more Evelyn spoke the less certain she became.

'People can't seem to look beyond themselves and realise that there is a reason why counterbalances like me exist. Do you really think Earth would be better without death? Do you actually believe that it would solve anything? By the gods, when will you all understand that the crops have to die so the seeds can grow? That the fish has to die so the bear can eat. That people have to die so that there's enough room on that crowded little planet for the rest of them. It's an unfortunate fact of nature that new life cannot bloom without death. That's what Darnigold could never wrap her head around,' Evelyn said with a hint of sadness in her voice.

Her words struck Allura like a lightning bolt.

She had assumed that Evelyn's refusal to allow her daughter to destroy the essence of death had been an act of selfishness. The tattered state that the argument had left the mother and daughter's relationship hadn't seemed even nearly enough punishment for Allura's liking.

Yet now she was beginning to see things very differently, as the true weight of Evelyn's impossible choice dawned on her.

'All this fuss over that 'Eviscero Charge'. They can call it whatever they like, but I see it for what it really is. Just another weapon. A bomb that kills these wonderful things inside of us. Nothing more, nothing less,' Evelyn said, tenderly pressing her hand to her own chest.

'And the greatest irony of all is that it was created by the Embodiment of Life... HA!' Evelyn slapped her knee as she laughed, then finally looked at Allura wistfully.

'Ah forget it, hate me if you want,' she said dismissively, mistaking Allura's ashamed silence for contempt. Sitting beside her on the rock, Allura cleared her throat and spoke with a softer tone.

'You really didn't do it to keep your powers, did you?' she asked as they watched the water race by.

'Power is like a tide, it rises and falls. My daughter and I are only rulers of The Cycle because we happened to be chosen as the Embodiments of Life and Death. It just as easily could have been anyone else and most days I wish it had been. But the way I see it, I could die tomorrow and someone else would be chosen to take my place on the throne of Acropalyptia the very next day and the world would move on quite gladly. So no, I don't care much for power, it is fleeting. People are where I put my stock.'

With the clicking of joints, Evelyn slowly turned to look at her again.

'Sometimes you have to look past your own needs, far beyond yourself, to see what the right thing is. It's not always easy, but if you really care, you do it anyways.'

Allura's mind turned to Noah and Ofelia. The people she would be leaving behind. If she disappeared now, they would always think she didn't even give them a second thought. She knew what she had to do.

I owe them a goodbye at least.

'So, do ya mind helping a frail old woman into town?' Evelyn asked, straining as she pulled herself off the rock.

'Alright, but as you might have guessed we need to avoid the main road,' Allura replied, wading into the water and pulling London back onto the riverbank. 'I would say we could fly there, but I can't risk anyone spotting her around town at the moment, so we'll have to go through the woods.'

'Fine by me, as long as we get there before the markets close. I prefer the road less travelled anyway,' Evelyn said as she pulled her hood up over her mane of grey hair. 'Maybe on the way you can tell me how an Earth girl ended up with an angelursi, hmmm?'

And so Allura did just that, recapping the entire story of her time in Orterra, although being sure to skip any mention of Horas' murder or Raven's nefarious schemes.

She had reached the end of the story when the

sounds of clanging metal and chattering townsfolk came into earshot.

'Those Kraw kids are nasty little biters,' Evelyn said. 'They're part of that 'Orterrans Only' movement. They think anybody who wasn't born here is taking power from those who're entitled to it. Course, that's just cause their father hasn't got any.'

'Really?' Allura asked as she balanced nimbly across a log.

'Yep. Carter Kraw. The sheriff of Endwood. One of the least exceptional people I've ever met and that's got nothing to do with him not being an embodiment. Though there seems to be less and less exceptional people nowadays, especially with Horas gone.'

'You knew Horas?' Allura asked in surprise.

'Oh yes. Whenever I was passing through Endwood he'd invite me to that old cabin of his and we'd have a few too many drinks together. Between you and me, I actually tried talking to his spirit in the Wilting Fields. I knew it wouldn't work, but I had to give it a whirl.'

'What do you mean?'

Evelyn shook her head and tapped her staff against the ground.

'Girly, what have you been doing these last few days that you haven't even heard of the Wilting Fields?'

'Trying not to die mostly.'

'Ah that's no excuse. It's a place in The Cycle where spectres from Earth and Orterra linger for a little while after death. But the thing is, if there ain't a blood relative around to see them, then the spirits are like echoes of the people they were in life. They can't anchor themselves to this world and not even I can get them to talk when they're like that.'

'Then why did you try it with Horas?'

'I don't know, suppose I felt I needed to at least give it a shot, but like I said, it didn't work and I ended up watching him fade away after a while, like all the others.'

'So, where do they go after they disappear?' Allura asked, but found no comfort in Evelyn's lack of an answer.

*

Eventually, they reached a fork in their journey with Endwood in one direction and the cabin in the other. Evelyn ran her hand along London's long face, muttering something or other before turning her attention to Allura.

'You are an unusual girl, but it was very nice meeting you.'

'Yeah, it was weird but nice meeting you too,' Allura replied, shaking the woman's scrawny hand.

'Hopefully our paths will cross again someday,' she said with a smirk.

'I doubt that. I already told you, I'm going back to Earth.'

'And why is that again? You missing that Olderman lady's warm hugs?'

'No, definitely not,' Allura laughed. 'But that doesn't mean I belong here and it definitely doesn't mean I deserve to be the Embodiment of Hope.'

'Girly, it ain't about what you deserve, it's about what you do.'

With that, she took the path to the left, leaving Allura and London to wander off to the right.

One quirk of the cabin that Allura had learnt during her sleepless night was that it made a distinct creaking sound in the wind, which made finding her way back to it much easier as the breeze picked up.

By the time she and London approached it, the entire structure was humming like a church choir and they were both all too happy to get out of the biting cold.

Allura locked the shed behind her then made her way out of the front door where she was immediately confronted by Noah who looked at her in shock.

'You're okay?' he asked in a flat and expressionless tone.

'I'm fine,' she said.

'Good, I'll go tell the others,' he replied just as coldly as before.

'The others?'

'Everyone has been looking for you Allura! You ran away and then the Kraws said they saw you in the woods with a bear! Only me and Ofelia guessed what actually happened, but everyone else was worried you might have been hurt!' Noah said angrily as Ofelia came running up the trail behind him, her eyes alight as she spotted Allura.

'There you are! I'm so glad you're alright,' Ofelia said as she scurried past Noah and pulled her in for a big hug.

'You used London to scare the Kraws off, didn't

you?' he asked.

'Noah!' Ofelia said sharply, breaking the hug. 'I kept telling him you wouldn't do that, they must have spotted you taking her for a walk, right?'

Allura so desperately wanted to lie to her, to keep that hopeful light in Ofelia's eyes alive, but then she thought of what Evelyn had said about doing what was right.

'No, Noah's right. I wanted to scare them.'

'What? Why?'

A lump formed in Allura's throat as she realised the extent of her mistake.

'They were the ones who broke into the cabin,' she said bluntly and both Noah and Ofelia's eyes and mouths widened in a shared 'o-o-o-ohhh' expression as everything clicked into place.

'So, it had nothing to do with Horas' murder?' Noah clarified.

'I guess not,' Allura admitted in embarrassment.

'Which means everything that happened this morning was for nothing? You got yourself all worked up and used London to make yourself feel better for no reason,' he said.

'That's not exactly what happened.'

'London could've been hurt, Allura! And now the whole town is hunting for her! I don't care what The Kraws did, why would you do something like that to her?' Ofelia asked with a deep disappointment in her voice.

'Because that's just what I do, okay? I make stupid decisions without thinking!' Allura said, feeling them both retracting from her as she grabbed Ofelia's hand. 'But look, I'm here now. I came back because I wanted to see you both one more time before I left,' she said in a foolhardy attempt to make everything better.

'You're running away again?' Noah asked in disbelief.

'It's for the best.'

'For who? Certainly not for London. Why are you so set on leaving? What is there for you on Earth that you cannot wait to get back to?' Ofelia asked, but Allura didn't answer.

She couldn't.

'I was so happy when Cognitius told us to take that carriage with you, but now-' Ofelia started to say, only realising her mistake after it was too late.

Allura wanted to believe that she must have misheard her or that she had misspoken as she thought back to that day at Cambium. She remembered their eager faces as they crossed the courtyard to tell her the good news and how lucky she had felt to have them want to ride with her, but now, it all made sense.

'Is that true?' she asked.

'I....uh....' Ofelia stammered.

'IS IT?'

'Yes, okay? Cognitius asked us to travel with you to Endwood, but it's not a big deal,' Noah admitted.

'Did she ask or did she tell you to?'

Their silence spoke volumes.

How could I be so stupid?

'You know what, I don't know why I even bothered coming back. You two never actually

226

wanted to hang out with me, you were just doing whatever Cognitius told you to.'

'That's not true,' Ofelia interjected.

'How can I believe you? You started lying to me from the moment we met.'

'Allura, we're your friends,' she pleaded.

'I don't have any friends!'

Ofelia was startled for a second, and then the doe eyed girl turned to run away as tears streamed down her face.

'Did that make you feel better?' Noah asked.

'I really don't need your opinion about it. You would've been happy to keep locking your doors every time the Kraws walked down the street for the rest of your life,' she said, utterly tired of his judgment.

Noah took a big gulp and Allura couldn't tell if he was swallowing his sadness or building up the courage to say what he did next.

'Y'know, my dad told me I should let the adults handle the search for you. He said that if there was a bear on the loose, he didn't want me going out there, but I told him that I'd made a promise. I told him that I had to help my friend, but now I can honestly say I don't know where she is anymore.'

'She went that way,' Allura said spitefully as she pointed in Ofelia's direction.

'Cognitius was right, you really can't get out of your own way, can you? By the gods, you can't even tell a dream from a nightmare,' he said, shaking his head as he followed after Ofelia.

Please don't go.

I didn't mean any of it.
I'm sorry.

The words she wished she could say swirled around her head until he was out of sight when finally she cried out:

'Wait!'

But the distance between them had already grown far too great.

13

An uninvited guest

The light seemed to drain from the world all too quickly that evening and Allura decided that any plans of returning to Earth would have to be put on hold until tomorrow.

Instead, she sat on the front porch of the cabin and tried to spot the giant moon she had glimpsed at Cambium. But the clouds were dark and impenetrable, making it impossible to see anything more than its shining outline sitting in the sky.

It was only moments after the wind and snow had picked up, and Allura had made her way back into the cabin, when there was a knock on the door. Her heart was aflutter with the faint possibility that it could have been Noah or Ofelia as she hastily opened it to find herself face-to-face with a monster.

The creature had bulging grey skin and twisted horns protruding from its forehead with three red eyes that were fixed on her, cold and lifeless. Clearly it had once been a formidable beast, but now it was nothing more than a head hanging from Abraham's hand.

'Is that where you've been all day?' she asked,

trying not to look the thing in the eye anymore.

He nodded.

'Well thanks for telling me,' she said, thinking of how she may never have needed to involve her former friends if she had known where he was.

I guess we'll call it even for the wedding, she thought as he stepped inside and inspected the carnage with a concerned expression on his face.

Slapping the head down onto the kitchen counter, he pointed at Allura and then did a circular motion with his finger around the room as though to ask 'Did you do this?'

'It was the Kraws,' she explained.

The look of disgust on his face told her that he had heard nothing of the day's events and with a simmering rage in his eyes, he pulled a massive knife from one of the drawers and began chopping wildly into the slimy meat.

She didn't know if it was her sour mood or the fact that the main ingredient was a giant head, but Allura didn't feel like cooking that night. And so, she simply gazed into the darkness while Abraham prepared the meal.

But as she watched the silhouettes of the trees swaying in the wind, she realised that there was another set of eyes staring back.

She leapt away from the window and her frightened gasp seemed to tell Abraham all he needed to know. Hammer in hand, he marched outside and lifted the unknown watcher off the ground.

The man dangled there, kicking his legs about

helplessly as Abraham refused to let his feet reconnect with the floor. Only then did Allura get a good look at him, and although it took her a moment, she realised that she recognised him by the quiver on his back and the three cuts across his forehead.

The hunter, she realised with a sickening dread as she ducked under the window frame so that he couldn't spot her.

'Put me down Abraham,' the hunter insisted, flailing about like a scared animal trying to wriggle its way out of a trap.

Allura stayed low, afraid that if he saw her then Abraham would surely find out what she had been up to in the woods. But Abraham must have also recognised the man as he released his hold and allowed him to drop to the floor with a thud.

'Now I know you're probably wondering what I'm doing here and I won't lie to you, I'm on the hunt,' she heard him say. 'You'll hardly believe it, but it's a big one lad... an angel bear.'

Allura's heart did cartwheels in her chest.

Please don't listen to him.

Please don't listen to him.

Please don't listen to him.

Thankfully, Abraham scoffed and she could hear their feet against the gravel as he began to guide the hunter back towards the gate.

'No, no, no Abe. Listen to me, no one has caught even a whiff of one of these things on the mainland in over a century, but I saw it with my own eyes! And what's more, I saw a girl riding the damn thing.'

The pounding rush of blood in Allura's ears was

becoming unbearable, she needed to see what was happening, to know if he had already figured out where she was keeping his target.

'It took me all day to figure out where she lives but-'

Allura remained quiet as she peered out the window, but his eye was drawn to her almost immediately.

'THAT'S HER!' he exclaimed as she ducked out of sight again. 'I SAW YOU!'

No, you didn't, she wanted to say.

'Listen lass, unless you want the rest of Endwood round to play with your little pet, I suggest you give me what I came here for,' he threatened and Allura heard the sounds of Abraham sighing deeply followed by the clang of his hammer hitting the ground.

Allura was puzzled at first because the footsteps she heard seemed as though they were moving back towards the cabin, but then she realised exactly where they were going.

Poking her head up again, she saw them walking towards the shed and rushed out ahead of them. Sliding her arms between the gaps in the two large handles, she barricaded the door as best she could.

'NO!' she yelled, kicking them away.

'Move,' said the hunter, positively giddy with excitement as Abraham gestured for her to step aside with a tilt of his head and a loud, sharp whistle.

'I WON'T LET YOU DO THIS!' Allura insisted, the freeze of the metal handles biting into her skin, but Abraham carefully plucked her out of the way with as much effort as if she had been made of paper.

He loosened the lock from the door and the hunter primed his arrow.

Allura's worst fear was about to come to life as the doors were thrown open to reveal London, still and silent on the floor.

That's not possible, Allura thought in horror, but there was no denying what they were all seeing.

The bear was already dead.

With tears in her eyes, Allura looked up at Abraham for answers, for some explanation of how this could be, but all he did was sigh as the hunter dropped his bow in disappointment.

Cautiously, the man stepped into the shed, poking and prodding at the mound of fur that had once been a living and lively bear, in search of even the slightest signs of life.

But none were found.

No breathing, no twitching, no growling.

Nothing at all.

By all accounts, the creature was dead.

'Oh, I see how it is! You had to take all the glory for yourself didn't you!' the hunter yelled, looking fit to burst with anger. Soon after, arrows were snapped and the bow was tossed to the ground with an impetuous bellow as the man mourned the loss of his greatest hunt.

'You embodiments are all the same! Always thinking you're better than the rest of us and taking whatever you want for yourselves!' the man cried like a spoilt child.

'How did you know I was an embodiment?'

Allura asked in surprise.

'I saw what you did in the woods. Only an embodiment could've done that, unless you're one of those magic freaks. Quite frankly I don't know which is worse,' he said in disgust.

Allura wanted to delve further into what he had seen, but the man quickly erupted into another tantrum. He continued to call Abraham unpleasant names for quite some time before dusting off his bow and storming back into the night.

Once the stomping of his feet had faded entirely, Abraham let out another sharp whistle.

Shaking herself awake, London sprung up off the ground, her chest filling with air as she stared at Abraham with big, needy eyes like a dog begging for their owner's approval.

Abraham patted her on the head while Allura dove in to cuddle the great big bear.

'You clever girl! I'm so happy you're okay! You had me so worried!' she said as they rolled around together before turning her focus back to Abraham.

'But how? How did you get her to do that? How did you even know she was in there?'

However, as soon as she asked the questions, she realised the answers. It was obvious really and she had felt silly for not putting it together sooner.

Although Horas might have looked after her, Abraham had been the one that trained her.

*

The food frothed and boiled with random cubes of meat floating across the surface as Abraham ladled a

234

large serving into Allura's bowl. She winced at the sight of it.

Bit of brain, sliver of tongue and a whole eyeball. Lovely.

Carefully selecting the spoonfuls of broth that she was actually willing to put in her mouth, she hated to admit that despite its appearance, it tasted amazing.

Abraham sat opposite her, both of them resting uncomfortably on the tattered sofas as they finally decided it was time to address the bear in the room.

'Sorry to ask again, but I want to make sure I have this right. You knew about her the whole time?' she asked.

As Abraham nodded, the excessive amounts of food he kept bringing to the cabin suddenly made a lot more sense.

'Huh, I guess I'd just assumed you were *really* hungry,' she murmured.

Abraham smirked before holding the bowl up to his lips and flinging his head back, emptying its contents down his throat. Slamming the bowl on the table, he pounded his chest and let out a deep, satisfied 'ahhhhh' then got up and walked to the bookcase.

Running his hand along the wall behind it, he stopped at a panel that was ever so slightly more faded than the others and pushed on it, popping it out of place.

Not a bad hiding spot, she thought as Abraham stuck his arm into the gap and rummaged around before pulling out a folded piece of paper.

He handed it to her and Allura opened it to reveal

another drawing of 'Rutherford, Abraham and I'.

In the sketch, Horas was sat on a tree stump in the foreground with a baby angel bear cradled tenderly in his arms. Over his shoulder, Orville was stood, smiling at the small cub, while Abraham remained tall and steady in the background, looking off towards the horizon.

Although it was hard to take her eyes off of the adorable bear cub, Allura's attention was pulled towards the armour wrapped around each of them and the sharp swords that hung at Horas and Orville's waists.

'Was this during the war with Malvus?' she asked and Abraham nodded in confirmation. 'How long did it go on for?'

He held up five fingers, one for each year.

'How did you get through that?' she asked and his eyes fell on the drawing. Allura looked at it again until finally she understood.

They had each other.

Thoughts of the way things had gone so wrong with Noah and Ofelia made it hard for her to look at the sketch any longer. She set it on the table and copied Abraham's technique for finishing the meal. Devouring the rest of the broth in one enormous gulp, she pounded her chest and released her own hardy 'ahhhh'.

In that moment, Allura felt closer to Abraham than anyone else in Orterra. And so, as he threw on his coat and made for the door, she decided she had to tell him that she knew about Horas' murder.

Even if it meant exposing that Orville was the one

who had told her, she felt she had to warn him about her suspicions regarding Raven's involvement before she left tomorrow. Regardless of the fact that she didn't exactly have proof.

However, before she could tell him, he bent down to put on his shoes and she noticed something.

It was a peculiar something. A terrible something. A something that she wished she had seen sooner.

Flashes of her first morning in Cambium flooded her mind as she remembered hiding in the kitchen while Raven spoke of something sinister.

She had wanted to know who he was talking to, but only managed to spy a pair of leather boots, scuffed at the edges with a gold line along the seam.

They were the boots of a co-conspirator, worn by someone who was helping or at least aware of Raven's actions against Horas and Orville.

And they were the very same boots that Abraham was now lacing up.

*

When he left, Abraham's giant stature had seemed more intimidating than before, as though at any moment he could crush her with one firm stomp of his incriminating boot.

She didn't want to be afraid of him, but it was hard not to be, especially after seeing first-hand what he had done to the tearer and that grotesque three-eyed monster.

Once he was gone, she tried to keep her mind from spiralling out of control by searching the false panel in the bookcase for potential clues, but there was

237

little to be found except for notes on angelursi and another vial of Abundantil.

Then, she checked the murmur paper to find that there was still no reply from the lord of Highdenhome regarding what she had seen during the wedding.

As much as she wanted to ask Orville for his guidance, she had clearly lost his interest.

What would I tell him anyway? That Raven and Abraham were having a private conversation about something I know nothing about?

Overwhelmed, exhausted and entirely disheartened, Allura reminded herself that soon none of this would be of any concern to her. She wouldn't even remember a thing about it.

I'm leaving in the morning, she reaffirmed in her mind as she readied for bed.

Oddly enough, the bedroom had been the least impacted by the Kraw's rampage. Not to say that it was untouched however, as the sheets had been torn and every pillow had been pilfered, but when compared to the truly tattered state of the sofas, the bed's mattress was relatively unharmed.

As much as Allura hated to do so, she knew she would have to sleep in it.

At least this survived, she thought, realising that the painting of the bear was still intact on the floor.

Lifting it up, she noticed a panel on the wall where it had hung, lighter than the others around it, just like the one at the back of the bookcase.

Overcome with curiosity, Allura pushed on it until it too popped open, revealing a space that was no bigger than a letterbox. Sliding her hand into the hollow wall, she felt nothing at first, only wood and a small insect that darted from finger to finger.

She brushed it away then reached further into the crevice, until she felt something leather and rectangular. Pulling it out, she confirmed what she had suspected.

It was a book.

Now why would Horas keep you in there? she questioned, running her finger along the unmarked cover and spine.

Opening it to the first page, it quickly became apparent that this was not just any book, but a journal.

Horas' journal.

Flicking through the pages, she found the final entry to be particularly enlightening.

R has requested I meet him tomorrow at Craven's Mountain. I believe it has something to do with the dark thoughts he mentioned last time we spoke. I know he is a good man, despite what others may say, but I am afraid that the path he is heading down is one I cannot follow.

Those close to him have kept me informed of his activities, but there are occasions when he is said to disappear for days at a time. Even those closest to him do not know where he goes, nor what he is up to.

I will leave Endwood tomorrow with hope in my heart that I can restore him to sanity.

This isn't fair. All I wanted was to go back to

Earth and forget all about this place, Allura thought as she collapsed against the bed and tried to forget what she had read, but once again Evelyn's words echoed around her head.

'Sometimes you have to look past your own needs, far beyond yourself, to see what the right thing is. It's not always easy, but if you really care, you do it anyways.'

It's up to me.

The list of people she trusted had grown even smaller, but she felt she owed it to Horas to find the truth. Unfortunately for her that would mean making a quick stop to Craven's Mountain.

Wherever that was.

Putting the journal aside, Allura decided that the secrets within would simply have to wait until tomorrow. Her immense tiredness had well and truly got the better of her.

However, as she felt her eyes grow heavy and her body go limp, a single question consumed her thoughts.

Who is R?

In her heart she knew the answer and as she drifted off to sleep, she felt an uneasiness set in, as though a familiar pair of dark, swirling eyes were watching her.

14

Atrilarium's Eve

The night was cold and restless, once again disturbed by dreams of darkness and a malevolent figure in a shimmering doorway.

Except this time the shadowy outline reaching out for her morphed and shifted, changing its shape as though it could not decide who or what it wanted to be.

Stranger than that however were the words it uttered.

Had it spoken before?

She couldn't remember, but when she woke, she tried to put a face to the voice. It had been eloquent and clear, but its tones and nuances faded too fast for her to recall, until all she could bring to mind were the words it had said:

'Come home Allura. Come home.'

With neither the time nor the patience to be haunted by nightmares, she pushed it to the back of her mind. After all, there were other things that required her attention, especially if this really was to be her last day in Orterra.

Having flicked through Horas' journal and finding

seemingly nothing useful inside, she slumped out of bed to begin riffling through what remained of her clothes.

A baggy pair of trousers and a cotton shirt was the best she could muster before placing a bowl of leftover broth in the shed and heading into town in search of the library.

If she was going to Craven's Mountain, she would first need to find out where it was.

The main street was more abuzz than usual with last minute shoppers and excited children rushing about. Musicians played festive songs from their windows and the smells of mulled wines and roasted meats hung thick in the air.

Noah had warned her that it could get busy on Atrilarium's Eve, but it seemed as though everyone in Endwood had spilled out onto the streets.

At the end of a short alley, she found the town's library, its grand marble exterior and tall pillars not at all reflecting the cosiness within. The inside was small and smelt slightly musky, but every inch was bursting at the seams with books, journals and parchments.

As she walked through, she was met by a tiny woman wearing bi-focal glasses and a pointy green hat. She popped out from behind her little desk and eagerly approached Allura, speaking in a high-pitched squeak.

'Hello, I am Tilda and can I just say, I'm happy to see you come our way. Have a look around and see what you see, and if you have any questions then please come to me.'

'Nice to meet you,' Allura said, unsure if she was also supposed to rhyme. 'If I asked, could you tell me where to find a specific book?'

Tilda let out a squeaky giggle then pushed her glasses down the bridge of her nose as she explained that:

'Oh yes, oh yes, I know every book, map and tome. Good memory's a perk of being a gnome. For thirty years I've been this library's clerk. Please ask away, put me to work,' Tilda said proudly.

'Well alright, do you know where I could find anything about Craven's Mountain?'

'Now that's a story of death and woe! Go up those stairs to the right if you want to know.'

Allura thanked her and headed up the creaky staircase. At the top, she found an entire section dedicated to Orterran history, including a thick book tightly bound in a muted red leather with the title hand-sewn in yellow silk:

The Fall of Craven's Mountain and Other Terrible Tales.

Slamming the heavy book onto a table, she skimmed through its endless pages until she found what she needed. According to the book, Craven's Mountain was a place on the border of The Balance and The Bliss that was mined by the people of both dominions.

However, after years of prosperity, the men of the mountain disturbed the things that lived far beneath their feet. The monsters that poured out of the depths led to the mountain being abandoned, while the mine was left to fester for centuries.

Until now, Allura thought before looking around to make sure that no one was watching as she carefully ripped out the map she needed.

As she returned the book to the shelf, she was startled as she accidentally bumped into someone, knocking the book they were carrying to the floor.

'Sorry,' Allura said as she bent down to pick it up, only to find herself reading the cover:

The Delicate Art of Growing Squilms by Horbadgery Yates.

From what she had gathered at the Donnelly's house, there were only two people in Endwood who were mad enough to try and grow squilms in winter when everything else was dead.

Allura looked up and standing there in a fleeced cardigan, was Faye Donnelly with a wicker basket hanging from her arm.

'You're not supposed to take the pages you like home with you,' Faye whispered, her eyes veering towards the map in Allura's hand.

'Please don't tell Tilda,' Allura whispered back.

'I won't if you won't,' Faye replied, tilting the basket to show a small pile of loose pages with ripped edges.

'If those squilms don't bloom, Lydia will never let me hear the end of it,' she said mischievously. 'I'm glad I ran into you though. I wanted to ask if you would be popping by the house at all today. Ofelia was in quite a state last night and when I asked her what happened she said you had a bit of a falling out.'

'I don't think she would want to see me,' Allura

said shamefully.

'Let me guess, you said some things you wish you hadn't?'

'How did you know that?'

'Because that's what happens. I remember when I was young, I couldn't stop doing stupid things to the people I cared about. Even Lydia was sick of me at times back when we were just friends. But I suppose that's the true test of a friendship really, finding out how to move past those mistakes.'

'But that's the problem, I don't know how,' Allura admitted, trying not to meet Faye's eyes. There was too much kindness in them, more than she felt she deserved. Usually, she didn't stick around this long after messing up to make things right.

'Well, there's an easy part and a hard part. The easy part is saying sorry.'

'And the hard part?'

'Forgiving.'

*

Faye and Allura left the library together and Ofelia's mother let her in on a little secret. It was a trick that she and Lydia had developed for dealing with each of their children whenever they were upset or angry or in need of some cheering up.

For Ofelia's brother, the solution was a new book while for Ofelia's sister the key was soft toys, but Ofelia herself had a much more edible solution.

'Sweets?' Allura asked as Faye led them to a colourful building with a big sign that flashed and sparkled – SUGAR & BLISS.

'They work every time,' Faye replied, holding open a rainbow coloured door. Allura stepped inside and found that the shop comprised of floor upon floor of sweet confectionaries and excited children.

On the ground level alone, there were erupting volcanoes of freshly packed fudge, glowing gumdrops that continued to shine brightly as they were swallowed, bubbles that solidified into delicious orbs of chocolate and lines of red liquorish so long and thick that children were playing tug of war with them.

'This place is amazing,' Allura gasped, 'but I haven't got any money.'

It was a fact that had not bothered her until this very moment, but her disappointment soon faded as Faye pressed a silver coin into her hand.

'Just don't tell Lydia,' she said with a cheeky grin.

The pair skipped around the shop, filling Faye's wicker basket with silly-whirl bubble gum, chocolate coins, floating jelly beans, fizzy unicorns, sherbet cauldrons and countless other sweet treats before heading back onto the main street.

Gnawing on candy canes as they walked through the snow, Faye told Allura all about her adventures as a treasure hunter many years ago. One tale in particular about the crypt of Farrion Vildor took up most of their journey, and before Allura knew it, they had arrived outside of the Donnelly's home.

Nerves gripped her and she hesitated to take another step. She desperately wanted to make things better, but her past experiences seemed to suggest that she could only make them worse.

Luckily Faye could see what was happening and stretched a supportive arm around her shoulder.

'Did you know that Cognitius asked us not to interfere with your time here?'

Allura looked at her confused, starting to think that the mad old woman had been sabotaging her from the very beginning.

'Why would she do that?'

'She said you needed to find your own way.'

'But you invited me to the wedding?'

'Well, between you and me. My wife is a big softy at heart.'

Allura was touched that they had defied their sovereign's requests for her sake, although a small part of her worried if that could be considered treason.

'So, why are you telling me now?'

'Because I think she was wrong,' Faye said, handing her the basket, 'I think you need someone to tell you that it's okay to mess up.'

Those were perhaps the exact words Allura needed to hear as her nerves swiftly hardened into determination.

I can do this, she decided and with a swift push on the door, she entered.

Upstairs, Ofelia's room was a sad sight indeed. In many ways it reminded Allura of the ransacked cabin. Much of the light was blotted out by heavy green curtains and dozens upon dozens of scrunched up balls of paper were scattered across the floor.

There was also an almost eerie silence, broken only by Ofelia's heavy breathing and the pattering of

TibbidyBoo's claws as he ran through the overhanging tubes from one enclosure to the other.

The crying girl herself however had hidden away under a blanket on her bed. Allura approached slowly before sitting on the edge of the mattress.

'It's me,' she said, but Ofelia remained quiet. 'London's safe… I thought you would want to know. A hunter came looking for her last night, but Abraham managed to trick him into thinking she was dead.'

The blanket shifted, but there was still no sign of Ofelia.

'Oh yeah that's the other thing, Abraham knew about her the whole time… can you believe that?'

Just apologise, Allura told herself, angry that she was finding it this difficult.

'Look, I understand if you don't want to talk to me… I wouldn't really want to talk to me either right now, but I have something I need to say. You can just listen in if you want.'

Allura was certain that the words would make no difference, but knew that they needed to be said. After a long and awkward pause, she plucked up the courage and finally said:

'I'm sorry.'

Upon hearing her own words, Allura realised just how much she meant them.

'I really am. I am so sorry,' she continued, barely able to contain herself anymore as the things she had been too afraid to say were suddenly pouring out of her.

'I shouldn't have ran away and I really shouldn't

have used London like that. I think I convinced myself that all of this was too good to be true, because usually it is, so I let myself ruin it just to prove that I was right. But I see now how wrong I was. So from the bottom of my heart, I am truly, deeply, completely sorry.'

There was no response, but Allura didn't regret what she had said. She was being more honest and open than she had ever been before and it felt great.

'Alright... well, that's all I wanted to say,' she mumbled before slowly making her way to the door. Lingering with her hand on the handle, she searched for anything else she could tell her.

Then it hit her.

'Oh, I also brought you some sweets.'

Fumbling through the murky blackness, she dropped the basket on Ofelia's desk.

'Okay, I'll get out of your hair now. It was really great getting to know you, even if it was only for a little while.'

Allura opened the door when suddenly the blanket rustled and after a second longer, it fell away entirely, revealing the heaped mess that was Ofelia. She peaked through a fog of knotted golden hair before asking:

'What kind of sweets?'

*

Reconciled and ravenous, the girls chomped and chewed on chocolates and sweets until their jaws ached. With the rush of sugar coursing through them, they were able to convince Ofelia's parents to allow them to visit Noah under the very strict condition that they were both to be back before dark.

'Both of us?' Allura had asked in surprise.

'Well of course dear, we can't have you spending Atrilarium's Eve all by yourself in that lonely old cabin, especially if it is to be your last day here,' Lydia replied.

I guess I could stay one more night, Allura thought, remembering her plans to visit Craven's Mountain and get back to Cambium before the day's end.

On their way to Noah's house, the girls continued to share what remained of the basket. Grabbing big handfuls of toffee, they stopped to watch a school of fish moving through the river Pale and to admire the pretty Atrilarium lights strewn across Endwood.

Allura wasn't sure if this was what forgiveness usually felt like, but all she knew was that she was loving it.

All too quickly however, they made their way to the Tanden's residence and Allura felt even more afraid to see Noah than she had Ofelia, the memory of their last encounter causing her to hesitate to even touch the big bronze door knocker.

But still, she knew it was the right thing to do (also Ofelia had already done it the moment they arrived). When it opened, they were surprised to be met by Elliott and Patricia, dressed in big winter coats and preparing to head out themselves.

'Is Noah with you?' Elliott asked swiftly.

'No, we thought he was here,' replied Ofelia.

There was a look of stricken panic in the couple's

eyes and before they could confirm it, Allura knew what was going on.

'We think Noah may be in trouble,' Patricia said, frantically wrapping a scarf around her neck. Allura found it a little unnerving to see the usually docile woman looking quite so animated.

'He'll be okay darling,' Elliott said, holding her close.

'What happened?' Allura asked.

'We're not sure. He didn't seem himself last night, but he wouldn't tell us why. Then this morning he rushed out the house and when I asked him where he was going, he said he 'had a promise to keep.' But that was three hours ago and if he's not with you two then I don't know where he could be.'

Oh no, this is all my fault.

'This is all our fault,' Patricia wailed, echoing Allura's thoughts into life as she burst into tears.

Allura was confused, certain that she alone was the one responsible. However, things became clearer as Patricia told them of a sickness that had made Noah frail when he was little.

A deep illness had poisoned him inside, making him so weak that he couldn't play with the other children or explore the outdoors like everyone else. For years, the only life he had known was one lived in other people's dreams, but things changed as he got older and his condition faded.

The real world opened up to him, but by then it was too late. By then he had learnt not only to be cautious, but to be afraid.

Hearing of Noah's past, Allura's guilt grew

greater for the things she had said to him and as soon as Mrs. Tanden was finished explaining, Allura offered to help in their search.

'Oh bless you,' said Patricia as they all stepped outside.

'Right. You two look around town and we'll have a look in the woods,' Elliott said without a trace of his normal jolly self.

'Stay safe,' he added sternly as they split ways.

'That plonker could be ANYWHERE,' Ofelia said, smacking her hand to her head in frustration, although Allura could tell she was only trying to mask her concern.

'No, not anywhere. You heard what his dad said, Noah's trying to keep the promise we all made to look out for each other.'

'So?'

'So, I think I know exactly where he is.'

*

On the far side of Endwood, a little-ways beyond a bridge that stretched over a choppier part of the river, an imposing house stood out amongst the trees.

It had a sloping tiled rooftop and despite its obvious age, it seemed well-kept with fresh paint and glinting clean windows. The manor house was grand and pristine, an ill-reflection of the crude and grubby Kraw children who resided inside of it.

But it was there, out on the snowy lawn at the front of the house, next to a black, horse-drawn carriage with the word 'SHERIFF' written on its side, that the girls spotted Noah.

They had approached 'Kraw Castle' from the woods and watched from behind the trees as Noah paced up and down beside the coach.

'What's the worst that could happen?' he asked himself as he headed towards the house. 'They could kill you. They could kill you dead that's what could happen,' he answered aloud as he turned on his heel and jogged back towards the woods.

Allura didn't think she would ever feel so grateful for Noah's fearful indecisiveness. At least, that was until he turned towards the house again.

'Can't be a coward forever,' he muttered to himself as he approached the front door.

'He's gonna get himself battered. We have to stop him,' Ofelia said as the girls leapt out from the woods and caught up to him halfway up the path.

He flinched as they tapped him on the shoulder.

'What do you think you're doing?' Allura asked in a hushed yell.

'I'm getting your stuff back,' he replied, clearly startled to see her.

'No, you're getting yourself in serious trouble.'

'Well, why do you care?'

'Because…' Allura paused, '…because you're my friend.'

'That's not what you said yesterday.'

Before anymore could be said, the sounds of locks unbolting boomed from the other side of the front door. They hurried into the treeline and ducked behind a bush.

From there they watched as a well-groomed man with combed brown hair, mutton chops and a thick moustache stepped out onto the porch.

He wore a white shirt with a wolf pelt draped over his shoulders and had a short sword hanging from his belt. In his hand was a half-finished glass of brown liquid.

Looking around with strangely bloodshot eyes, he descended the porch steps, wetting his fine leather boots in the snow.

'Who's there?' he called out and Allura could tell that Ofelia was fighting the instinct to answer as the man she assumed to be Carter Kraw approached the carriage.

'Faded Widow? Are you here?' he asked as he pulled out his sword. 'Or is it you? After all this time.'

What is he going on about? Allura wondered as Carter dropped to his knees and stabbed wildly underneath the carriage with his silver blade.

It was almost comical, until he rose to his feet and his eyeline was drawn to the woods. Allura, Noah and Ofelia dropped even lower behind the bush as the sound of crunching snow grew louder and louder.

He approached their hiding spot with a worryingly quick pace and given what he had just done to the underside of the carriage, Allura was frightened to discover what he would do if he found them.

Suddenly, the sound of shattering glass echoed from the house and with unblinking eyes, Carter returned his sword to its sheath and ran his hands down his face, letting out an exhausted sigh as though it were a sound he was all too familiar with.

'What was it this time?' he howled as he turned in

place and charged towards the house. 'I swear to the gods, if either of you have even touched my storm clock, you'll *both* be spending the night in the stocks!'

After one more check of the tree-line. Carter returned to his manor and slammed the door, hard. Together, the three bush-dwellers waited until they were certain that the coast was clear, then sprinted as far as their feet could take them away from 'Kraw Castle'.

While Ofelia burst into fits of nervous laughter and Noah let out multiple sighs of relief as they ran, Allura was left with the distinct impression that something more than them had got the sheriff spooked.

Eventually, they came to a much-needed stop outside of Noah's house, having sprinted full speed through the woods, across the bridge and back into town.

'That was… crazy,' Ofelia uttered slowly through huge gulps of air, but Allura quickly noticed that Noah was dead silent on his doorstep with his head in his hands. She sat down next to him on the cold stone and placed a hand on his shoulder.

'I'm sorry about what I said yesterday. I didn't mean any of it,' she said softly.

'I wasn't upset because you said it, I was upset because it's true. I'm scared of everything. I always have been. You probably thought I was going to knock on Kraw's door, but I was just about to turn tail and run away when you two showed up. I don't want to be afraid all the time. It's like I can't help but see the worst possible outcome of everything.'

Allura recognised those same feelings in herself. The nagging voice in her head constantly telling her that things were never going to turn out well.

In many ways, his fears were her own and understanding that compelled her to confess.

'Well at least you always stick around. Everyone I've ever met seems to realise sooner or later that I'm no good so I take off at the first sign of trouble. '

'Is that why you disappeared for so long yesterday?' Ofelia asked.

'Yeah, I heard what Noah said about me. How I should go back to Earth.'

'You idiot!' Ofelia said, smacking him on the back of the head.

'OW!'

'Don't be mad, he was right,' Allura said.

'No, I wasn't,' Noah was quick to reply. 'I thought someone was trying to kill you so I wanted you to be safe. But believe me the last thing I want is for you to leave.'

'That goes double for me. We really are very happy that we took that carriage ride with you.'

Without thinking, Allura found herself pulling them into a hug. The warmth of their arms tightening around her was all the forgiveness she needed.

*

Midday had rolled around and after Noah received a firm telling off from his parents, Allura and Ofelia begged them to let him stay out with them, promising not to take their eyes off of him if they did.

Allura had to play the 'it's my last day' card to convince Elliott and Patricia, but once they agreed to grant Noah his freedom, the trio made their way to the gnarled tree at the end of Ofelia's garden.

Sat on the bulging roots with their shoes pressed tenderly against the chunks of ice drifting down the river, Allura finally got to recount her adventures since last they saw each other.

Noah was particularly interested in her chance encounter with Evelyn, while Ofelia was far more concerned with reading the contents of Horas' journal. She flipped backwards and forwards through it, but always found herself drawn to the final entry.

'THREE?' Noah said in disbelief. 'You have been here less than a week and you have already met three of Orterra's leaders! I know I've said it before, but you *really* must be something special.'

'It's not about who I am, it's about who I replaced, trust me. Cognitius, Orville and Evelyn probably wouldn't give me the time of day if not for Horas.'

'Still! It's unheard of,' Noah argued.

'What's more important is that you think Abraham might have had something to do with all this,' Ofelia interrupted in a saddened tone.

'I don't know for sure,' Allura admitted, 'but I can't take the chance of telling him what I found in case he is.'

'But that's assuming that Raven definitely has anything to do with it,' Noah replied as Ofelia handed him the journal. Allura rolled her eyes at him, unable to imagine how he could possibly think Raven wasn't involved after what they had overheard at the castle.

'Alright fine, for arguments sake, let's say Raven is behind all this. Why don't you tell Orville?' he asked.

'Because, he still hasn't even replied to my first message.'

'We could tell our parents,' Ofelia suggested.

'They wouldn't believe us and even if they did, they'd want to tell Cognitius,' Allura explained.

'But she'll still be travelling back from Giant's Peak, they won't get a message to her until midnight at the earliest,' Noah said, realising the fatal flaw in Ofelia's plan.

'Exactly, which just means more time for someone else to be killed.'

As they spoke, Noah examined the map Allura had taken from the library. He gave her an unimpressed glare for vandalising the book, but pushed past his personal opinions on the matter to answer her question about how long it would take to get to Craven's Mountain.

'By carriage, an hour, maybe two, why?' he said, his eyebrows furrowing as Allura gave him a suspicious smile. 'No. No way,' he said, shaking his head.

'Come on! Orville told me the last time anyone ever saw Horas he was leaving Endwood and now we know where he was going. This could be the last place he went before he died. I would be really quick. In and out. Just to see if there's anything there.'

'Hey if you're going, we're going too,' Ofelia interjected, positively beaming with excitement.

Noah anxiously rubbed the back of his neck as Allura stood up and offered her hand out to him. He sighed as he used it to lever himself up and off the snow.

'Alright fine. Maybe you're right. Maybe we're the only ones who can do this, but even if we wanted any part in this madness, it would take us all day to walk to the mountain.'

Allura could almost see the knot tightening in Noah's stomach as she replied:

'Who said anything about walking?'

15

A cold reception

THIS IS INCREDIBLE!' Ofelia shouted as they soared through the air.

Although it had taken them a little longer to get off the ground, London hardly seemed phased by the extra weight on her back once they were in the sky.

If anything, the bear appeared to relish the company, purring loudly as Ofelia stretched out her arms and shouted for joy.

The only one bothered by them being there was Noah, who clung to the straps of Ofelia's overalls for dear life. Fortunately, he was blinded by her long hair billowing into his face. Not that there was much to see anyway as a thick snowy mist had rolled in, consuming everything beneath them in a hazy whiteness.

'You might want to hold on tight,' Allura advised them as she felt London's head drop low and the speed picked up.

The girls laughed and Noah let out a little yelp as they swooped through a falling stream of frosty water that dropped from a cliff face. TibbidyBoo caught cool droplets of icy water in his mouth before burrowing back into Ofelia's pocket and as they flew, Allura admired the serene stillness of the cloudy fog below them.

It was like flying over a blank canvas that moved with gentle wisps and curls, interrupted only by the tallest treetops and the peaks of snowy mountains in the distance. But as they got closer to Craven's Mountain, they heard a sound, like the echoes of rocks smashing together.

'Was that a landslide?' asked Ofelia.

'Sounded like it, but there's something weird about it,' Noah said meekly.

Allura had to agree with him, she had heard plenty of landslides on their way to Highdenhome, but there was something different about this one, as though it was orchestrated, controlled.

Then everything went quiet again.

Suddenly, a gigantic boulder emerged from the mist, hurtling towards them at startling speed.

They all screamed as London instinctively swerved to avoid it. Continuing on its trajectory, the boulder reduced a nearby tree to splinters as it tumbled to the ground.

'WHAT WAS THAT?' yelled Noah as another boulder spiralled towards them.

'DOWN!' Allura screamed, pushing into London's fur.

They dropped closer to the mist as the boulder whooshed overhead, narrowly missing them while Allura desperately pulled on the rope. She had barely managed to get London under control when two more humongous lumps of jagged rock came into

261

view.

Smashing into each other, they sent shattered stone exploding in every direction as a churlish laughter echoed from the valley.

'Sounds like trolls!' Ofelia realised.

'TROLLS?' Allura asked, alarmed.

She'd seen lytes, tearers and stone golems, but the reality of trolls still took her by surprise.

'They're trying to knock us out of the sky!' cried Noah.

'Don't worry, I've got an idea!' Ofelia said as she sat up straight and held her hands around her mouth like a megaphone.

But before she could do whatever she was planning, a pair of enormous, three-fingered hands covered in spots and boils rose out of the fog and flung another chunk of rock towards them.

London veered sharply, sending Ofelia tumbling off of her back.

With a blood-curdling scream, she dangled precariously from London's side, with only Noah's tight grip on her overalls stopping her from plummeting into the fog.

While one of his hands grasped onto Ofelia, the other clasped around London's fur to stop him from falling too. The determined bear hardly noticed as she and Allura were all too busy trying to avoid the boulders.

'OFELIA, GRAB MY HAND!' Noah cried.

'I'M TRYING!' she yelled back as she reached up to him, but London swooped and swerved, causing Ofelia's arms and the satchel hanging from her shoulder to flail about wildly.

Meanwhile London's wings were beating hard and fast, and Allura could tell it was becoming too much for her.

'Just a little further!' Allura hollered into London's ear as she spotted the peak of Craven's Mountain, looking as distinctly curved as it had been on the map.

We're going to make it, Allura dared to think when a sharp rock sliced along one of the bear's outstretched wings.

London jolted, causing one of Ofelia's overall straps to snap. The hanging girl dropped lower as Noah was left with only a single piece of fabric to cling onto with all his strength.

'PLEASE DON'T LET GO,' Ofelia begged.

'I WON'T,' he swore, but Allura could see his hold on London was loosening and within seconds, both of her friends would be lost to the fog.

To make matters worse, a shower of rocks was raining down on them, each one hurled with sickening laughter from the trolls. Bloodied and exhausted, London persevered, dodging and weaving as best she could.

The mountain itself was so close now, but it seemed they would never reach it as a dozen more speckled hands rose from the mist, each one wielding even more boulders.

We're done for, Allura thought as her friends let out a terrified scream.

Behind her, Noah's hold on London's fur had finally broken and he too was sliding off of her back.

With her friends seconds away from falling to their dooms, Allura reached back and grabbed his hand.

Thinking quickly, she hooked her free arm around the bear's neck for support and pulled at Noah's hand with every morsel of might in her body. Yet still, she could not hoist them all the way up.

Completely and utterly powerless, Allura watched as the grotesque trolls readied to throw their boulders, lifting the rocks high above their heads, like catapults ready to fire.

Her friends hung onto her for dear life and London's blood dripped into the misty chasm below, leaving Allura to do the only thing she could think of.

She shut her eyes and ignored the agony in her arms as they were stretched to their absolute limits, focusing instead on that unplaceable yet powerful feeling that had saved her and London from the hunter's arrow.

Come on, come on, Allura begged, not only to herself, but to the light that brought her here and anyone else who might have been listening.

Reaching as far into herself as she could, she felt a flicker of that elusive power surging within, but each time she tried to summon it, to stoke the fire that swelled inside of her, it was extinguished by her own despair.

It won't work, she told herself.

It's hopeless. We're going to die.

Then something truly miraculous happened.

From seemingly nowhere, a deep and powerful

voice boomed throughout the valley. It sounded raspy and ancient, and spoke in a language that Allura did not recognise, but most important of all, it did *not* sound happy.

As its words echoed around them, the boulders fell from the troll's hands and one by one they retreated back into the depths of the fog. After that, the only sound was the heavy stomping of the trolls' feet as they clambered over one another to get back into their caves.

'WHAT WAS THAT?' Allura asked.

'I DON'T KNOW, BUT CAN WE LAND ALREADY!' Noah screamed as London came crashing down onto a tall hill that led directly onto the mountainside.

There, Ofelia fell to her knees and dug her hands into the snow, swearing to never take solid ground for granted again. Meanwhile, Noah planted himself firmly under a nearby tree, his motion sickness finally getting the better of him.

'Is everyone okay?' Allura asked, rubbing her aching arms.

Noah was too busy trying not to throw up and Ofelia had simply fallen silent, the shock of what had happened taking its toll. Allura decided to give them a minute while she checked on London, gently stroking the bear's head as she inspected her wound.

The cut was long and thin, carving out a line of featherless flesh across the full-length of her wing, but thankfully it had not gone too deep.

Allura comforted the injured bear until her whimpering came to a stop while staring back at the way they had come, finding no trace of any trolls amongst the mist.

'What was that all about?' she asked.

'That was just one of the things those horrible bloody trolls like to do for fun,' Ofelia answered.

'THAT was a game to them?'

'Everything's a game to them,' Noah replied in disgust as the colour started to return to his face.

'Bloody trolls,' Allura muttered to herself as she continued to survey the blanket of mist, overhearing Ofelia and Noah's conversation as they spoke softly underneath the tree.

'Thank you for not letting go,' Ofelia said with an embarrassed mumble.

'It was the least I could do,' he replied.

'You could've let me fall.'

'No, I couldn't,' he said with more sincerity than either of them were comfortable with.

Allura smiled to herself at the sound of them awkwardly getting along. She was about to make a joke about it when she found herself oddly drawn to the tree above them.

It was drooped over and obviously dead for the winter, with a thick pile of brown and gold leaves sat in a circle around it. From the shape of its long hanging branches, she recognised it as a willow and although it was impossible for her to know why, she felt a deep sadness at the sight of it.

Pressing her hand against the bark, she thought she could hear a whispered voice calling her name, if only for a moment, but she quickly dismissed it as nothing more than a trick of the wind.

'We should get going before whatever scared the trolls off comes after us,' she said, pulling herself away from the trunk.

'I wouldn't worry about that,' said Ofelia.

'Why not?'

Holding her hands up to her mouth again, she said: 'BECAUSE I DON'T THINK IT WILL BOTHER US!' in the same deep voice that had saved them.

'Woah, how did you do that?' asked Noah in astonishment.

'I may not know much about maths or Earth history, but I do know ogres,' she said proudly. 'And lucky for us, if there's one thing that trolls are terrified of, it's ogres.'

'What's the difference?' Allura asked.

'The number of legs mostly,' Ofelia replied.

And so, with everyone still in one piece, they set out for the mountain while Ofelia explained how fortunate they were that one of the very few words she knew in ogrish was 'run'.

The foothills connected directly to the mine with the once grand entrance carved into the stone itself. Except now, the rocks had collapsed, leaving only a small sliver through which they could enter.

'You'll have to wait out here,' Allura said to London, pressing her head softly against the bear's.

'Are we really doing this?' Ofelia asked in a mixture of uncertainty and anticipation.

'I don't think we should,' Noah said, his hands shaking. 'I'm getting a really bad vibe from this place.'

'It's an abandoned mine, what sort of vibe did you

expect?' asked Allura.

'But that's the thing, it doesn't feel abandoned.'

'Noah, if you don't want to come, you don't have to. You've helped us plenty already and I'm sure London would love the company anyway. But this could be our only chance of finding out what happened to Horas.'

'You don't know that,' he said, searching helplessly for any way to stop her.

'We know he was coming here, he said so himself in the journal.'

'Okay fine he *probably* was here, but need I remind you, he also probably died here. For all you know we're going to find his corpse in there and if we do, what makes you think we're going to turn out any different? By the gods, we were nearly killed just getting here.'

'But we survived.'

'Barely! And whatever is in there could very well be worse.'

'That's why I wanted you with us,' Allura said before slipping out of sight through the crack in the mountain.

It was a tight squeeze made of rough and slimy stone, but after some shimmying and wriggling, she made it to the other side. Allura stopped, not wanting to take another step deeper without her friends and watched from there as Ofelia positioned herself by the opening to follow.

'Ofelia, please. I'm-' she heard Noah say.

'It's okay to be scared,' Ofelia said, 'as long as you remember to be brave when it matters.'

With that, she joined Allura inside the mine shaft. Together they peered through the gap as Noah paced back and forth along the mountainside with London looking at him curiously.

'I know, I know. I made a promise,' he said with a sigh.

Kicking a stone in frustration, he pushed up his glasses and made his way into the mountain, entirely unaware of exactly how right he had been.

16

The monster of the mountain

How is it that Ofelia of all people remembered to bring her satchel, but not one of us thought to bring a lantern? Allura wondered as they fumbled through the darkness.

Apart from the fragments of light that snuck through the broken stone entrance behind them and a faint luminescence that glowed way off in the distance ahead, the mine was pitch black.

Luckily, some good had come from Allura's time in the basement as her eyes had grown accustomed to finding their way through the dark. As they took one cautious step after the other, she was able to make out the shapes of fallen rubble and fractures in the floor for them to avoid.

Unfortunately, her friends were not quite so adept.

'Ah!' cried Noah.

'What is it?'

'I walked through a cobweb,' he whined.

'I've swallowed about three,' said Ofelia.

'It's not a competition.'

'I know. Although if it were then I'd be-' she choked on her words (or more accurately, on another spider's web) before she could finish her sentence.

'Would you both be quiet?' Allura whispered as they ventured further into the mine, the ground starting to crunch and snap beneath their feet while a musty stench filled their nostrils.

From up, down, left and right, the occasional splash of a puddle or crack of stone caused them all to gasp and tighten their grip on one another. The endless possibilities of the unknown caused their bodies to clench in fearful anticipation at every turn.

Allura even thought she could hear the clanging of metal, like an echo from the once operational mine's past. Ofelia tried to reassure her by explaining that at worst it would only be a remnant, the accursed ghost of someone who's life had been lost due to blighted magic, but for some reason that didn't make Allura feel any better.

Eventually, after a few more minutes of stumbling and shaking in the dark, they found the source of the light they had been following. Thin sunbeams shone through tiny cracks in the ceiling, illuminating a decrepit, but no less grand hall which they entered through a large rotting doorframe.

There, Allura realised where that terrible smell had been coming from as she spotted four large wooden tanks filled to the brim with old lamp oil in each corner of the room. Tattered banners hung from the walls with the insignias of The Bliss and The Balance on them, while tall piles of rocks and shattered pillars littered the room and cloudy cobwebs filled the eroding ceiling.

Including the one they had entered through, there

were seven large doors around the room, but Allura could see that four of them had been buried by fallen debris, while another had been blocked by a truly gigantic skeletal hand (the thumb alone was almost twice Allura's size). However, the other remaining door was stuck open and seemed to lead into another dark corridor.

Noah and Ofelia rushed off to investigate the remains of the hall, while Allura continued to take in the enormity of it all. As impressive as it was, she felt a sadness at the thought of how much time and effort would have gone into constructing such a place, only for it to be left in ruins.

'BY THE GODS,' Ofelia said from behind a mass of fallen stone.

'What is it?' Allura asked, hurrying over, but quickly having her question answered when she caught sight of something disturbing.

It was a huge skeleton (although not nearly as big as the one whose hand blocked the door) hanging upside down from an ancient web. Its upper half resembled that of a large human, but the rest of its body looked more spider-like, with eight legs splayed out across the rocky ceiling.

'What is it?' Allura asked in disgust.

'It's an ogre,' Ofelia replied with sorrow in her voice, 'or at least it was.'

A monstrous half-human, half-spider hybrid was not how Allura had imagined an ogre to look, but then again, she hadn't really put much thought into the matter.

It was whilst Allura examined the dead creature

that Ofelia climbed a tumbled heap of rocks and pried one of its large clenched hands open, revealing a second skeleton inside.

A human one adorned in fine gold armour.

'What happened here?' Allura asked.

'When they decided to leave this place to the monsters, some miners and a few warriors tried to take it back for themselves. The stories say they were never heard from again, but I guess now we know what happened to them,' Noah explained.

As he spoke, they all started to notice skeletal arms and legs sticking out from the stacks of collapsed stone. With each one Allura saw, the snapping and crunching sounds they had heard in the dark earlier made more and more sense.

'Be at peace,' Ofelia muttered, placing her hand on the human's skull, but as she reached up to do the same for the ogre, Allura spotted something lodged in its ribcage. Something that glistened in the flecks of sunlight.

She reached up and tried to wrestle it loose, tugging at its leather-wrapped handle as hard as she could, until finally, it slid out of place.

Raising it high into the light, she confirmed her suspicion that it was a sword, as sharp and shiny as the day it was forged despite the many centuries it had spent buried in the ogre's gut.

'I guess that must've been what he used to kill it,' Ofelia said, gesturing to the man in the ogre's hand.

'Do you want it?' Allura asked, holding it out to her, but Ofelia shook her head.

'Noah?' Allura offered.

'I wouldn't know what to do with it,' Noah replied, although his eyes lingered on it as Allura tested the weight of the weapon in her hand.

The handle was light and short enough to fit nicely in her palm, while runic symbols ran along the length of the blade. Before she could become more acquainted with it, a scratching sound demanded her attention.

She turned towards the noise with the sword pointed, only to find that it was Noah scraping a flat rock against the metal edge of an axe that had been imbedded into a wall.

He repeated the action over and over again.

'What are you doing?' Ofelia asked.

'Gimme a second,' he replied as he found an old torch with a white rag wrapped around the top and coated the tip in lantern oil.

Bringing his unlit torch up to the axe, he once again skimmed the stone along its edge with greater force and sent sparks flying. The golden embers caught onto the rag, igniting it instantly, and Noah held the flaming stick up proudly.

'That was annoyingly impressive,' Ofelia admitted.

'Thank you very much,' Noah said smugly, using the torch to guide them towards the door that would take them deeper into the mountain.

Armed with a guiding light and the sword of a dead man, they moved through the next passageway with renewed confidence. Unfortunately, in the light of the fire they could see more than just the way through, they could also see in clear detail the dark pools of dried blood that stained the floors.

It was unsettling to say the least, but they did their best to ignore the marks of those who had gone before as they explored the corridor's many diverging rooms for any sign that Horas had ever even been there.

As they searched each room, they discovered that half of them had been used as makeshift homes for the miners, while the other half were filled with tools, equipment and mine cart rails which led into the greater mine below.

Never straying too far from one another, the three friends felt as though they had searched under every stone, over every mound and in every rusted mine cart as they reached the end of the corridor, still without any trace of Horas or his killer.

The corridor itself ended rather abruptly, stopping at a point where the mountain had split in two, ripping the last room away from the corridor and leaving a deep and dreadful abyss between them.

They all gazed down into the darkness, which in its prime, when all the fires were lit and the miners were at work, would have been a truly magnificent sight to behold. Now however, it was long-dead and the closest thing to life was the sound of a whistling breeze flowing through the cavern.

'Think of all the gold and jewels they left down there,' said Noah.

'I'd rather not,' replied Ofelia.

'Maybe we could pop down and have a quick look,' Allura suggested.

Noah and Ofelia shot her an unimpressed glance.

'Kidding,' she said, but only because there seemed to be no way down. The railway was far too steep for them to walk on and they would have to be mad to get in one of those rickety old mine carts.

Noah stretched the torch as far across the gap as he could and they peered into the pitch black ahead of them, trying to spot any sign of where to go next, but there was nothing to see.

It was a dead end.

'We must have missed something,' Ofelia said.

'Or there was nothing to miss. Maybe this whole thing was just a stupid wild graver chase,' Noah said, kicking a piece of rubble hard into the abyss with an immediate *clunk!*

Allura's ears pricked up.

'Did you hear that?' she asked excitedly.

'Hear what?' Noah asked, but she was too busy collecting more stones and metal fragments to answer him.

One by one, she tossed them into the void and waited to hear them *thud* and *ping* and *clank* against an unseen surface.

'What are you doing and how can we help?' Ofelia asked, kicking a broken bucket into the hole without exactly knowing why.

'Just listen,' she said throwing a metal bolt as hard as she could. They listened intently, expectantly, until they heard it *clang!*

'It didn't fall!' Noah said in astonishment, finally catching up on what Allura was up to. Although there was a deep and ancient pit between them and whatever awaited in the darkness, they had managed to confirm that there was indeed something on the other side.

'Brilliant. Now we just need to find a ladder or something to get across,' Ofelia said looking around for anything suited to the task, but Allura was all too impatient to find out what was waiting in the abyss.

Passing the sword to Noah and securing her hair in one of the many bows Ofelia kept with her at all times, Allura moved further back into the corridor and took a runner's pose.

I better be right about this, she thought before darting forwards like a rabbit out of a cage.

'WAIT! DON'T!' Noah yelled, but he was far too late to stop her.

She barrelled towards the end of the corridor, ignoring her friends' protests as she leapt off the edge and vanished into the darkness.

A rush of butterflies filled her stomach as she soared over the gap. The stale air and a pungent taste, like rotten eggs overwhelmed her senses as the pitch black, that had once seemed so absolute, suddenly gave way to torchlight.

She quickly realised that it wasn't darkness at all, but an inky veil of fog. As thick as the snowy mist outside, it had been used to surround the entrance to a secret room, hiding it amongst the inky blackness of the empty mine.

Allura landed with a tumble, sending plumes of dust into the air.

I'm alive! she thought to herself in relief as her friends cried out.

'ALLURA?'

'ARE YOU OKAY?'

'I'M ALRIGHT!' she called back. 'YOU TWO HAVE GOT TO SEE THIS!'

Dusting off her skinned knees she began to inspect wherever it was she now found herself, finding that the room was a surprisingly well-lit square with two walls made of hard stone and one that seemed equally as dense, but with an odd, fuzzy quality to it.

The floor was covered in a layer of the dark fog and around the room, chests and metal carts filled to the brim with translucent gems and shining gold sat ready for the taking.

Under normal circumstances, they would have garnered Allura's attention, but her focus was drawn to one of the corners of the room where a desk had been carved into the wall.

It wasn't the desk itself that interested her, but the odd assortment of curiously new-looking objects that rested on it. Before she could take a closer look, Ofelia came bursting through the curtain of blackness, landing gracefully like a cat before embracing Allura in a strong hug.

'Please don't do anything like that again.'

'I'll try,' she replied and while Ofelia took in her surprising new surroundings, Allura looked back towards the fog.

'You not coming Noah?'

'It's okay,' he called back, 'I'll keep lookout here.'

'Alright well, try not to get eaten by that troll behind you,' she said.

Although they could not see him, the rapid

shuffling of his panicked feet made the girls giggle.

'Oh very funny,' Noah said sarcastically as Ofelia started to interact with the fog, waving her hand around in it and watching it move like water.

'I've never seen anything quite like this,' she said, astounded.

'I have,' Allura replied.

'Really? Where?'

'The first night I came here. When Raven took me to see Cognitius he left a trail of smoke behind him just like that.'

'You seem pretty sure he's involved, but none of it makes any sense. Why would he want to kill Horas? Or Orville? He's served him loyally for years?'

'And you don't think that after all that time he wouldn't do anything for more power?'

Ofelia wanted to say 'no', but the thought of the skeletons in the hall and the people who had died for a few pieces of gold made her go quiet.

She was so lost in that thought that she didn't notice TibbidyBoo wriggle free from her pocket and sprint around the room before turning his attention to the strangely textured wall.

Allura also hadn't noticed him as she returned to the desk and investigated the three objects resting on it.

The first was a small bag containing a bundle of yellow petals, the second was a thin manual filled with schematics (but for what, she did not know) and the third was a dagger with a gold handle and a twisted blade, stained at the tip with blood.

Her heart skipped a beat at the sight of the weapon.

Shaken by her extreme fear, she turned away from the desk, but before she could ask for Ofelia's thoughts on the items, she felt something snap under her foot.

Looking down, she saw that she had trodden on the leg of another skeleton, but it was different from the ones they had seen in the hall.

It was neither human nor ogre, and it had a shimmering complexion to it. Picking up one of the bones, she immediately recoiled in disgust as she felt that it was coated in a slimy liquid.

'What are these?' Allura asked, pointing to the lion-sized skeleton.

'Hmmm, looks like it could be a tearer to me.'

As they spoke, TibbidyBoo nuzzled into the soft wall, brushing his fur against it.

'Tearer? Like that thing that attacked us in the woods?'

'Exactly, but I don't know what that gooey stuff on them is. It almost looks like slobber,' she said, crouching down to get a closer look. 'These bones seem fairly new, as though they didn't decompose, but were-' she trailed off; the thought too terrifying to express aloud.

'Were what?' Allura insisted.

Ofelia took a nervous gulp.

'Licked clean.'

It was at that precise moment, as Ofelia spoke the words that made Allura's hair stand on end that TibbidyBoo decided to sink his sharp teeth into the fuzzy wall.

As if on command, the room shook and a deep, throaty sound rumbled around them. Suddenly, the wall began to expand and retract and the scraping of something against the ceiling caused centuries of dust to rain down on them.

'GET OUT! GET OUT!' Noah screamed from beyond the fog.

'What's happening?' Ofelia asked.

'I don't know, but take these,' Allura said, hurriedly stuffing the objects from the desk into Ofelia's bag.

With the items secured, Ofelia grabbed TibbidyBoo as they made for the exit. The black fog vanished and the furry wall detached itself from the room as the girls stood at the edge of the precipice, finally able to see the full extent of the chasm they would have to clear.

It's bigger than I realised, Allura thought as the room quaked again and a huge chunk of the ground fell into the ravine, causing them to hop back even further.

'Come on!' Noah pleaded from the corridor.

'We won't make it,' Ofelia said.

'Yes, we will,' Allura insisted as she grabbed her hand. 'We have to.'

Behind them, there was a terrible boom as the ceiling began to cave in, flattening the desk and the metal carts.

'THREE!' Allura said.

'TWO!' Ofelia joined in.

'ONE!'

They jumped...

…and came crashing down on the other side.

Coughing up dust, the girls lay flat on the floor, laughing in shock at what they had just done, but Noah remained stern and frightened.

'We need to go,' he said, quickly helping them both to their feet.

'Give us a minute at least,' Ofelia said, trying to catch her breath.

'We don't have a minute.'

'Why not?'

A loud thud caused them all to look back into the darkness. What little light remained revealed a creature roughly the size of a bus, perched on top of the rubble of the room it had been sleeping against.

It had fuzzy dark fur across its slender body and a black fog flowing from its flat nose as it stretched on its back two legs. Still stirring from its slumber, its big, bulging eyes fixated on them and its sharp teeth started to grind together.

Shockingly, Allura actually recognised the creature. Its creepy thin fingers, long pointed tail and soulless yellow eyes had left quite an impression on her in Cambium's library.

She thought back to the first book she had inspected, remembering the monster's name as she spoke it aloud:

'The clawing kross.'

'Ofelia what do we do?' Noah asked, but Ofelia could only bring herself to mumble a reply that caused the creature's bat-like ears to prick up.

'What was that?' Allura asked.

'Run,' Ofelia said.

'RUN!'

The pounding of feet and the beating of her own heart was all Allura heard after that as the three of them sprinted down the corridor. They only made it halfway to the main hall when the creature gave chase on all-fours with a horrid shriek.

It scuttled around the walls of the corridor, barely able to fit, but still moving at mesmerising speed. Allura heard its terrifying cries, but was determined not to look back, certain that their only chance was to outrun it.

Ofelia swiftly pulled them both to the ground, narrowly avoiding the creature's swiping talons as it continued to scuttle overhead before dropping from the ceiling to block their path into the hall.

'In here!' Allura said as they ran into one of the side rooms.

Inside were rows upon rows of rail tracks which were mostly buried under fallen rocks. Miraculously however, one set of tracks had been left untouched and still had a mine cart in place.

There was no time to think as they all leapt into the cart and tried to make themselves as small as possible.

They all held their breath and waited, each of them tensing as the sound of talons cracking through stone announced that the clawing kross had entered the room.

Allura peered through a small hole in the side of the cart and watched as the fearsome creature took big sniffs of the air with a bloodthirsty madness burning in its eyes.

She gripped Noah and Ofelia hard, as if to silently tell them to remain completely still as the black fog poured from its nose and filled the cart. After a long minute surveying the room, the clawing kross turned to leave.

Allura prepared to release a relieved sigh when the creature's swooshing tail knocked into the cart and the wheels started to creak into motion.

Oh no, no, no, no, no.

Inch by inch, the mine cart crawled slowly along the track, approaching a drop that would take them down into the belly of the mountain.

Squeaks of old metal against metal caught the creature's attention and it spun around quickly towards them.

They were approaching the point of no return and either they would be plunged deeper into the mine or have to face the monster head on.

There was no time to decide however, as seconds later the choice was made for them. They were fired down the track and into the cave.

Ofelia popped her head out over the edge of the cart as they dropped, screaming, almost joyfully, as though it were a rollercoaster and not an ancient mining track that could send them hurtling to their doom with every sharp turn and loosened bolt.

'WHAT DO WE DO?' Noah shouted, but there was nothing to be done. Even if they could find some way to slow it down, they would then be at the mercy of the monster that was following close behind.

The track continued to descend deeper and deeper into the tunnel until they were freed from the confines of the cave and found themselves travelling along a shaky bridge hundreds of feet above the ground.

Allura quickly realised that they were now in the enormous mining chamber itself, and from what little they could see, the miners had hollowed out most of the mountain.

As they whizzed through the remarkable mine, they passed countless support structures and platforms made of decaying wood, as well as endless walls of rock encrusted with emeralds, rubies and other jewels that glittered in the torchlight.

Under different circumstances it all would have been incredibly alluring, but with the clawing kross gaining on them, none of it held Allura's attention for long.

With the flat and straight surface of the bridge giving the creature a clear run at them, things were looking dire and Allura was struggling not to drown in the same despair that she had felt when the trolls attacked.

But that feeling of dread gave her an idea.

'What're these things afraid of?' she asked Ofelia.

'Not much!' Ofelia replied.

'What about ogres?'

'Oh, that's brilliant!' Ofelia said as she turned to face their pursuer.

Holding her hands up to her mouth again, she performed the ogre's call. The emptiness of the mine amplified the sound and it was as deep and booming as before, except she had somehow managed to make it even scarier than the first time.

Yet it had no effect on the creature.

If anything, it seemed more determined than ever to catch them.

'It was worth a shot,' Allura said, patting Ofelia on the shoulder and snatching the sword from Noah who was overwhelmed by panic.

I need to try to scare it off, she thought, standing as tall as she could in the cramped metal cart.

It was difficult to keep her balance, but she did her best and lifted the sword high above her head.

She felt as though she understood what the dead man in the ogre's grip would have felt, facing down a mighty beast in his final moments without fear or hesitation. Yes, if she too was to die in this forsaken place, then she would at least take this monster down with her.

Releasing a warrior's scream as the clawing kross lunged at her with its claws and teeth bared, Allura was not prepared for what happened next.

In an explosion of blood and fur, the clawing kross was tackled off the bridge by some barbaric force.

It was difficult to make out, but Allura quickly realised that although Ofelia's ogre call had failed to scare the clawing kross away, it had caught the attention of something else.

While Noah continued to hide at the bottom of the cart, the girls watched in bewilderment as the beast that had been chasing them now battled with a monster that matched it in horror and size.

The gigantic ogre they had accidentally summoned from the depths looked much like the skeleton they had seen, only with flesh and fur across its half-man, half-arachnid body.

'By the gods! I guess it worked a little too well!' Ofelia squealed as the two creatures fought atop man-made platforms and tall rigged structures.

Meanwhile their cart had entered a spiralling descent into the heart of the mine, which gave them a full view of the fight as they circled around and around like water down a plug hole.

The clawing kross was rabid, ferociously scratching and gnawing while the ogre swung powerful punches and struck with its pointed stinger. Even Noah brought himself to peek through the holes in the cart and watched as the two goliaths collided.

Then they came to the end of the track.

The cart hit a sudden halt in the centre of a ludicrously tall room at the very bottom of the mine. Hanging from the ceiling were giant chains hardly withered by age, which Allura assumed were once used to carry materials up to the surface.

'There!' Allura said, pointing to one of the large receptacles attached to the chains.

She pulled down hard on a lever and heard the sounds of cogs and gears whirring to life in amongst the screeching and roaring of the two monsters in the other room.

After a moment longer, the chains rattled and shook before slowly starting to pull empty bucket after empty bucket all the way up to the top.

'Go!' Allura commanded and Ofelia hopped in the first bucket, followed soon after by Noah who took the one beneath her.

Finally, Allura made for her bucket and was lifted

off the ground just in time to watch the ogre and the clawing kross' fight burst through the walls and into the room below.

Allura continued to watch them pummel and slice at one another, but the higher she got, the less she could see. Until, all she could do was listen to their yells and growls echoing through the mountain.

'We're almost out!' Ofelia called down as she nimbly jumped from her bucket and onto a pile of debris at the top. Noah copied her and by the time Allura joined them they had already dug out enough space to squeeze through the rubble.

Hopping from her bucket and onto the pile, Allura prepared to follow when, from far below, she heard a bloodcurdling cry followed by a sickening *snap!*

She knew that one way or another the fight was over.

Crawling through the gap her friends had carved out in the doorway, Allura realised that they had made their way back to the hall of skeletons.

'This way!' Noah remembered, hurrying towards the door on the other side of the room.

Too eager to escape, they ignored the sound of shifting stone behind them and felt the fresh breeze blowing in from the tunnel ahead as they ran for the exit.

Then all at once, as if from nowhere, a black fog rolled in ahead of them.

Frozen in terror, all three of them looked up to see the furious face of death staring back. It was bleeding now from a deep cut across its cheek, but the clawing kross looked as terrifying as ever as it clung to the wall above the door.

Tackling her friends out of the way of the beast's snapping maw, Allura watched as the clawing kross chomped through the ground and sent rocks flying.

There, for only a moment, it violently thrashed its head around, trying but failing to loosen its teeth from the bedrock.

Thinking quickly or barely thinking at all, Noah plunged the torch fire into the creature's eye and it let out a shrill scream that shattered Noah's glasses.

Seizing the opportunity, Allura swung with the sword, swiping at the monster's hand to try and force it out of their way. But instead of yielding, the clawing kross continued to wail and shriek before batting them all away with its free arm.

Skidding across the ground, Allura felt the sword fling from her hand and pierce one of the barrels of oil. The foul-smelling liquid leaked out onto the ground as Noah and Ofelia helped Allura back onto her feet.

Scrambling into the corner, they stepped up onto a collapsed pillar while the flood of oil covered the floor in front of them.

'What now?' Ofelia asked.

'I don't know, but it's not going to keep crying like that forever,' Allura said, only noticing then that it had already stopped.

In fact, the clawing kross wasn't making any noise at all.

It had vanished.

'THERE!' Noah shouted, but by the time he'd pointed his trembling finger, the creature had already disappeared again into the dark.

Sounds of skulls toppling over and rocks sliding across the room told them that the monster was still there. But with only the thinnest beams of sunlight to guide them, they could hardly tell which direction it was coming from.

All they knew was that the danger was close.

Very close.

The monster was toying with its prey, purposefully frightening them until they were utterly petrified, and once they were... it stepped into the light.

There, its grotesque features were highlighted as it bathed in a sunbeam before dropping down and crawling towards them, scuttling from shadow to shadow.

Allura looked at the bony hands stretching out from piles of fallen rocks and feared that they would suffer the same fate, becoming just another set of forgotten skeletons in that horrible dank hall.

I never should have brought us here, she thought as Noah did the last thing she had expected, pulling the sword from the barrel and standing at the edge of the collapsed pillar they were on.

'What're you doing?' she asked, but he ignored her.

Pointing the sharp end to the ground, he kept a close eye on the clawing kross as it skulked towards them, both of them waiting for the exact right moment.

It was as the creature's muscles rippled and its jaw unhinged that Noah said:

'I really am sorry about this.'

The clawing kross sprung towards them and with all the strength he could muster, Noah scraped the sword against the floor.

Golden embers flickered from the touch of metal on stone, then the flickers became sparks and the sparks became fire.

In an instant, the oil ignited in a pool of flames.

Helpless to stop itself, the clawing kross dove head first into it, setting its bristly fur alight. Within seconds it was bolting around the room in a frenzy, desperately trying to extinguish the blaze while, Allura, Noah and Ofelia jumped across fallen debris and made a mad dash for the tunnel.

'THAT WAS INSANE!' Ofelia said as they ran.

'BUT GENIUS!' added Allura.

'PLEASE DON'T TELL MY PARENTS ABOUT THIS!' Noah pleaded as they approached the cracked stone through which they had entered.

The fresh breeze and natural light were like a beacon, drawing them out of the dark and Noah was the first to hurriedly squeeze through.

Outside he found London, right where they had left her. She growled uncertainly, unnerved by the tremors inside that were causing the mountainside to shake.

'Hope your wings feeling better,' Noah said, patting her on the head while inside the mountain, Ofelia prepared to follow.

As she did, Allura looked back and spotted something awful behind them. It was a warm glow that grew brighter with every passing second as they heard the noise of four legs scurrying after them.

'Hurry! It's coming!' she yelled, forcefully pushing Ofelia through the gap.

Allura turned sideways and started to edge her way out, step by step, ready to leave the cursed place behind. But the clawing kross had other ideas.

Crashing around the corner, it squeezed its way through the cave, crushing stones with its claws as though they were made of sand as it charged towards her.

Fur smouldering and its mouth hanging open in a silent scream, the clawing kross outstretched its frog-like tongue through the crevice and wrapped it around Allura's arm.

'LET GO OF ME!' she screamed at the monster as Ofelia grabbed her hand from the other side, trying as best she could to pull her free.

But the young girl was no match for the clawing kross and Allura could feel her grip slipping. She was moments from being plunged back into the darkness when a shattering roar eclipsed everything else.

The clawing kross drew back in fear as London made herself known, snarling ferociously and pressing her furry face as far into the gap as possible. It was only when she clawed at the monster's tongue that it loosened its grasp on Allura's arm and scampered back into the pitch black.

At long last, Allura was free.

Exhausted and overwhelmed, she slumped down on the mountain's edge with London's head resting in her lap and her friends sat beside her.

There, they remained for some time with their legs

dangling over the side, until eventually, Noah let out a single, triumphant shout over the mountains.

Yeah, Allura thought, *that probably sums it up.*

*

By the time they took off, the mist had disappeared, revealing grand verdant valleys and thick forests wrapped in coats of fresh snow. Allura welcomed the cool air as they flew and she felt like she could finally breathe again as they made their way back to Endwood.

Most of the journey was spent excitedly discussing their daring escape and even Noah could hardly believe the things he had done.

'I guess we finally know why that tearer was in the woods. If a clawing kross came to my house, I'd probably move out too,' said Ofelia.

'That's great to know and all, but it's not really worth nearly dying for,' said Noah.

'No, but the stuff in Ofelia's bag might be.'

'What stuff?' he asked, reaching for the bag, but having his hand slapped away.

'These were in that secret room,' Ofelia explained as she handed it to him with a cheeky smile. He rummaged through it with one hand and firmly grasped onto London with the other.

'But what has this stuff got to do with what happened to Horas and Orville?' Noah asked incredulously.

Allura pondered that very question for the rest of the journey, realising that she had left the mine with more questions than she had arrived with.

17

Petals and plots

Endwood seemed as warm and welcoming as a fireplace in winter when they returned from their expedition. The very sight of it causing a sense of calmness and ease to wash over them as they came in to land.

'Don't worry, angel bears heal much quicker than us,' Ofelia reassured her as they walked London to the shed of Horas' cabin.

Allura inspected the clipped wing to find that she was right, the cut had already begun to smooth over, leaving only a bald line amongst her feathers.

I wish I was an angel bear, she thought, feeling the sting of her own scuffed knees and bruised shins as she placed the sword up on a high shelf.

But there was no time for self-pity as the sun had already begun to drop from the sky, leaving them only an hour or two until they had promised to be back at the Donnelly's for dinner.

Quickly formulating a plan, they decided that one of them would go to the library and try to find out what the schematics were for, while the other two would either visit Boliver's Blacksmiths or Potions and Poisons for answers regarding the dagger and the petals.

Noah was all too eager to go to the library and Ofelia had a fascination with the petals. This of course left Allura to carry the dagger, which made her feel inexplicably uneasy, as though something inside of her knew the weapon all too well.

Before they split up, Noah held out his hand to Allura and in complete confusion, she awkwardly cupped it with her own.

'The map,' he said bluntly.

'OH!' Allura blurted out, slightly embarrassed as she quickly jerked her hand away and reached into her pocket to pull out the torn piece of paper, now crinkled and barely legible.

'Good as new. You'll be able to put that back no problem,' Ofelia joked as Noah looked at it in dismay.

'This is why you're not supposed to take the pages home with you,' he hissed before storming off towards the library.

'We all nearly died and he's worried about library books,' Allura tutted as she and Ofelia headed down the main street and stopped at the top of an alley a few shops away from Potions and Poisons.

Allura could feel the weight of the dagger in her hand, it seemed to be getting heavier with every step.

'What's wrong?' Ofelia asked.

'I think – I think this dagger was used to do something... terrible,' Allura stammered, her heart racing and stomach churning.

'How about I go to Boliver's instead and you go

ask about the petals?' Ofelia suggested, snatching the dagger from her.

Allura immediately felt liberated by its absence, as though an anchor had been lifted off her chest, but it didn't seem to have the same impact on Ofelia. Instead, she dropped the bag of petals into Allura's hand and skipped off to the blacksmiths before Allura could even say 'thank you'.

Bursting with curiosity and feeling light as a feather without the blade, Allura entered Potions and Poisons optimistically, only to find that it was equally as decrepit on the inside as it was on the outside.

It was the only shop on the main street not flooded with last minute shoppers, in fact it was completely empty. Allura could see why however, as the shop was dingy and shrouded in shadow with dust and dirt coating every surface, and tall candles with feint flames dripping pools of wax onto the grimy floor.

Each wall was covered in shelves lined with potions of every kind, from tall skinny bottles with bubbling liquids, to small round jars filled with shimmering elixirs.

The sounds of brewing magic emanated from gold and silver cauldrons that boiled in each corner with mysterious concoctions. Although she couldn't be sure, Allura could have sworn that if she looked hard enough, she could see unsettling screaming faces in the vapour they released.

As Allura tried to spot another one, an unusually wide man with blackened teeth and deep sunken eyes appeared behind the counter.

'You looking for something?' he asked as Allura approached him with a cheery smile, a tactic which she had always found to be useful whenever she needed something from one of the sellers at the station market.

'I was hoping you might be able to tell me what this is,' she said, placing the small bag on the counter.

With a suspicious wariness, he leant away and tugged the bag open, gritting his teeth as though he expected something to shoot out at him. She noticed small scars across his chin and neck and started to wonder if his caution was the result of some terrible prank gone wrong in his past.

Realising that there were no tricks at play, he peered directly into the bag then grabbed a small set of pincers from his desk and carefully pulled out a single petal. He held it up to the dim light and examined it with great interest, his jaw falling open as he held it up to his nose and took a sniff.

Calmly, he placed the petal back inside the bag and refastened the string around the top. After some thought, he leant forwards and said:

'Where'd you get this?'

'Does it matter?'

'I'd say so. That's Ultima Oscula, one of the most toxic poisons known to man.'

The same poison used at Orville's wedding, Allura immediately recalled.

'What do you know about it?' she asked.

'Only that it's rarer than a cyclops and ten times as deadly. They grow it in some fancy garden in The

Balance, but that's just so it don't go extinct.'

'Is there anyway someone could survive eating it?' Allura asked, wondering how Orville had done exactly that. The shopkeeper scratched his head, racking his brain for any possible answer.

'Tarkiss root,' he said with a snap of his fingers. 'If you ate some tarkiss root before ingesting Ultima Oscula, it could make the poison a touch less lethal.'

Allura thought back to her time with Orville, vaguely remembering that he had mentioned something about eating 'a great many things' without knowing what they were that day.

'Thank you. You've been a great help,' she said reaching for the bag, but the shopkeeper slammed his hand down on the countertop.

'Hang on now missy, I don't work for free.'

'What do you want?' Allura replied, taken aback.

'I think I'll keep the bag,' he said with a smug smile as pretty as a tar pit. 'You have a good day now.'

'That's not fair,' Allura argued.

'Not fair huh? Well, I charge six silver pieces for my services, so unless you have that on you, I suggest you bugger off.'

I can't let him keep them, Allura thought.

They were too important, possibly acting as evidence that could tie this whole conspiracy together. And so, she imagined she was back in the London markets, haggling over a punnet of fruit and allowed her instincts to take over.

'You could keep the whole bag,' she said calmly, 'but there are a lot of petals in there and something tells me that they're not exactly legal to have around here.'

'What's your point?' he asked.

'Well, all I'm saying is, I hope I don't happen to run into Sheriff Kraw. And if I do, I pray I can manage to keep all twelve petals a secret,' she said, coming alive at the chance to bargain and barter.

'Of course, it would be much easier for me to keep quiet about them, if there was just one secret to keep.'

The shopkeeper's smile twisted into a scowl.

'You threatening me girl?'

'Of course not, I'm trying to give you what you asked for,' she said cheerily. 'One petal.'

They argued for a while, proposing offers and counter-offers until eventually, Allura had him right where she wanted and they agreed on a number:

'Three petals? THREE? You're practically robbing me!' he said as he returned the bag to her and watched with furious eyes as she counted out three petals on the table.

'When I came in here you didn't even have one. Now you have three for pretty much nothing,' she said with another cheery smile stretched across her face. 'You have a good day now.'

*

Boliver's sat between a tall bell tower and an even taller blissul tree that stretched far above the rooftops of Endwood. There, by the cobbled steps of the blacksmiths, Allura planted herself on a barrel and waited impatiently for Ofelia to emerge.

Thoroughly bored, she decided to rummage through her pockets and pulled out the murmur paper which she had completely forgotten to check since they left for the mountain.

It'll be blank anyway, she told herself, trying to temper her own expectations as she unfolded it.

But to her surprise, there was a message which read:

Allura,

I am deeply sorry it has taken me so long to reply. Darnigold and Raven have not afforded me a moment alone since I received your message and I hope you will agree that this is something that requires discretion.

I will look into the woman you mentioned at the wedding, but if she is who I think she may be, then it certainly complicates matters. If you see her again, I urge you to keep your distance and contact me.

Orville

Allura fought the impulse to reply immediately, despite all that she wanted to tell him. There was her chance encounter with Evelyn Dormé, her suspicions about Abraham and her discoveries in the mines of Craven's Mountain to name a few.

But after she had reread his message more closely, she could not shake the feeling that anything she wrote would also be read by Raven as well. As much as she disliked him, she had to admit that he seemed rather cunning.

I bet there's no secret that can be kept from him.

A heavy thud from inside the blacksmiths interrupted her thoughts and she tucked the paper back into her pocket before rushing through the doors to find a large man in a leather apron lying prone on the floor.

He was unconscious, but in one hand he held a magnifying glass, while the other had the dagger in a tight grip.

Allura swiftly crouched down to help him when she spotted Ofelia just a few feet from him. She was also on the ground, but her eyes were very much open.

'What happened? Are you alright?' Allura asked, helping Ofelia to her feet.

'Just a bit woozy, it takes a lot out of me,' she replied as the man stirred in his sleep. 'We should go before he wakes up.'

'Did you do that to him?'

'I had to wipe his memory,' she answered as though it were no big revelation.

'You can do that?'

'Barely. I only took the last few minutes from him,' she said, retrieving the dagger from his grasp.

Allura felt a piercing shot of paralysing fear in the dagger's presence, but it quickly passed as the blade dropped into Ofelia's bag.

'Why did you take his memories?' Allura asked.

'I'll tell you on the way. Let's go,' Ofelia insisted as they hurried out the door.

Her head hung low as she sluggishly followed

Allura through town, constantly bumping into people on their way to the library, but despite her worn out state, she managed to explain what had happened.

According to the blacksmith, the dagger was one of twenty-four, gifted by the giants centuries ago to the twelve leaders of Orterra and their conferants. The blades were forged from the metals and minerals of their owner's territories and this one in particular was made from starlight stone; a mineral found only in The Balance.

'So both the dagger and the poison were well within Raven's reach,' Allura said, yet there was still one thing she didn't understand.

'If the blacksmith helped us, why did you have to make him forget?'

'He was going to tell Sheriff Kraw what we'd found,' Ofelia explained.

'And you couldn't have told me that you can do that before I gave up three of the petals to keep that creep at the potions shop quiet?'

'I told you I was the Embodiment of Forgetfulness. But trust me, I wouldn't have done it if I didn't have to. It doesn't feel right, taking someone else's memories. It makes me feel like a thief.'

'You're not a thief,' Allura said, giving her a reassuring smile. 'You're just a good friend.'

And so, once Ofelia's strength had returned, they hurried to the library with a sense of excitement as two of the three mystery items had now been solved.

After halting at reception for another of Tilda's rhymes, they made their way to the back of the building, to a small nest of desks crammed between columns of wide bookcases. There they found Noah, silent and slack-jawed.

'What's wrong?' they asked and his eyes pointed to the book in his hands.

Taking it from him, they began to read it for themselves. The book was titled *The Loves and Losses of The Cycle by Rowan Heatherheart* and it told of the stories, rumours and myths about the domain ruled by the Embodiments of Life and Death.

Among the tales of the Wilting Fields and the Era of the Dead, was the altercation between Evelyn Dormé and her daughter, Darnigold.

The girls examined it with confusion at first, unable to understand what had put Noah in such a frightful state.

But then they saw it.

Allura couldn't believe it at first, certain that what they were seeing could not possibly be what it seemed. But other than a few missing bits and pieces, the book contained an exact copy of the schematics they had found at Craven's Mountain.

The fact alone that the book had incomplete copies of the plans did not shock them all that much. However, the title printed in a fanciful font above it made their hairs stand on end.

THE LOST SCHEMATICS OF THE EVISCERO CHARGE.

'By the gods,' Ofelia muttered.

'I can't believe it,' said Allura. 'You found it Noah, you really are a genius.'

'I don't know about that – anyone could have done

it I suppose,' he replied, a deep blush filling in his cheeks.

They quickly caught him up to speed on everything they had learnt, including Orville's reply on the murmur paper which Noah read with great interest. As he did, Tilda popped out from one of the bookcases.

'Ever so sorry to be a bothersome weed, I just want to check you have all that you need,' Tilda said in her sweet little voice.

Allura and Ofelia stepped away from the desk to talk with her, hoping she wouldn't notice what they were looking.

'How I love to see young curiosity thrive, but we're closing soon, it's nearly five.'

'Nearly five!' Ofelia said as Tilda walked away. 'It'll be dark soon, we need to get home!'

There was a genuine fear in her voice, no doubt caused by the thought of being on the receiving end of her mother's angry tone. Allura couldn't blame her, even she was a little scared of Lydia when her lips pursed and nostrils flared.

But still, she was hesitant to leave, it felt like they were on the cusp of putting everything together. As though they were only missing a single piece that would make sense of it all.

'Well, what do we do with all this?' Allura asked, gesturing to the petals, dagger and schematics.

'Don't worry, I'll keep it at my place if you want,' Noah offered, returning the murmur paper to her. 'Then we can give it all to Cognitius when she comes to collect you tomorrow.'

'Alright,' Allura agreed, painfully aware that she was now doomed to never see the look on Raven's face when she exposed what he had done.

'Just remember, you can't tell anyone,' Ofelia said.

'I won't,' Noah promised, although Allura noticed a tremor in his voice.

A slight quiver of nerves... or guilt?

*

The Donnelly household celebrated Atrilarium's Eve in a way that Allura had always dreamt of celebrating a holiday.

They sat by the fire, sung songs of legendary heroes, played board games with funny names, ate tiny cakes and chocolate covered biscuits, built snowmen and snow-monsters, and told stories way into the evening.

'You can't do that,' Cameron said as Ofelia made up her own rules to one of the games.

'Sure I can, watch,' Ofelia said, cockily knocking his piece off the board again.

As they erupted into an argument, there was a bang at the door. Allura watched Faye answer and although she couldn't see his face, she recognised Abraham's big hands pressed against the doorframe.

He had come to find out where she was and Faye was quick to tell him.

For a moment, his head peeked inside and Allura snapped her gaze away, knowing she would find it hard to even look him in the eyes. Faye invited him in, but he declined and Allura watched him wade through the snow towards town.

She would have felt saddened to see him go if she hadn't been so suspicious of him.

In truth, her mind was heavy with worry and questions about the plot she and her friends had been unravelling, yet she still managed to find joy in the festivities. She learnt the lyrics to the songs and the rules to the games, until she felt as though Atrilarium had been a holiday she had enjoyed every year before and perhaps, would enjoy every year after.

But of course, that was not the case and fate was primed to remind her of that fact.

It was while Faye and Lydia were putting Abigail to bed and Ofelia had run upstairs to find her 'people pencil' (the one she used when drawing a person rather than creatures or places), that Allura felt a strange compulsion.

She didn't know why, but something about the way Noah had spoken earlier caused her to check the murmur paper just one more time.

Glancing up from her big cosy chair, she made sure that Cameron wasn't watching. He was too busy losing at a game of self-playing cards to pay attention and so she unfurled the note. That was when she saw something that made her blood turn cold.

The page now contained no remnant of Orville's previous message, but instead there was a single line that read:

Thank you for telling me. Do not worry. I will handle it.

At first, she wondered what Orville could have possibly been talking about, but then she remembered that while they had spoken to Tilda, the paper had been left unsupervised with Noah.

Just like that the guilty crack in his voice came into perfect focus.

No wonder he offered to look after the stuff. He told Orville everything, she realised, not that she could blame him. Besides, it wasn't like she was going to be around to help much longer.

But then she had a truly frightening thought.

What if it wasn't Orville who wrote back?

In that second, the sound of hooves thumping outside followed by the screeches and yells of carriages and their drivers drew Allura to the window. Her stomach felt tight, as though it were being suspended in place.

Like the tension in the air before a cataclysmic storm.

She peered out the foggy glass and watched as two carriages charged past, the first of which was led by Carter Kraw. The second however, was pure silver with a large open window on its side. Watching as it passed, Allura flinched at the void-like eyes that glared back at her from inside.

He's here.

'Who was that?' Cameron asked as he joined her at the window.

'Nobody good,' she replied as she hurried to the front door, gripped the handle, then stopped as the sizzling of food and the sound of raucous laughter in the kitchen gave her pause.

Ignore him. Forget about the dagger and the poison and the embodiment destroying bomb. Forget about Raven and Horas. Forget about it tonight then forget everything tomorrow. Just let go of the handle and enjoy the rest of the evening.

She could feel her hands unclenching when suddenly a vivid image became clear in her mind. It was Raven with his smug grin and wicked soul, plunging the dagger into Horas, a man who had only wanted to help him.

That was all she needed to make her rush out into the cold.

There was a feeling of stillness outside with only the sounds of the carriage wheels against the cobblestones disturbing the otherwise tranquil night. Allura followed the tracks onto the main street and as she crossed the bridge, she saw exactly what she had feared.

The two carriages came to a stop outside of a tall, thin terraced house that blended in with the row of equally tall, thin terraced houses. She hurried over, trying to remain light on her feet so that they wouldn't know she was coming.

As she did so, Carter Kraw swung the door knocker with a heavy hand and after a moment, the door clicked open. Inside stood Elliott Tanden, looking very confused in his fluffy dressing gown.

'Can I help you sheriff?' he asked.

Without a word, Carter barged past him, as though he wasn't even there. Two more officers followed him inside and the house erupted with clanging and banging as they searched through each and every room.

'What in Yragshall do you think you're doing?' Elliott asked loudly.

'Only what we have to,' Raven said in a controlled voice as he finally stepped out of his carriage.

'Raven? I should've known you would have something to do with this.'

'I am only acting on my commander's orders. We've had some, disturbing reports,' Allura heard him say as she hid in the shadows across the street.

'Your commander? You mean Orville? He would never do this to us! What reports are you even talking about?'

'Someone poisoned Orville with Ultima Oscula on the day of his wedding. The only way that could have happened is if someone inside of the castle, someone he trusted, had slipped it into his food,' Raven explained.

'And you think I did it? This is madness!'

'Do you deny it?'

'Of course!'

'Then you won't mind us having a look around.'

Moments later, Patricia emerged in a groggy haze with Noah held closely at her side. They tried to reason with Raven, but he held firm in his silence, making it as effective as pleading with a statue.

'Dad, I need to tell you something,' Noah said, but by then it was already too late. Carter and his guards marched out of the house carrying something wrapped in cloth.

They held it out to Raven and he meticulously took it apart. Allura seethed as the petals, the dagger and the plans were all laid bare in front of him. Unlike Elliott, Raven seemed entirely unfazed by the objects and with a nod of his head, the guards grabbed Noah's father.

'I don't know what those are!' he yelled as they shoved him violently into the silver carriage.

'STOP,' Noah begged while his mother shouted at them with the same desperation.

Allura however had remained undiscovered and was poised to leap to Elliott's defence when a hand stretched across her shoulder. She turned to see the face of Evelyn Dormé staring back at her.

With a single look, Allura could tell that she had heard everything.

'Sit tight girly,' she said quietly.

'But I can help.'

'Look at them,' Evelyn replied, nodding towards Carter and Raven. 'Something tells me they don't care much for what you got to say. So, stay here and keep quiet.'

Evelyn then stepped out of the alleyway and moved across the street where Raven spotted her immediately.

'Lady Dormé? What are you doing here?'

'I've been in town since yesterday, came to collect my knick-knack for the meeting didn't I,' she said, holding up a necklace with a glistening jewel at its centre.

'So, seeing as I was here first, I suppose I ought to be the one asking you what exactly it is you're doing here?'

'Official business,' he answered dismissively.

'Is that right? A fella from The Balance like you arresting a citizen of The Bliss? You wouldn't mind if I have a little looksie at Orville's written orders, would ya?'

'I'm afraid I have none as this was a time sensitive matter, but you need not concern yourself with it, after all, shouldn't you be making your way to Tetricore? The Counter Club will be meeting soon.'

'The meeting's not for another few hours and you know how I like to be fashionably late. Besides, I'm sure I'll get there in no time in a fancy carriage like that,' she said, eyeing up Raven's silver cart.

'I'm afraid under any other circumstance I would gladly let you share my carriage my lady, but I will be transporting the suspect with me,' he said.

'And what is it that he's done?'

'As I said, it is official business so I cannot divulge that information. Even to you.'

Evelyn's smile quickly turned sour and the lights along the entire street seemed to flicker as the air turned a harsher type of cold.

'I am the Embodiment of Death, boy. While I really do get a good kick out of watching you pretend to have any actual power, you'd do well to remember who you're talking to.'

The lights returned to their normal glow and the freeze vanished as the biggest smile stretched across Allura's face. She could tell by Raven's expression that he had not been expecting to run into someone with more authority than him in this little town.

'We believe he may have been responsible for Orville's poisoning and possibly Horas' murder.'

'Now that is serious,' Evelyn said, feigning surprise. Then she went quiet for a second and looked away, as though deep in thought. 'I know! Why don't we let him tag along with us and have The Counter Club decide what to do with him?'

WHAT? Allura thought, still lingering in the shadows.

'A splendid idea,' Raven said with a false smile, 'but those aren't my orders. Orville would be rather upset if I did not follow his exact commands.'

'You let lil ol' me worry about my son-in-law. There are more leaders of Orterra in the Counter Club than at any trial you could whip up for him. Surely you're headed that way anyway, unless you were planning on skipping out on the meeting entirely?'

Raven stalled for as long as he could until finally, he sighed deeply and agreed to her terms. Even Allura could tell that he really had no other choice.

'Mr. Solmen, sir. You- you'll put in a good word with Orville for me, won't you?' Carter Kraw asked pitifully as Raven hoisted himself into his carriage.

'Don't you worry, I'll be sure to mention just how adept you are at searching houses,' Raven replied as Evelyn climbed into the other side.

The old woman looked back into the darkness where Allura was hiding and gave a reassuring nod that did anything but reassure her.

Then, with a crack of the reins the horses began to trot, leaving Noah and Patricia to watch helplessly as Elliott made his way towards damnation.

The coach disappeared around a corner down the

street and Allura was wrought with the overwhelming sense that she had just made a terrible mistake.

18

The Counter Club

The night turned dour when Allura returned to tell Ofelia and her family what had happened. Where there had once been laughter, there was now only a quiet uncertainty. Patricia arrived soon after to ask them to look after Noah while she headed to Tetricore to plead her husband's innocence.

'I'll come with you and we'll have Elliott back before its time to open presents,' Lydia insisted, leaving her wife to look after the children.

'But... there's five of them,' Faye said dubiously.

'I have complete confidence in you,' Lydia replied before kissing each of her children goodbye and stepping out into the cold.

'We should go with her,' Ofelia whispered.

'Why bother? They won't listen to us,' Noah said with his head in his hands. 'This is all my fault. We were running out of time and I thought telling Orville would make everything better. I should've known Raven would see it.'

'Maybe the Counter Club will figure out that Orville never gave Raven those orders. I mean they're some of the most powerful people in Orterra.

Leaders and conferants from almost every region. I know they embody negative forces, but surely they'll want to find the truth,' Ofelia said hopefully.

'Maybe,' Noah mumbled, but Allura could tell that with his father's life on the line, 'maybe' wasn't nearly good enough.

And so, as they spoke, Allura tried as best she could to put herself in Raven's shoes, to outsmart him for once. But every time she attempted to piece his plan together, she found herself at one insurmountable question:

Why did Raven reach out to Horas?

She had originally assumed he simply wanted his help in killing Orville, given how the two had fallen out years ago, but then she thought of the wedding.

Specifically, how perfect a murder the poison would have been if it had only worked as intended. A murder that required just one person, which would have made Horas an unnecessary risk for a plan that was bound to succeed.

Then it hit her.

What if his plans didn't end with Orville?
What if he didn't just want to rule The Balance?
What if he wanted... more?

She thought of the Eviscero Charge, the bomb uniquely capable of destroying not only an embodiment caught in its blast, but the very essence of what they embodied, forever.

With that firmly in her mind she considered the members of the Counter Club, each of them high-ranking cogs in the Orterran system. If even one of them was removed without an immediate replacement there would be chaos, but all of them vanishing in one swoop, well she didn't want to even think about what would happen then.

'We have to go to Tetricore,' she blurted out, unwittingly interrupting Ofelia and Noah's conversation.

'What?'

'We have to go to Tetricore, right now.'

'To the meeting? I already told you they won't listen to us.'

'We don't need them to listen to us. We're going to catch Raven red-handed.'

'What are you talking about?'

'Please, just trust me. I really think we might have a chance to make this right.'

She watched pensively as they considered it. Then, after a few anxious moments, Noah looked Allura in the eyes and boldly said:

'I trust you.'

'Me too,' Ofelia agreed.

'Whatever you're thinking, we're in.'

Great, now all we need to do is sneak out of here.

Ofelia was clearly thinking the same thing as her eyes lit up with the spark of an idea.

*

'We're going out to water the squilms,' Ofelia said in a loud and stilted voice as she held up a tin watering can.

'Really?' Faye responded suspiciously.

'Yes,' Ofelia replied.

'In the middle of all this?'

'Yes.'

'All three of you?'

'Yes?'

Faye pursed her lips, looked off into the distance and tutted then examined the three of them with a smile.

'I imagine you'll be a while,' she said, folding her arms.

'Quite a while,' said Noah.

'Maybe even a few hours,' added Allura.

'And what you're doing is important?' Faye asked softly.

'Very,' all three of them replied.

'Alright then, but please, please, be careful,' she said with a sigh as she coddled them in warm coats and wrapped them in long scarves, before sending them on their way.

Out in the backyard, Ofelia in fact did water the squilms as they ran through the wilted farm and out the back gate.

As they dumped the watering can by the base of the thick tree, Ofelia and Noah giddily celebrated their plan's success. Allura remained quiet however, happy to let her friends believe that they had actually tricked Faye as they sprinted as fast as they could towards the cabin.

When they arrived, Ofelia tried to wake London from her slumber while Allura retrieved the sword from the shelf.

'We should give it a name. All the swords in the stories had names,' Noah said excitedly.

'What about Stabby?' suggested Ofelia.

'Or you know, anything else,' said Noah.

'For all we know it could already have a name,' Allura said, showing them the runes along the blade.

'Huh,' Noah smirked.

'What?'

'It's written in Old Orterran. I don't know a lot of it, but I think this says 'Trai'.'

'What does that mean?'

'Beam.'

And so, they agreed, whether Noah had misinterpreted the runes or not, the sword was called Beam.

But even as they loudly discussed it, London remained curled in a ball in the corner, keeping as far from the cold as she could. Allura approached her, stroking her wing which was now completely healed.

'I'm sorry girl, but we need you,' Allura urged London, causing the bear's head to poke out from under her wing. With a heavy snort, she shook herself awake as Allura pushed open the shed's double doors to see a shocking figure blocking their way.

Abraham stared down at them sternly with his hammer at his side.

'Are you here to stop us?' Allura asked, to which he nodded.

'Because where we're going is dangerous or because you don't want us to stop Raven?'

She could tell that she had lost him at that point or at least he wanted her to think she had.

Either way, he wasn't moving.

Allura was torn, something inside of her

desperately wanted to trust him, but she didn't know if she could. Instead, she chose a third option, handing Beam to Noah and approaching the silent man without any means of defending herself.

She moved towards him without a word and even Abraham couldn't tell what she was about to do. Then calmly, she reached into his coat pocket and pulled out the drawing he had shown her of him, Horas and Orville.

'If you ever cared about them, then you have to let us go,' she said.

Abraham scanned the sketch through glossy eyes and looked up to see the three of them staring back at him. Then, after a long pause, he stepped aside.

'Thank you, Abraham,' she said as she climbed onto London's back.

No turning back now, she decided as she tugged on the rope and felt the world fall away beneath them. Allura looked back to see Abraham waving them off and she could tell from the pained look on his face that he was already regretting his decision.

*

As they flew, Noah told them the history of Tetricore, a place that had once been the tallest castle in The Balance, built at the heart of the region's deepest valley.

A place where people from every corner of Orterra had gathered to reject the system that ruled them. With one voice they had declared Tetricore as an independent state, free from the control of any other realm.

It had been a dream forged from a need to live without leaders, but like all dreams, it eventually came to an end.

What little remained of Tetricore now stood as a testament to the lengths some rulers would go to in order to maintain their hold over the lives of others. The event had been so significant that it formed the basis of the Orterran calendar, with every date thereafter being referred to as either BT (Before Tetricore) or PT (Post Tetricore).

In return for Noah's history lesson, Allura filled them in on what she now believed were Raven's true intentions. The Counter Club's meeting was a powder keg, filled with some of the most important people in Orterra and primed to explode.

Horas and Orville had only been the first in Raven's plan to clear the board for his own rise to power and now he would use the Eviscero Charge to take out the rest. Worse still, it would all be blamed on Noah's father, unless they got there first.

It was harder flying at night and had it been snowing they wouldn't have stood a chance. But the winds were fair and the speckles of light that shone from clutches of small huts and goblin colonies guided their journey, keeping them in line with Raven's carriage.

It was only as they approached their destination that Noah voiced a question that none of them had thought to ask.

'What exactly is the plan?'

'We get to Tetricore. We find Raven. We stop him,' Allura answered like a master tactician.

'Yes, but *how* do we stop him?'

His question was met with silence.

'We've got a sword,' she eventually replied.

'He can turn into smoke,' Ofelia pointed out.

'Well... I'm sure we'll think of something.'

*

By the time they arrived at Tetricore, it was almost midnight. The moon hung huge and heavy in the sky behind rippling black clouds as London came down to land on one of the cliffs overlooking the battered ruins.

Allura stood in awe of the remains, which looked as though someone had piled thirty colosseums on top of one another, before bringing them all toppling down like a child's plaything.

From what she could tell, whatever had actually happened in that place was far worse than she could ever dare to imagine.

After a few moments of taking in all that was left of Tetricore, Raven's silver carriage emerged from between the trees below and made its way towards the collapsed tower. The bottom layer was glowing with torches and candlelight, and his carriage came to a halt outside of the entrance.

Allura pulled out her spyglass to get a better look.

Clear as day, she watched as Evelyn stepped out of the carriage and gestured to two guards in black armour who sprang into action, dragging Elliott out from the backseat.

'Is that my dad? Is he okay?' Noah asked.

The chains on his arms looked uncomfortably

tight, but Allura was glad to report that he seemed otherwise unharmed.

She continued to survey, expecting Raven's dark outline to manifest from the coach, but even after they had taken Elliott inside, he was nowhere to be seen.

Where is he?

Scanning the area around the tower, she spotted something shifting in its glow.

A silhouette seemed to slide up the huge mass of stone on which the structure was built like a snake. It approached the tower until it was at the edge of the ruins and then vanished entirely, as though sinking into the rock itself.

'There!' she said, pointing at the spot. 'But he just disappeared.'

'You lost him?'

'No, he literally disappeared.'

'Where could he have gone?' asked Ofelia.

'Maybe he's in the under-tower,' Noah suggested casually.

The girls looked at him and once he noticed their expressions, he looked back at them in confusion.

'We're waiting for you to explain what that means,' Ofelia said.

'I told you, this was once the biggest tower in the entire Balance. But they didn't just build it up into the sky -'

'They built it into the ground,' Allura realised.

'We need to get down there.'

As stealthily as they could, they drifted to the bottom of the valley, leaving London safely out of sight amongst a cluster of trees before sneaking to the bottom of the foundations on which the tower was built.

'I saw him by the edge of the tower,' Allura whispered as she pointed to the top of the mound of stone.

Remaining as quiet as possible, they dug their fingers into the crooked rock and started to climb. Armoured guards continued to patrol the area, with some wandering directly underneath Allura and her friends as they scrambled to get to the top.

With each elevation, Allura held her breath, knowing that one wrong move could alert the guards. However, as they approached the spot where she had spied Raven, her hand clasped onto a rock, only to feel it come loose.

Please don't, she thought, but watched in horror as it ripped away from the wall, tumbling towards the ground.

Her eyes shut and her teeth clenched together as she waited for an inevitable 'what was that?' from the guards... but it never came.

Daring to open one eye, she glanced down to see Ofelia a few feet below her, clinging to the wall with one hand and holding the loose stone in the other.

'Nice catch,' Allura mouthed as the small rock was lodged into another crack in the wall.

Together, they completed the climb and found themselves by the smooth side of the tower. From outside, they peered through a gap between the enormous pillars that ran the full length of the circular room.

Inside they saw an ancient table with six chairs arranged along the sides and one at each end. Allura also noticed a small pile of trophies, gems and knick-knacks huddled together in the centre.

Evelyn did say they had to bring a gift, she recalled.

'By the gods,' Noah said in astonishment, 'they're all here.'

Although Allura didn't recognise most of them, Noah gladly filled her in on who exactly she was looking at.

In attendance were:

- Evelyn Dormé – Embodiment of Death and co-ruler of The Cycle
- Sydney Harrow – Embodiment of Evil and co-ruler of The Duality
- Lowell Mendelson – Embodiment of Chaos and co-ruler of The Balance
- Marr Shaw – Embodiment of Hate and co-ruler of The Line
- Cassandra Rome – Embodiment of Selfishness
- Adrik Undertell – Embodiment of Cruelty
- Lyla Verensworth – Embodiment of Jealousy

The only one that was missing was the Embodiment of Deception himself; Raven Solmen.

'Nice of you to show up Evelyn,' said Lowell in an unpleasant and gravelly voice. 'I see you've brought a guest.'

'Well, you know, I get to skip out on all the small talk this way,' she said, smirking as she took her place at the head of the table.

'But this is no ordinary dinner guest. This is Elliott Tanden. Supposedly the man responsible for Horas' murder and the attempt on Orville's life.'

They all leant forwards with intrigue, taking a good look at Elliott who squirmed uncomfortable with so many eyes on him.

'Sssssoooo, what'sssss he doing here?' Lyla asked.

'I convinced Raven to let us cast our judgement on him. I thought it would be a better use of our time than nattering on about my daughter's wedding dress or what shade of purple we thought Orville's face turned,' Evelyn explained.

They whispered amongst themselves, then in turn they nodded in agreement.

'Finally, something half interesting,' said Sydney, the youngest and most bored of the group. 'Let's play.'

'We can't,' Lowell interrupted. 'Our party is not yet complete. Where is Raven?'

'He said he had some business in a nearby town he had to deal with, but he assured me we should start without him.'

An obvious lie, Allura thought as she noticed Noah was shuffling nervously beside her, like an over-wound toy ready to spring to life.

'Whatever you're thinking of doing, don't,' Allura said.

'But my dad's right there.'

'I know, but the best way we can help him is by stopping Raven.'

He considered her words, then took a final gaze at

his father before turning away. Examining the stone floor, he looked up and down at its smooth surface, then stopped as his eyes fell upon a person-sized hole in the rock.

'There,' he said. 'That must be where Raven went.'

'Good job,' Allura said before shuffling her body through the gap and down into an unlit tunnel.

'I guess it was too much to hope that we were done with dark, scary crevices,' Noah moaned as he and Ofelia dropped down behind her.

'You can hold my hand again if you like,' Allura joked, but she immediately felt both his and Ofelia's fingers intertwining with hers.

As they followed the tunnel downwards, they had to support one another across the slippery floor, damp with moss and foul murky water. A slimy mildew covered the cavern's walls and jagged stones protruded from the ceiling.

After a series of tight fits, they reached the end of the tunnel and found themselves in the remnants of another large circular room.

It was identical to the one above, except the structures and pillars around the edges were crumbled beyond recognition.

The biggest difference however, was that sat on a podium in the middle of the room was a cylindrical object that pulsated with a radiant energy.

Not much bigger than Allura's hand, the device let out a deep humming sound as entrancing lights shone from it, burning away the darkness around the room. It looked more powerful in person than any of them could have imagined.

'The Eviscero Charge,' Allura said, awestruck by its devastating potential.

'Incredible,' said Ofelia.

'Terrifying,' said Noah.

Tearing her eyes away from the device, Allura scoured the room for any sign of the man who had placed it there.

'Can anyone see Raven?' she asked before a pained yell echoed around them.

Suddenly, Raven appeared from a small doorway across the room from them. He didn't move with his usual tempered pace, instead he stumbled with a manic clumsiness, before tripping over the uneven floor and falling onto his back.

The room shuddered as a giant stone golem came charging in after him, far bigger and meaner looking than the one Allura had seen at Highdenhome.

I was not expecting that, Allura thought, confused as the stone monster swiped its arms at Raven.

He turned to smoke before it could strike and reformed behind the creature to stab at its legs with a shining dagger.

Splinters of rock chipped away, but with unimaginable speed, the golem twisted its entire body around and snatched him off the ground.

Wriggling and squirming, Raven tried to break free, but the monster's vice-like grip only grew tighter around his throat. For the first time, Allura saw fear in Raven's contorted face as the life was squeezed out of him.

More than that however, she noticed the dagger in

his hand, the way its blade familiarly spiralled into a point, exactly like the one they had found in Craven's Mountain.

Although she didn't entirely understand why, Allura found herself saying:

'We have to help him!'

'How?' asked Ofelia.

'And why?' asked Noah.

Both good questions, she thought, but despite her certainty that Raven was responsible for all this, she couldn't stand back and watch him die.

Wracking her brain, she tried to think of what they could do when Raven's eyes met hers, as though he had always known she was there.

With a weak voice, he used what little breath remained in him to say:

'GO!'

'Who are you talking to?' a voice called from the other room.

It can't be, Allura thought, telling herself that she must have misheard, but her fatal error soon became clear as a figure emerged from the doorway.

Only then did she realise that her biggest mistake had been convincing herself that the person in Horas' journal known as 'R' had been Raven.

She had fooled herself so fully, so completely, that she had never even stopped to consider it could have been anyone else.

But now she finally understood how terribly wrong she had been.

'You shouldn't be here,' the figure said as he spotted them.

Neither should you, Allura thought as she locked eyes with the man who had claimed to be Horas' friend.

The co-ruler of The Balance and the Embodiment of Order.

R as in Rutherford, she realised.

Orville Rutherford.

19

Battle of the under-tower

Raven's body turned limp in the unbreakable grip of the stone golem as Orville moved towards the podium in the centre of the room.

He walked slowly and didn't take his eyes off Allura or her friends for a second, ensuring that they couldn't make a move without him knowing.

But his fixation on them also meant that he didn't seem to notice as something scuttled in the shadows towards him.

Once he had positioned himself firmly between them and the Eviscero Charge, he rubbed his temples and let out a beleaguered sigh.

'I must admit I did not expect to see you here tonight,' he said irritably.

'This doesn't make any sense,' Allura said, 'Raven was-'

'Spying on me,' Orville interrupted. 'It seems even from beyond the grave Horas still had his eyes on me. I had thought I could distract him with Elliott and the meeting tonight, but I should've known he would have those damn twins watching me too.'

Raven's words in the kitchen at Cambium

repeated in her head: 'I think he may know what I've done, what I am' and suddenly, Allura was filled with rage.

'I don't know why you're doing this, but you need to stop,' she said, shakily pointing Beam at him.

'Oh Allura, you know exactly why I'm doing this.'

Thinking back to the day they had met, Allura recalled the shining faces of Orville's wife and daughter dangling in the memormist. How happy they had looked together. How his daughter had reached out to him as the train took him away.

But more than anything else, she remembered the devastation on Orville's face when they were taken from him, his family's home reduced to ashes.

'You want to destroy death because of what happened to your family?'

'Not just death. Evil, selfishness, cruelty, chaos. They're all up there and I can finally free Earth from their influence.'

'Killing everyone upstairs won't bring them back Orville.'

'No, but it will stop anyone else from having to feel my pain ever again!' he yelled, his prim and proper façade falling away to reveal him as a man possessed by revenge.

'It was all you,' Allura realised aloud, still putting it all together. 'And you let me think it was Raven.'

'After you figured out Horas was murdered, I needed to give you a suspect to chase. But really Allura, use your head, of course it was me. Did you really think it was just a coincidence that I ate the one thing that could save my life from Ultima Oscula?' explained Orville, causing Allura to wonder how she could possibly have been so foolish.

'But I never lied to you. What I said about the negative embodiments is true. You should hate them. They are greedy and selfish and they do not care about people like us. If they did, they would have allowed their essences to be destroyed centuries ago.

'So, yes. I pretended to love Darnigold to acquire the schematics and poisoned myself to throw Raven off my trail. But none of that, not one bit of it, even comes close to what those monsters above us have done to the people of Earth.'

'What about Horas?' Noah asked, causing Orville to stop for a moment. It had clearly been a relief to get this all off his chest, but the mention of Horas gave him pause.

'I knew that once my plan succeeded, this world would find itself suddenly in need of leadership. Cognitius and the rest of my co-rulers are capable, but even they would struggle to contain a power vacuum like that.'

'What Orterra will need is people of strong will and character. That is why I invited Horas to Craven's Mountain, away from Raven's sight, to ask him to help me.'

Allura recalled Horas' journal, how only a day before his own death, he had thought of Orville as 'a good man, despite what others may say'. She wondered if he had still thought as much after learning of Orville's plan.

'I thought we could mend our friendship and lead

this world into a brighter future together, but he accused me of madness. He said I had lost my way. I did all I could to convince him to see reason, but he refused.

'I knew I couldn't let him leave Craven's Mountain after that, so I tried to trap him in the mines. But he fought back and I had to-' he trailed off, unable to speak of his evil deed.

'You killed him,' Allura spat through gritted teeth.

'I did. And for the rest of my life there will not be a day that goes by that I won't regret it.'

As he spoke, a fire ignited inside of Allura, her grip tightening on Beam's handle as she battled the urge to charge at him. Orville looked at her as if he could read her thoughts and said:

'There is no need for hostility, Allura. I was hoping that you and I could be allies in the new world that is coming. That's why I told you about what happened to Horas in the first place, to prove that you can trust me.'

He's completely insane, she decided as a blood red anger started to consume her. But before he could say anything else, his words swiftly morphed into a sharp yelp.

Droplets of blood trickled down his fingers as he clutched his throbbing hand. Pain overwhelmed his mind and in his distraction, the stone golem's grip loosened, dropping Raven's body to the floor.

Still unconscious, Raven took shallow sips of the air as he laid with his face flat on the ground. A chirping sound drew Allura's attention towards the outline of something small and fuzzy hopping away from Orville.

It scampered towards them and once it was up close, they recognised its baggy cheeks and round black eyes.

TibbidyBoo chirped cheerfully as his pointed fur returned to its naturally soft state and he ran up Ofelia's leg before securing himself inside one of her pockets.

'Had he been in there this whole time?' Noah asked, but not even Ofelia was entirely sure.

Meanwhile, Orville pulled a handkerchief from his pocket and wrapped it around his injured hand, muttering threats and warnings in his pained rage as the Eviscero Charge began to hum and shake with overwhelming energy.

'ENOUGH!' he barked and with a flick of his wrist, one of the walls crumbled away, creating a large opening back into the valley for them to escape through.

The clouds above Tetricore had parted and rays of moonlight flooded the under-tower, causing Beam to emit a low humming sound of its own.

'I will not let any of you die here, but we have to leave, now!' he demanded.

Yet Allura and her friends stood firm and unmoving in front of him.

'We're not going anywhere,' she said defiantly. 'And neither are you.'

Orville tutted disappointedly, then finger by finger his hand clenched into a fist. Sharply, he stretched out his arm towards them, causing the floor to shake and sections of the ground itself to come alive, twisting and rising around them.

'Keep the golem away from Raven! I'll take care of the rest!' Allura yelled to her friends.

'Good luck!' Ofelia replied as she and Noah ran unsteadily towards the stone monster, shouting insults and throwing pebbles to catch its attention.

Orville however, focused on Allura, just as she knew he would.

Stone pillars blasted out the ground in front of her, blocking her path to the Eviscero Charge and forcing her to run along the edge of the room while the device continued to flash and judder in the centre.

Dodging and diving out of the way of Orville's concrete barricades, Allura hadn't even noticed as the sword in her hand continued to soak in the ethereal glow of the moonlight.

'There's no time for this!' Orville growled in frustration.

Instantly, Allura found herself trapped in a stone prison that stretched several feet above her head. She attempted to climb, but the walls grew and grew until they became unscalable.

Trying not to panic, she realised to her horror that her prison was beginning to close in around her, getting tighter with every passing second.

Think. Think. Think.

But it was hard to remain calm and focused when beyond the wall, she could hear her friends struggling to evade the golem.

'What did you think would happen here? I mean really? That you and your friends would be able to stop me with a can-do attitude and that little sword of yours?'

As good a plan as any, Allura thought, lifting Beam high over her head.

The runes shimmered with iridescent light and after a deep breath, she swung down. To her shock, the strange shine of the blade dissipated into a blast of energy, reducing the stone to rubble.

Woah!

'That's not possible!' Orville wailed as he balled his fists again.

But this time, Allura was ready.

Leaping to the side, she avoided another circle of rock as it burst from the ground. Orville tried again and again to catch her, but each time she was just a moment too quick.

Beads of sweat ran down his forehead and Allura was happy to see he was starting to panic.

It's now or never, she thought, as she strode directly towards him.

She knew he outmatched her in every way when it came to tactics or strategy, but she was young and sharp, whereas decades as ruler of The Balance had dulled him.

He had grown too comfortable behind a desk, surrounded by hired help and nice things. Whereas, until only a week ago, Allura had only ever dreamed of having nice things.

Orville's panic clouded his focus as she approached him, dragging Beam behind her as she darted from side to side.

She barely avoided the stone pillars that sprung up like geysers and she could tell he was becoming wise to the pattern of her movements.

And so, she did something entirely unexpected.

Jumping to the side at the last second, she stood on the edge of one of the rising structures, riding it up into the air. Before he could react, she leapt at him with the shining sword in hand.

Orville dove out the way, just as Allura had planned.

With him gone, she was on a direct course for the Eviscero Charge itself. Feelings of calm and serenity built inside of her once again as she was filled with a certainty that they were going to win.

Then, she struck the device.

But Allura realised her mistake all too late.

Instead of shattering to pieces, the Eviscero Charge released a wave of purple energy, sending both Allura and Orville flying across the room. With a loud thud, they crashed into the walls at opposite ends from one another.

Of course it would defend itself, she berated herself, nursing her injuries as Ofelia and Noah rushed to her side.

'Are you okay?' they asked, but Allura couldn't answer, her head felt foggy and slow.

She wanted to tell them to 'LOOK OUT!' but all she could do was watch as the monstrous mountain they had been battling hoisted each of them into the air.

Allura reached out helplessly as her friends were trapped in the golem's tight grip. Squirming and shouting as it squeezed them harder and harder.

Yet all too quickly did they realise that it was no

use fighting as each breath became weaker than the last.

'Don't worry about them,' Orville said as he pulled himself up off the floor.

'I'll ensure they wake up miles from here, a little worse for wear perhaps, but give it time and it will be like all of this was just some horrible nightmare. They'll be safe, happy and free to go about the rest of their lives with no one ever believing what they saw here. Just like you.'

Allura rattled her head until the screeching in her ears disappeared. Then, when she found the strength to rise to her feet, she instinctively reached for her sword, only to find that it had slipped from her hands during the blast.

I just have to keep him talking, she thought as she tried to spot Beam amongst the blinding lights of the Eviscero Charge.

'I spoke with Evelyn you know,' Allura called across the room to him.

'She's not as evil as you say she is. She refused to let Darnigold destroy death because she wanted to protect the people of Earth. Don't you get that? There's a natural order to things. You of all people should understand that!'

'Lies!' Orville yelled furiously. 'Every word that leaves that woman's mouth is poison.'

'It's the truth Orville. But even if you're right, even if you do make a better world without death or cruelty or evil, when will you stop? When will it be good enough for you?'

'You're right, my vision for both worlds does not

end here. But do not worry, there will be no more needless deaths. There are ways of separating an embodiment from the essence within them, and after I have restored order to this world, I will systematically strip every counterbalance of their powers and destroy that which they embody.'

'You want to stop needless deaths? Why don't you start with the people upstairs? There's at least twenty guards up there, not to mention Noah's parents and Ofelia's mum! Don't they matter?' Allura asked as she pointed towards the chamber above them.

'I never meant for anyone else to get hurt. It is a shame to lose good people like Elliott, but someone has to take responsibility for what's about to happen. However, I vow to you that it will be worth it. When you weigh the costs, a world without imagination is a small price to pay for a world without death. We all have to make sacrifices for the greater good,' he said sternly, but Allura couldn't stomach what she was hearing any longer.

'Easy for you to say, you're not sacrificing anything. You've just given up hope,' she said in disgust.

'You haven't the faintest idea what I have sacrificed,' he replied before taking a quick breath that sounded like a whimper.

'Horas always told me to keep hope alive and I tried, I really did, but the war with Malvus was too much to bear. All those people, *my* people, dead in some fool's crusade. It showed me that hope is nothing but a tool used to convince us to do nothing to fix what's broken.'

'Then why not kill me too? If hope is just a tool then why not let that bomb take me and hope with it?'

'Because every tool has its uses,' he replied and with a nod of his head, the entire wall shifted forwards, slowly entombing Allura.

Protruding lumps of stone closed in around her throat as she gasped helplessly and watched her friends similarly struggle in the stone golem's grasp.

Through choked breath, Ofelia reached out to her and sputtered:

'He's... wrong... Allura.'

'Hope... is all... we've got,' said Noah before falling eerily silent.

Orville looked at them, not with hatred or anger, but in a disturbed way that Allura found hard to place.

Until she recognised it as envy.

'The innocence of children,' he said solemnly. 'Yet the truth is, hope didn't save my family or yours Allura. But now we have a chance to save billions of people, billions of families. Imagine that. They will get to live the lives we should have had. Can't you see? Just think of how much greater your life would have been without all of that unnecessary tragedy.'

As much as she wanted to hate him, Allura struggled to see Orville as anything more than a man broken by grief in that moment.

And as much as she didn't want to play his game, she found herself imagining an entirely different life for herself. One that she had dreamt of countless times before.

It was an utterly ordinary life with two caring figures whose names she did not know, but whose love was true and unconditional.

They would tuck her in at night and build sandcastles with her on the beach. They would hug her when she was sad and tell her silly jokes for no reason other than to hear the sound of her laughter. When she did something wrong, they would teach her not to do it again, not through cruelty, but through kindness.

She would know that they were proud of her, even when she wasn't proud of herself, and teach her how to cook and dance and sing.

But most importantly of all, they would never abandon her.

This other life, the one that fate had denied her, was almost too enticing to cope without and Allura could have gladly slipped into that daydream forever.

But then another thought wriggled into her mind. A memory that she didn't even realise she had remembered. Yet there it was, plain and clear in her head, the last words that Cognitius had said to her before her grand adventure had even begun.

'Hope is not important because it's easy. It is hope's endurance in the hardest of times that gives it power.'

Then, in a flash of images streaming through her mind, she saw Cognitius saving her from the lytes and Noah catching TibbidyBoo as he hurtled to his certain death.

She felt the wind in her face as she soared through the air on the back of a winged bear and the warmth in her heart as Lydia and Faye invited her to join them at the wedding.

The smells of food cooked by her and her stoic friend Abraham, and the words of wisdom Evelyn had imparted.

She remembered the most scatterbrained girl she had ever met making voices that tricked a party of trolls and the boy who was afraid of everything facing off against the clawing kross.

And as her extraordinary week flooded her mind, she realised that she had been dreaming of another life, just as the one she had was really beginning.

'It's okay Allura,' Orville said softly. 'Drift away and know that when you wake, I will have made a better world for you.'

It all faded to grey as painful breaths turned her vision cloudy, yet Allura felt as though she had never seen so clearly. Her life had once been a tale of misery and heartache, but not anymore.

Now it was full of opportunity, freedom and love.

Hope was no longer an empty promise. It was real and palpable and for the very first time, she allowed herself to be consumed by it.

A comforting calmness spread throughout her body as her mind slipped away. She felt completely at ease, as though she were sitting around a warm fire at Christmas, in a cosy house on a quiet street in London with a quaint ornament shaped like a bear hanging from the tree.

It's not too late, she told herself.

We can still stop him.

Her skin felt itchy with boundless energy, as

though lightning was pounding through her entire body.

I know that we can.

Clenching her fists, she heard her knuckles crack like gunshots in her ears and her heart thumped like a war drum as her eyes shone with a silver light.

I believe that we can.

Fragments of her shining aura flickered through the stone that held her prisoner.

I have hope that we can.

With a thunderous scream, she unleashed a forceful storm of pure energy that broke Orville's hold on her.

He was thrown to the ground by the blast and the stone golem was shattered to pieces, dropping Noah and Ofelia to the floor.

Awestruck, Orville glared up at Allura as she emerged from the wall like a butterfly from its chrysalis, radiating with unfathomable power. She was the Embodiment of Hope and she had finally learnt what that meant.

'You're right,' Allura said with an echoing bass to her voice, the air tasting like sweet nectar after so long without it.

'Life would be easier without all the bad stuff, but those things are just a part of who we are. I'm sorry that you couldn't move on from what you lost, but I'm done letting my past control me.'

Orville rose unsteadily onto his shaking legs, only to collapse against the wall. As he did, the Eviscero Charge's blue and purple energy caused huge stalactites to drop from the ceiling and crash down around them.

'So, this is new,' Ofelia exclaimed with a goofy smile at the sight of Allura.

'Pretty cool, right?' she asked, admiring her own glowing hands. 'Are you two okay?'

'Just about,' Noah said, wiping the golem dust off his clothes.

'You should get out of here,' Allura said, gesturing towards the opening in the wall.

'Not a chance,' said Ofelia.

'Yeah, we're with you until this is done.'

Allura pulled them in close and although she was hot to the touch, they both hugged her back.

But they didn't have long as behind them, the stone golem reformed, its pieces pulling themselves back together until it was whole again.

With a raspy roar, it charged towards them. But as it approached, Noah spotted Beam soaking in the moonlight on the floor.

Wisps of magic emanated from it and he was drawn in by its ghostly aura. Without hesitation, he grasped the handle and swung upwards towards the creature, unleashing a bolt of unfiltered light.

Empowered by the moon, the resultant beam tore through the mindless monster. It staggered for a moment, reaching towards them with each shaky step before crashing to the floor in a pile of pebbles.

'You're pretty good with that thing,' Allura said as Noah clumsily spun it in his hand with a smile.

'LOOK OUT!' Ofelia warned as another sharp rock broke from the ceiling and dropped above Noah.

She barely managed to push him out of the way, but was too slow to save herself as the chunk of stone crushed her flat.

Or at least it would have, had the stalactite not stopped in mid-air.

There, it twirled and glistened in the moon's radiance, only a few inches from Ofelia's nose. She was frozen with fear, but Allura was quick to pull the frightened girl out of the way before the suspended rock finally hit the ground with a *crunch!*

Still holding Ofelia close, Allura spun around to look towards Orville. His clothes were tattered and trickles of blood ran down his forehead as he dropped his arm, the effort of controlling so much earth clearly exhausting him.

'I only ever wanted to help,' he said weakly.

'I know, but now I have to fix what you've done,' she replied.

Leaving Noah to look after Ofelia, she approached the Eviscero Charge. It made a phenomenal whirring noise, getting louder with every step she took, and it shone as though it contained the sun itself.

The immense power it exuded was volatile and unpredictable, striking the walls and ceiling while leaving the immediate area around it untouched, like the eye of a hurricane.

There has to be a way to stop it, she thought as she forced her way closer.

'There's nothing you can do. I made sure of that,' Orville said. His tone could easily have been mistaken for gloating, but Allura could sense that there was a hint of shame to it.

Determined to prove him wrong, she raised her hand up to the Eviscero Charge and unleashed every ounce of power that flowed within her.

The silver light she exuded tangled and danced with the colourful energy spewing from the device as the entire room quaked from the force of their struggle.

Until finally, with an exhausted scream, Allura released the last of her hopeful power and dropped to the floor, feeling her silvery glow fade away.

It had taken everything she had, but when she looked up, only the podium had been burnt and fractured. The Eviscero Charge itself remained entirely unscathed.

I can't do it. I can't stop it, she concluded, on the verge of admitting defeat, when suddenly she was struck by an idea.

But maybe I don't have to.

With a plan forming in her head, she plucked the weapon from its position on the podium. Where she had expected it to scorch her skin, she only felt its violent energies tingle and vibrate in her hand.

Ofelia was still in shock on the floor, staring at Allura while Noah leant against her in exhaustion. With the Eviscero Charge in hand, Allura made sure to take a long hard look at her friends, uncertain if or when she would ever see them again.

'Thank you,' she said before sprinting through the hole in the wall.

'For what?' Noah yelled after her.

'EVERYTHING!' she shouted back.

Allura struggled to keep her balance as she traded

the sturdy stone of the under-tower for the thick and slippery mud outside.

· Yet still, she did not slide nor stop as she ran faster than ever before, armed with the distinct notion that she was finally running towards something rather than away.

Torchlight weaved its way down the rocks behind her as guards and members of the Counter Club emerged from the tower, frantically searching for the source of the terrible commotion. Amongst the many panicked voices, Allura was certain she heard Lydia and Patricia, which only hastened her pace.

'There you are,' she said, coming to a halt at a memorably gnarled tree at the base of which London stood, looking very happy to see her.

'What do you say girl, quick ride and then home?' she asked, waving the pulsating device.

The great bear dropped low and Allura climbed onto her back. Then, a few powerful flaps of her wings later and they were rocketing into the sky.

All too quickly, they found themselves above the misty clouds, finally revealing the full moon in its complete, luminous enormity.

It took up much of the night sky and shone with a cold light that danced across the clouds. Most of its surface was scarred by craters, some bigger than The Bliss itself, but they only added to its delicate beauty.

With the moon in clear view and the tower below reduced to the size of a ring she could wear on her finger, Allura decided that they were probably high enough.

I really hope this works, she thought, stretching

her arm back like a pitcher in the most important game of their life.

The Eviscero Charge ticked and whirred louder and louder until Allura knew it was now or never. Springing her arm forwards so hard that it felt like it was going to pop out of its socket, she catapulted the device out into the midnight void.

'GO! GO! GO!' Allura yelled, pushing London into a nosedive.

They fell so fast that the biting wind tore at her skin, but Allura ignored the pain as all she could think of was the fact that any second now the bomb was going to-

BOOM!

It exploded somewhere above them, igniting the sky in a tantalising rainbow of colours and obliterating the clouds.

The resultant blast of displaced air fired after them, lapping at their heels as they dropped from the sky.

'FASTER LONDON! FASTER!' she yelled. 'WE CAN STILL-'

They were struck by the shockwave, immediately knocking them unconscious and sending Allura hurtling away from London.

They became two free falling objects, battered by the rush of the wind and plummeting inevitably downwards towards the ground.

*

'Come home,' the voice at the door said. 'Come home, Allura.'

No! No please! Somebody help me!

She was back in the nightmare, the same one that had haunted her since her very first night in Orterra.

Pointlessly struggling, Allura cried and fought with every ounce of strength, but still she was stuck in place, doomed as she always was to be pulled back into Mrs. Olderman's clutches.

Then she heard a familiar voice from behind her.

'It's okay Allura. I'm here,' Noah said as he emerged from the pitch black, carrying himself with a more confident swagger than he ever dared to in real life.

What are you doing here? she wanted to ask.

'I'm here for you,' he replied, as though reading her thoughts. 'Listen, usually I can only enter dreams when I'm asleep or near the dreamer. It's taking everything I've got to do this from this far away so I'm really going to need you to work with me,' he said, grabbing her by the hand.

With that one act, Allura suddenly felt control of her body returning to her.

'Noah, I don't know what's going on. I'm scared,' she admitted.

'Then I suppose we'll both just have to be brave,' he replied warmly as he gestured towards the light where the silhouette of a person continued to reach out to her.

As they approached, Noah let go of Allura's hand and walked through the doorway. Although hesitant for a moment, she knew she had to trust in her friend and warily accepted the figure's hand in her own.

Then, she stepped through as well.

The light was blinding at first, a severe brightness that forced her to cover her eyes, but they soon adjusted. Where she had expected to see the miserable interior of Mrs. Olderman's home, there was a forest.

A wide wood, crisp and calm in the golden sunlight. But it wasn't just any forest.

It was Endwood.

'There you are,' the silhouette said with a chuckle, revealing itself to be Cognitius.

Alongside her, visions of Ofelia, Abraham, Lydia, Faye and all the others Allura had come to care for joined them in the woodlands. They congregated around her, each one of them looking overjoyed to see her.

'You're safe. You're home,' said Cognitius.

'I'm sorry it took me so long to realise,' Allura replied tearfully as Noah placed his hands in hers again and smiled.

'I told you. You can't tell a dream from a nightmare,' he said, his hand instantly turning cold against her skin. 'But now we really need you to wake up.'

'What?' Allura asked, as a powerful wind blew through the trees.

'It's time,' he said, his voice fading into a distant echo as the forest crumbled and disappeared around her.

'WAKE UP!'

*

Fast and frantic, Allura's eyes fluttered open.

Her brain was scrambled again, as though trying to hold onto any one thought was as elusive as trying to catch a butterfly.

She could grasp it for a moment, but all too quickly it would slip through her fingers. The only thing she could tell for certain was that she was flying.

Wait, flying or falling?

Looking down, she realised that she was spiralling out of control towards the remnants of the dilapidated tower below.

Definitely falling!

The very air around her was illuminated by the dazzling light of the erupting Eviscero Charge. She looked over her shoulder, up towards the moon, only to see that the sky itself was seemingly on fire.

Then it all came back to her.

The flight, the explosion, the fall.

Looking back towards the ground, she was terrified to see that the distance between her and the treetops was shrinking faster and faster while the wind pushed against her like a wall of ice.

'LONDON!?' she screamed. 'LONDON!?'

Where is she?

Desperately searching around her, she spotted her falling friend below, spinning as she fell with her wings dangling limply. Allura made herself as narrow as possible, holding her legs together and pinning her arms close to her body to fall faster.

As she drew nearer, Allura reached out her hand and tried to take hold of the rope, but it bobbed and weaved in the air as though purposely evading her grasp.

When finally she did catch it between her fingers, she used it to pull herself onto the bear's back and held on tightly as they continued to spin uncontrollably.

Tugging at her fur, Allura screamed at the top of her lungs into London's ear:

'WAKE UP!'

A set of big brown eyes sprung open and Allura screamed at her to go upwards as the confused bear startled back to life.

Then suddenly, as though she knew exactly what she was meant to do, London flexed out one of her wings to counteract the dizzying tailspin, then stretched out the other at the perfect time.

For one glorious moment they steadily rode the wind, but they were still moving too fast as they approached the treetops.

The sounds of a falling forest rung out across the valley as they crashed through the canopy. Snapping twisted branches on their way down, they plunged into the earth in a wave of upturned dirt and moss, coming to a stop in a troop of giant mushrooms.

There, sat in a small crater of their own making, Allura summoned all the strength she had left to press her forehead against London's and let out a weak, but joyful chuckle.

'Well done girl,' she said, exhausted, but grateful to be alive.

'Well done.'

Her vision blurred and she could feel herself slipping back into unconsciousness once again as a figure hurried towards them. It was only when she knelt down in front of her that Allura recognised it as Ofelia.

'They're over here!' she called out.

'Did it work?' Allura whispered.

'Yeah, it worked! You did it! It's over!' she answered excitedly.

It's over? Allura thought, struggling to believe it and too tired to speak anymore. But it was true. Against all odds, they had won.

Now, at long last, there was one thing left to do.

It was time for Allura to go home.

20

Atrilarium Day

In Earthly terms, it was 25th December 2010, and to the best of her memory, there had been twelve times in her life that Allura Saint-May was uncertain if she would make it out alive.

This most recent brush with death had by far been the most elaborate and had left her in a haze.

Each time she tried to wake, she was lulled back into a deep and dreamless sleep, catching only brief glimpses of concerned faces coming in and out of focus.

But eventually, still tired and sore, her eyes opened in earnest. Initially it seemed too good to be true as she woke to the soft touch of a well-sprung mattress beneath her rather than the wet dirt and splintered wood of the forest.

Where am I?

Paper snowflakes and butterflies hung above her. Their thin wings flapped in the cool draught that flowed in from the window, through which Allura could see the welcome sight of Endwood sitting peacefully beyond the treeline.

Beside the bed, Ofelia gently rocked back and

forth in a creaking wicker chair. She wore red tartan pyjamas and had her ridiculously long hair tamed into pigtails as she sketched absent-mindedly into one of her books.

'Good morning,' Allura croaked, trying to sit up.

'Now what time do you call this?' Ofelia joked. 'How're you feeling?'

'I'm actually okay, I think,' she replied, almost believing the words as she built up the courage to ask: 'What happened?'

Ofelia took a moment to remember every detail and after a great deal of thought, she recounted the story from the very moment after Allura lost consciousness.

She was relieved to learn that London had scampered off into the woods before anyone could catch her, although it worried her to learn that she had yet to be seen again since.

Meanwhile, the full force of the Counter Club had come crashing down on Orville. In fact, at that very minute he was being escorted by Evelyn and Raven to the impenetrable fortress of Igramel, which housed Orterra's most wicked and dangerous.

He had gone with them willingly, any fight that was left in him had been destroyed alongside the Eviscero Charge.

'Poor Darnigold, she's going to be heartbroken,' Ofelia commented.

Poor Orville, Allura found herself thinking.

'I still can't wrap my head around why he would do all this,' Ofelia said, but Allura felt she could understand it all too well.

'You know at Highdenhome, when I first met Orville, he told me that he felt lost when he was chosen to come to Orterra. I think he meant that he'd left a part of himself on Earth and he'd never be whole without it.

'Horas helped him find his way, but after the war, when he pushed the people who loved him away, he lost himself again. He lost hope,' Allura explained.

'I wish I could say I didn't understand him, but before I came here, I didn't have much myself.'

'And now?' Ofelia asked as she squeezed Allura's hand.

'Now I have something to be hopeful about.'

Bright smiles stretched across their faces for a calm and quiet moment, but it didn't last long before Ofelia shouted: 'OH!' as though remembering something important as she reached into a bag on the floor.

'They found this on Orville when they arrested him,' she said, handing over Orville's half of the murmur paper. 'It was actually Raven who suggested they give it to you, so it seems we had him figured all wrong.'

'Hmmm,' was all Allura had to say.

'What?' Ofelia asked, recognising the unconvinced look on Allura's face.

'Don't you think it's interesting that he was suspicious of Orville the whole time?'

'Well no, because he was Horas' spy. By the gods, I overheard him bragging to the Counter Club that he was the one who told Cognitius that Horas had been murdered in the first place! Which like I said, means we were wrong about him.'

'Maybe. Or maybe it means that Raven knew exactly what Orville was up to all along and chose to wait right up until the last minute to try and stop him.'

'Why would he do that?'

'To make himself look like a hero. Think about it, with Orville in prison and no new Embodiment of Order to take his place, something tells me his second-in-command will have to take over as head of Highdenhome.'

Ofelia smacked her hand to her forehead.

'Raven just got everything he's ever wanted,' she said, feeling slightly nauseous.

'And we helped him get there.'

They sat in silence, stewing in their failure until they heard the faint sounds of music and laughter downstairs which pushed any thoughts of Raven or his potential victory to the back of their minds.

'Well anyway, I have something else for you,' Ofelia said excitedly. 'Your Atrilarium present.'

My present? Allura thought, taken aback and slightly confused as Ofelia didn't move an inch to pick up a gift or hand her a card.

Instead, Ofelia gave her a unique gift, one that could not be unwrapped or held, but only spoken of and agreed upon.

It was the best present Allura had ever been given and afterwards she decided she had a gift of her own. Spotting her hooded cloak sat beside Beam on Ofelia's desk, Allura hopped out of bed and rummaged through the pockets until she found what she had been looking for.

'Hold out your hand,' Allura said, hiding the object behind her back while Ofelia did as she was told with her palm open expectantly.

After a few seconds of mounting suspense, Allura placed the spyglass in her hand.

'I can't take this,' Ofelia insisted.

'Oh, go on. Imagine how much faster you could fill in your book of creatures with this thing.'

It didn't take much more to convince her and Ofelia graciously accepted, laughing giddily as she peered out the window with it.

'Wow,' she said breathlessly, instantly spotting an elusive breed of bird perched in a tree miles away.

'Happy Atrilarium Day, Allura,' Ofelia said with an uncontrollable smile.

'Happy Atrilarium Day, Ofelia.'

*

Rapturous applause filled the house as Allura descended the staircase with Ofelia's mothers and siblings, as well as the whole Tanden family, gathered at the foot of the steps to celebrate her recovery.

As much as it warmed her heart, she suffered a realisation as their applause settled down.

'I'm so sorry. You should be enjoying the day, not worrying about me,' she said, her fear of ruining everyone else's fun coming to life in front of her.

'We won't hear it,' Faye said with a smile.

'Absolutely not. I owe you a great debt of gratitude young lady,' Elliott said, shaking her hand vigorously.

'Me too,' agreed Patricia.

'And me,' said Lydia.

'It's hardly like I did it alone,' Allura said, turning her head and flashing Ofelia and Noah a broad smile. Then her heart sank as a trail of black smoke wafted into the hallway and lingered in the air.

She thought it was Raven, here to sour the day and scold her for ever accusing him of Orville's crimes, but she felt an immense relief when Lydia shouted:

'The bacon's burning!'

Ofelia's mothers darted into the kitchen and scrambled to salvage the first of the day's many meals while Allura playfully ran her hand through the smoke, grateful that it wasn't what she had thought.

As everyone moved into the kitchen, she slung her arm around Noah.

'You know, I had the funniest dream about you last night,' she said and they burst into laughter.

*

Slightly charred bits of meat and over-done poached eggs were served for breakfast with the two families once again barely managing to fit around the Donnelly's kitchen table.

It wasn't the most comfortable of arrangements, nor was it the most delicious food any of them had ever tasted, but with hope in her heart and friends at her side, Allura felt that it was the best meal she had ever had.

Unfortunately, she didn't get to savour it for long.

Knock! Knock! Knock!

Everyone fell silent… well, almost everyone.

'Who there?' shouted Abigail.

'Shush,' hissed Cameron.

She's here, Allura realised as she got up from the table.

'You don't have to answer it on your own,' said Lydia.

'Yeah, we could come with you,' offered Ofelia.

'No. It's okay,' Allura said, tugging at her clothes in a vague attempt to make herself look more presentable. 'I think I have to do this myself.'

Making her way into the hall, she reached for the handle and swung the door open. There, looking up into the sky with her feet sunken deep into the snow, was Cognitius.

If she had stood any further away, Allura would have struggled to recognise her. The old woman wore a coat that hung baggy over her small frame with a bulky knitted scarf wrapped several times around her neck like a constricting snake.

'It's going to snow again,' Cognitius said very matter-of-factly.

Allura peeked her head out and glimpsed the grey clouds.

'Looks like it,' she agreed as Cognitius trained her eye on Allura, seemingly taken aback by the sight of her.

'Well would you look at you!'

Have I got something on my face? Allura worried, checking the mirror by the door. Her clothes were a little scruffy and her hair was once again full of knots, but she couldn't see what could have elicited such a reaction from Cognitius.

'What do you mean? I look like... myself,' she said with a smile.

'Yes and it's about time,' Cognitius replied as she unravelled her scarf and stepped out of the cold.

'Wait, how did you know I would be here?' Allura asked, realising that she had never told Cognitius she would be spending the day with the Donnellys.

'I assumed that when I told Faye and Lydia to leave you be that they would ignore me completely. Was I right?'

'More or less,' Allura admitted.

'Excellent. Although from what I've been told, neither they nor Abraham did a very good job of keeping you out of trouble this week.'

'You heard about that?' Allura asked, sheepishly.

'I'm the ruler of The Bliss, of course I heard about it. It's all anyone in Cambium could speak of this morning. The wood gnells in particular were enthralled by the story of Allura Saint-May, the Earth girl who saved the lives of not just one, but four Orterran regents in a single night.'

When she heard it like that, even Allura found herself astounded by what had happened.

'And like ten other embodiments!' Ofelia said as she hurried in from the kitchen with Noah close behind.

'It's true, we were there your majestic... majesty... highness,' Noah said awkwardly as he bowed and tried to pull Ofelia into a curtsy.

'Ms. Donnelly. Mr. Tanden. Do not worry, there

has been plenty of talk about the tremendous courage that you two showed last night as well,' Cognitius said, before looking directly at Noah.

'The boy who felled a stone golem.'

She then turned to Ofelia.

'And the girl who was willing to sacrifice herself for her friends.'

They all stood proudly, basking in the magnitude of what they had accomplished.

'But that's all over now,' Cognitius reassured them. 'Igramel's warden will ensure that Orville never so much as lifts another stone again, and although her heart may take some time to mend, the schematics for the Eviscero Charge have been returned to Lady Darnigold. From what I gather, she has decided to destroy the plans so that they may never be exploited again.'

Good riddance, Allura thought, although there was still one thing that she didn't quite understand.

'What about the dagger? The one that Orville killed Horas with. When I saw it I felt like I was dying. Do you know why that might have been?' she asked.

'Now that is interesting. If I were to theorise, I would say that perhaps it has something to do with these things inside of us. The very essence of our embodiments. They are more alive and more a part of us, than we ever dare admit. That essence of hope inside of you spent decades with Horas. After so long, maybe the sight of the weapon that killed him caused it to lash out within you.'

Allura nodded, wondering then why she hadn't

felt the same uneasiness around Orville, but ultimately realising the great tragedy of it.

He and Horas had been allies for so long, trusted one another so completely, that even the essence inside of her couldn't bring itself to see him as anything other than a friend.

'Now, if you two wouldn't mind, I was just about to ask Allura a very important question,' Cognitius said, sending Noah and Ofelia back into the kitchen as she looked Allura in her eyes and said:

'Are you ready?'

The question sat heavy in her mind as she glanced towards the kitchen where Noah and Ofelia's peeking heads disappeared from the doorway and the shadows of their eavesdropping families were cast onto the walls.

'Yes... well, no,' she stammered, trying to find the best way to say what she wanted to.

'The truth is, when I first arrived here, I wanted to leave because I thought I didn't belong. But if this last week has taught me anything it's that maybe no one really belongs anywhere.

'Maybe home is just wherever we decide it is. Wherever we feel it. And if I'm honest, I've felt more at home here in a week than I did in my whole life on Earth.'

She could hardly believe the words were leaving her lips and yet she meant them completely.

'So no, I'm not ready, because I'm staying. I am staying in Orterra for good.'

Excited whispers from the kitchen told her that she had made the right choice, but Cognitius didn't say a thing.

Instead, she simply reached into one of her coat pockets and pulled out a small box, wrapped in beautiful blue tissue paper with a white ribbon tied across it.

'I meant, are you ready for your gift?' Cognitius chuckled. 'Though I am glad to hear that you found your way.'

'You knew I was going to stay?' Allura asked.

'From the moment we met. Just like little Lucy Lummens, climbing that mountain to find the Embodiment of Courage only to learn it was her all along, I knew that you already had what you were looking for.'

Allura didn't know whether to laugh or cry, but instead she chose to simply tug at the ribbon and watch as the box disassembled in her hand.

Revealed inside was a delicate glass bauble with a proud bear stood supremely at its centre.

'Welcome home, Allura.'

'Thank you, Cognitius,' Allura said tearfully. 'Thank you.'

*

'I'm telling you, there were twice as many gifts on the pile last night,' Cinder said accusingly.

'So, what you're saying is that they just grew legs and walked away?' Raiph spat back as they trudged down the main street.

Their arguing hit an abrupt stop as they noticed Allura, the only other soul on the entire road. It was Atrilarium Day and while everyone else was inside, warm and cosy, enjoying the holiday with their families, the Kraws had chosen to spend the day staggering around Endwood in search of their mysteriously missing gifts.

They locked eyes with Allura and stood up straight, puffing out their chests and clenching their fists as they strode towards her. Allura narrowed her eyes as they approached and a silver glow flickered in the blackness of her pupils, the sight of which ignited a fearful shock on both of the Kraw children's faces.

With that, they quickly changed course, turning around and running in the direction they had just come from as though it had always been their intention to do so.

I could get used to that, Allura thought as she finished her journey to the inn Abraham was staying at. Once again, he didn't answer, but something told her that she knew exactly where to find him.

When she arrived at the cabin, Abraham was sat expectantly on the porch, surrounded by a mound of crudely wrapped boxes. He gestured to the presents with a wide sweep of his arm like a proud child at show and tell.

'Are those for me?' she asked unable to hide the excited rise in her voice, but as she eyed the presents, she noticed that many of the tags had been suspiciously torn off.

'This wouldn't happen to have anything to do with the Kraw's vanishing gifts, would it?'

He shook his head, but a slight smirk betrayed him.

'Well, thank you,' she said, wiping away the snow off the porch and planting herself down next to him.

'You knew Raven was Horas' spy, didn't you?' she queried, even though she didn't need to see him nod to know the answer.

'But you didn't want to believe he was right about Orville?'

He shook his head.

'I'm sorry I didn't trust you. I'm trying to get better at that,' she said and Abraham pointed to himself, which she took to mean 'me too.'

'Anyway, I've decided to stick around a while longer,' she told him and Abraham's big hand patted her on the back as gently as he could manage.

'The thing is I can't stay here,' she brought herself to say, glancing over her shoulder at the cabin. 'Ofelia told me this morning that her parents don't want me living out here all on my own, so they offered to put another bed in her room for me.'

With a raised eyebrow he glared at her as though in suspense about what her answer had been.

'I said yes, obviously.'

It had been an easy decision, one that she could only have dreamt of. Theirs was the family she had always wished for, and now that she dared to hope again, it felt like the only choice was to join them.

Abraham forced a smile, but Allura could tell he was hiding his sadness, no longer having an excuse to visit his friend's former home ever again, especially now that London had run off.

'It's not my home, it never was,' she said. 'But it could be yours. If you want it that is?'

The discomfort on his face told her that he had a lot of memories in that cabin, good and bad, all of which just reminded him of the life he used to have and the friends he used to love.

But she saw something else in his demeanour as well; opportunity. The chance to make new memories with new friends in a place that cared for him and that he cared for in return.

'You don't have to take it, but I think this could be a new start for both of us,' she said, offering him the keys. After glaring at it for a moment, Abraham's gaze seemed to be caught by something else, something beyond her.

Following his eyeline, she found herself staring into the forest where the trees and bushes rustled in the wind.

But I don't feel any wind, she realised.

Suddenly, with matted fur and dirty paws, a great winged bear emerged from the woods.

'London!' Allura called in elation as she and Abraham sprinted over. The bear's eyes sparkled as they approached and she let out a contented purr as they wrapped her in a huge hug.

'You found your way back! You clever girl!' Allura said, overcome with joy. Abraham seemed especially happy to see her, letting out a laugh as she licked at his face.

'You know, she'll really need someone to look after her if I'm going to be moving out,' Allura said, posturing London's head so that her big brown eyes looked up innocently at Abraham.

With a restrained smile, he took the keys from

Allura's hand.

'Horas would be proud I think,' she said and after a moment, Abraham nodded in agreement.

But as they stroked and clung gleefully to the bear, a question popped into Allura's head.

'When you found her as a cub all those years ago, did you name her?' she asked not really expecting an answer, but after a moment of thinking, Abraham chuckled to himself.

Then, in a deep and husky voice, he said:

'Allura.'

HE CAN TALK! she thought in disbelief.

But when finally she recovered from the shock, she began to really acknowledge his answer. Horas had named the bear 'Allura' which only left her with a greater curiosity.

*

Once all of Abraham's pilfered presents had been opened, Allura made her way back to the Donnelly's just in time to see off Noah and his parents. They were ready to celebrate the rest of the day in their own home and after she had exchanged festive pleasantries with Elliott and Patricia, Noah took Allura aside and shoved a book into her hands.

The History of Orterra by Ravaforth Hedley.

'I was planning on giving you this so you could remember us when you went back to Earth, but I think it works even better now that you're staying. We can go over it together before next term starts at The Stump. Oh, and don't tell Ofelia I said it, but I've bookmarked a section about choir whales in there that I think she'll probably like.'

'Thank you,' Allura said, truly excited to start reading (although she had the niggling feeling that it was more of a homework assignment than a gift).

'And don't worry, Ofelia will have no idea that you actually like her.'

'I'm not sure if I'd go that far,' he laughed. 'But honestly, I really am glad that you're staying. I guess you and her will be getting up to all sorts of adventures now that you're living together. Probably for the best, I know I can be a little unhelpful,' he said with a laugh, but Allura could tell he was worried.

'What are you talking about? You fought a clawing kross and a stone golem on the same day. I think you might just be the bravest person I've ever met. I've had my fill of adventures, but if something did come up, it's good to know you're just down the road,' she said comfortingly as she pulled a sheet of murmur paper from her pocket and offered it to him.

With a reaffirming push of his glasses, Noah accepted it and said:

'I suppose I could help out if you really needed me. I did make a promise after all.'

*

The rest of the day flashed by like a dream with the harmonious sounds of ripping gift-paper, crackling fires and sizzling hot food.

Abigail squealed joyously at the reveal of her new dolly while Cameron feigned disinterest in his books (although he seemed all too eager to start reading them). Meanwhile, Faye and Lydia fired off 'you shouldn't haves' and 'how did you knows?' throughout the day as they exchanged presents.

The look of sheer elation on Ofelia's face as she unwrapped a pencil set was one of the highlights and Allura could have gladly watched her draw the clawing kross and other frightening monsters in her big book of creatures all day.

The Donnellys had even bought Allura her own set of pyjamas that were emerald green, like her eyes, and had a similar chequered pattern to the rest of the family's.

After she threw them on, Lydia told them all the story of Aterosk and the history of Atrilarium Day, just as she had done every year before, followed by a ninety-minute mantelpiece concert from The Box of Misfits.

In the late afternoon, Cognitius sipped at danderlily wine then fell fast asleep by the fire while Allura, Ofelia and Cameron slurped down huge mugs of hot chocolate and watched as Abigail chased TibbidyBoo around the room.

The little marlee was in burrowing heaven as he dug and rolled through discarded sheets of paper, letting out playful chirps each time Abigail caught him.

Finally, Abraham popped by for a feast of roasted graver, crispy potatoes, soft squash, crunchy carrots, cuckoo-pigs in blankets, chestnuts and steamed squilms (which had bloomed that very morning).

'Told you there was still life in them,' Ofelia said smugly.

In the end, it was a perfect day filled with thoughtful gifts and delicious food overseen by the great glass bear that hung resplendently on the tree.

*

As Allura's first Atrilarium Day came to a close, she and Ofelia sat on the ledge of their now-shared bedroom window, dangling their legs over the pitched roof of the house as the delicate winter breeze rolled in.

Resting her head on Allura's shoulder, Ofelia sighed blissfully at the setting sun which barely continued to shine through the billowing clouds.

'Merry Christ-Mass, Allura,' she murmured.

'Don't you mean happy Atrilarium Day?' Allura asked, but Ofelia just shrugged lazily.

'Who cares what you call it? As long as you had a good one.'

Allura nodded contentedly as the light sunk below the trees and snow once again began to fall over Endwood. Her heart was filled with hope as the sleepy town welcomed each snowflake like an old friend, and for the first time that she could remember, she thought:

It's good to be home.

The End